"Val Penny has pro
cracking read, and
She is fully engage⌐
and it shows."

Michael Jecks – *best-selling author of unmissable historical mysteries including the 'Jack Blackjack' crime series including 'Rebellion's Message' and the 'Knights Templar' mysteries including 'The Last Templar' and the contemporary spy novel 'Act of Vengeance'*

"The Hugely talented Val Penny has delivered yet another pacey, tense read featuring Edinburgh's most famous detective, DI Hunter Wilson."

Stuart Gibbon – *Former Murder Squad DCI & co-author of 'The Crime Writer's Casebook'*

"A gripping novel about power, politics and revenge. Hunter Wilson is a compelling detective and Val Penny is an author to watch."

Erin Kelly – *best-selling author of psychological thrillers including 'Broadchurch', 'The Poison Tree' and 'He Said/She Said'*

"A compulsive read! DI Hunter Wilson and a cast of characters that will be familiar to those who are already fans of the series - as well as some fascinating new ones - appear in this complex, gritty and engrossing tale. Val Penny deals with the shocking issue of human trafficking, yet weaves magnificent warmth into her story. I can't wait for the next one!"

Katherine Johnson – *best-selling author of 'The Silence' and 'The Secret'*

"Val Penny has put together a crack team of detective investigators trying to keep Edinburgh safe, and fortunately for mystery lovers, their work is never done. Fans of the first two books in her Edinburgh Crime Mysteries will be delighted to find many of the same characters — good and bad — in Hunter's Force. After a shocker of a start, this mystery keeps going at a steady pace. I dare you to keep up with DI Hunter Wilson and DC Tim Myerscough as they work to solve this case. Hunter's Force is a gripping read to the end."

Joan Livingston – *best-selling author of Chasing the Case' and 'Redneck's Revenge'*

"Hunter finds himself in a case which is far too close to home and soon comes even closer. Crackling with vibrancy, life and tension, this book will pull you in to its pages and on a whistle stop ride."

Wendy H. Jones – *award winning author of her police procedural series of novels featuring Detective Inspector Shona McKenzie.*

"A great read, which had me hooked from the very start and hungrily turning the pages. I love Hunter, and all his cast of supporting characters, both good and evil. Such a rich and fascinating group, who rise from the page to live real lives. The plot was pacy, imaginative, and full of twists and turns, and the settings so evocative you could almost taste, smell and feel them. I'm looking forward to the next episode of Hunter's adventures already."

Simon Hall – *best-selling author of The TV Detective Novels and lecturer at University of Cambridge, Cambridge Judge Business School.*

To Gordon,

Hunter's Force

The Edinburgh Crime Mysteries #3

Val Penny

Also available:

Hunter's Chase
Hunter's Revenge

with best wishes
Val Penny

CROOKED
CAT

Discover us online:
www.crookedcatbooks.com

Join us on facebook:
www.facebook.com/crookedcat

Tweet a photo of yourself holding
this book to **@crookedcatbooks**
and something nice will happen.

To Dave,
with all my love.

About the Author

Val Penny is an American author living in SW Scotland. She has two adult daughters of whom she is justly proud and lives with her husband and two cats. She has a Law degree from Edinburgh University and her MSc from Napier University. She has had many jobs including hairdresser, waitress, lawyer, banker, azalea farmer and lecturer. However she has not yet achieved either of her childhood dreams of being a ballerina or owning a candy store. Until those dreams come true, she has turned her hand to writing poetry, short stories and novels. Her crime novels, 'Hunter's Chase' Hunter's Revenge and Hunter's Force are set in Edinburgh, Scotland, published by Crooked Cat Books. The fourth book in the series, Hunter's Blood, follows shortly.

Acknowledgements

Writing a novel is often said to be a solitary endeavour and, although a book is written by one person, the finished product is definitely not the achievement of that individual alone.

I am most indebted to my publishers, Crooked Cat Books, who showed faith in me when I was a completely unknown author and have nurtured me with the remarkable team in which they cocoon me. These include Laurence whose remarkable talent and patience are legendary and Steph whose generosity and kindness are unsurpassed. Now, what to say about my editor: Sue Barnard is a gifted author in her own right and, in addition to that, she has taken time out of her busy schedule to share her expertise and critical eye in order to help me bring my story and the characters in it to life. Sue, I cannot thank you enough.

My thanks also go to Alex Gillon, Scott Penny, David McLaughlan, Avril Rennie, Liz Hurst, Simon Hall and all those at Swanwick Writers' Summer School for their encouragement and enthusiasm.

I remain eternally grateful to Dave, Lizzie, Vicky, Lisa and my Mum for their unswerving support and unfailing belief in me. I must also thank everybody who encouraged me to write, but most of all, I thank my readers: each and everyone of them. Without you, The Edinburgh Crime Mysteries could not exist.

I must also acknowledge the following resources:

The Real CSI: A Forensics Handbook for Crime Writers by Kate Bendelow
The Crime Writers Casebook (Straightforward Guides) by Stephen Wade & Stuart Gibbon
Forensics: The Anatomy of Crime by Val McDermid
Human Trafficking by Mary C. Burke

Any errors, of course, are mine.

Hunter's Force

The Edinburgh Crime Mysteries #3

Chapter One

"You can all come back to my place!" Cameron shouted to his new friends. "It's only at Frederick Street, above the new betting shop."

It was a chilly night and he was sure they wouldn't want to walk too far. The apartment he now occupied, courtesy of his job, was just a couple of blocks west of the club.

"Lead the way!" Harry said.

"You got beer?" Gavin asked.

"Aye, I've got some cans in the fridge. And we can find out what happened to Xristina, my beautiful girl with the flowing Titian red hair, you'll see."

"Ha ha! Xristina stood you up – or she doesny exist ya chump," Harry laughed.

Harry Hope had his arm draped over the shoulder of the pretty brown-haired girl named Symona, and Gavin MacGregor was fancying his chances with the blonde called Olena. They all followed Cameron Wilson along to his place.

"Who knows why his girl didn't turn up at the club?" Harry bellowed.

"Who cares?" Gavin laughed.

"My landlord moved Xristina into the other bedroom in my place. Me and Xristina have a special connection. You can imagine that, can't you, Symona?" Cameron sought confirmation from the brunette.

"I am sure it is what you say, Cameron." She shrugged.

"And you are really brave soldiers?" Olena asked Gavin.

"You believe it, Olena. Big and brave and bad as they come" he smiled. "Although, if I'm honest, I'm glad to be home, at least for a bit."

"A bit?" she asked. "What you need a bit of?"

3

"Yes, that too." Gavin grinned and hugged her. He fancied his chances with her just a little more now.

**

The soldiers were on leave after a tour of Afghanistan and were glad to let their hair down. The lads had met Cameron and the young women in the queue to get into *Why Not?* (the night club in the basement of *The Dome* in George Street). They could have chosen *Shanghai* or *Lulu's* or any of the city centre clubs, but the massive queue outside *Why Not?* sounded lively, and they were attracted by the girls at the back end of it. They were chatting to Cameron and handing out vouchers to meet with them again at The Edinburgh Massage Suite in Lothian Road. Harry and Gavin tried to be subtle, and asked Cameron for a light for their cigarettes before introducing themselves and starting to chat to the girls.

Harry and Gavin had both already decided to take advantage of the vouchers that Symona and Olena had given them. And they were glad that Cameron didn't seem to mind them hogging the pair.

He told them that the girl he thought of as his was planning to join them in a few minutes. But as minutes became hours and hours became pints and pints became shots, Harry and Gavin began to tease Cameron about whether his date really existed or had he just lost the other two girls to better men.

The five of them linked arms and weaved along the wide pavement on George Street until they turned down into Frederick Street. The New Town of Edinburgh is always beautiful, but at that early hour of the morning, when the clubs were emptying into night buses, taxis and long walks home, the clear sky, sharp air and new friends made it even more magical.

**

"I'm on the second floor, boys," Cameron said as he fished his keys out of his pocket.

"I think we can manage the climb," Harry said lifting Symona over his shoulder in a fireman's lift and running up the stairs as she squealed in mock terror.

The door swung open as Cameron led the way into the apartment. "Why's the door open? My doors been kicked in! Xristina? Xristina? Where are you? Are you okay? We have visitors. Are you not feeling so well?"

Cameron got no reply.

"Beer?" Gavin asked.

"Through there in the kitchen." Cameron nodded absent-mindedly to the right as he went into the living room and switched the light on. There was no sign of his missing squeeze there either, but a girl with unnaturally red hair, not like Xristina's beautiful locks, wandered out of the second bedroom. Cameron had never seen her before.

"Who the hell are you? And what the fuck are you doing in my flat? Why was my door open and where is my girlfriend?"

The girl did not reply. She looked in his direction but her eyes did not appear to focus. Her mouth hung open. She had been crying. Cameron pushed past her and moved along the corridor to his own bedroom, but was stopped in his tracks by Olena's high-pitched scream.

"Holy fuck!" Harry shouted. "Cameron ! Who the fuck is this? What the bloody hell has happened here?"

Cameron stormed into the kitchen. Olena was screaming. Symona was cradling Xristina's head in her lap. She had been so badly beaten around the head that her features were almost unrecognisable, and the tops of her fingers were missing. The kitchen floor was stained with blood.

"Jesus!" Cameron exclaimed. "What the fuck?"

The unknown girl followed Cameron into the kitchen. As she caught sight of Xristina's body, she started to cry again.

"Anichka!" Olena said when she saw the weeping red-haired girl. "Why are you here?"

"No wonder this poor bint stood you up," Gavin whispered. "She's dead."

"I'm calling the police," Harry took his phone out of his pocket.

5

"No! No police!" Olena said, in a panic.

"We have to. This is mental. Whoever did this might come back," Harry said.

"We cannot with police," Symona sobbed.

"Hell's teeth, woman. She's had her fuckin' fingers chopped off! Anyway, I'm out of here!" Gavin shouted.

"No you can't leave! It'll look bad. See, I'll sort it. My Dad's a copper. He'll know what to do," Cameron stood in the blood-spattered kitchen and dialled his father's number.

"I know what to do: get to blazes out of here. I don't need this," Gavin said.

"No! We can't. Cameron's right. That'll make us look bad." Harry shook his head. "You know that, Gavin," Harry said as he opened the fridge and handed Gavin a beer. The two soldiers flicked open the cans of beer and wandered through to the living room, trailing Xristina's blood on the soles of their shoes.

Chapter Two

DI Hunter Wilson looked at the time on his phone before he answered the call. 4.03am. If this was some comedian from the sub-continent calling to tell him about putting in a claim for the accident he hadn't had... Then he noticed it was Cameron calling him.

"What's the matter, son? This is a hell of a time to phone." Hunter whispered.

"I didn't know who else to call."

"What's the matter? And it had better be good."

"It's far from good." Cameron told his father of the scene that had met him and his new friends when they got back to his flat.

"She's had what cut off? Bloody hell!"

"I know, Dad, I know. And her head has been bashed in too. What do I do?"

"Well, now we have Police Scotland in place there is a Major Incidents Team, imaginatively know as MIT, that deals with cases like this."

"Oh Dad no! The other girls'll go mental. You come. Please? At least at first. I need your help."

Hunter thought back to the days when Cameron used to ask for his help regularly: tying his shoelaces, drying him after swimming, learning to ride a bike. Those had been the golden years. It had been a long, long time since his son had sounded so desperate and pleaded for his help. It made Hunter feel good. He could help Cameron again. Brilliant!

"You're not back on the cocaine are you, Cameron? You're not hallucinating?" Hunter said suddenly.

"No I'm bloody not! But thanks for the vote of confidence. Believe me, I will be if you don't get your arse over here pronto!"

"And that's how you ask for help from your dad? A favour? Stuff you!" Hunter shouted back.

"What is it?" a bleary voice beside Hunter said.

"Please, Dad. Just come. I need you." Cameron sounded like a little boy about to burst into tears. "Another person's in my flat too. I've never seen her before. Just come, quickly, please Dad! I can't tell you how awful it all is here."

Hunter got out of bed and patted Meera' s arm. "Go back to sleep, pet. I've got to go and see Cameron. It's an emergency."

"At four o'clock in the morning? What's wrong? Is he using again?"

"No. But he was out for the evening and got back to his flat to find his flatmate dead on the floor"

"Why does he need you? Shouldn't he call an ambulance?" Meera asked.

"It's a bit late for that. She's been mutilated; her head has been bashed in and the tops of her fingers cut off."

"I'd guess she's probably dead, right enough. But doesn't Cameron need me more than he needs you? I'm coming with you," Meera said in a determined voice that brooked no contradiction.

"Thank you, Doctor Sharma," Hunter said softly.

Hunter smiled as the petite pathologist swung her legs out of the bed, dragged on the clothes she had worn the night before, and still managed to look beautiful. How did she do that?

"He's living in that flat in Frederick Street. It belongs to that Lord somebody or other. A young bloke that Tim Myerscough knows."

"Then phone Tim. I'll drive. We're going to need all the help we can get." Meera grabbed her car keys and they ran down the stairs from Hunter's flat.

DC Tim Myerscough was a relatively new member of Hunter's team. Hunter had little time for Tim's father, his former Chief Constable, but he did like Tim a lot. He was a polite, incisive and highly observant detective, who missed little and was very popular with his colleagues. He was the kind of man Hunter always felt, he wanted on his side, covering his back in a tight corner. And the man knew everybody who was anybody in the city.

***

When Tim was woken by his phone ringing, he noticed it was his boss on the line. He ignored it, deciding that at that time in the morning it must be an unintentional pocket call. He rolled over and nuzzled into Gillian's warm body.

The phone rang again, but Tim pretended he had fallen back to sleep.

Gillian's phone rang. Tim guessed the call was from Hunter because he knew they were dating and he would have looked up her number from his contacts list. Tim knew Hunter often contacted Gillian if he needed something translated. She was a talented linguist. However, she did not sound talented to Tim at that time in the morning. She just sounded tired.

"What is it?" she said sleepily. Tim glanced at her and smiled when he saw her answer the call without even opening her eyes.

"Gillian, I'm sorry to bother you."

"Detective Inspector Wilson? It's half past four in the morning!" Gillian grumbled.

"I know, Gillian. I'm looking for Tim Myerscough. Do you know where he is? It's an emergency."

"It'd better be. Tim, it's your boss," she said drily, handing the phone to Tim and snuggling back under the duvet.

"Boss? Do you know what time it is?"

"Indeed I do, young Myerscough," Hunter said seriously.

"Then, how can I help?" Tim asked. He heard the anxiety in Hunter's voice and Tim suddenly felt wide awake and alert.

"Can you meet me at Cameron's flat in Frederick Street, Tim? There's an emergency and we'll need to contact the landlord. You know him?"

"Yes, but I'm hardly Lord Lachlan Buchanan's favourite person."

"Is he the one they call Lucky?"

9

"That's him. Anyway, what's the emergency? "

Tim listened carefully to the revolting image Hunter painted for him.

"Cameron's flatmate had what cut off? I don't like to ask, Boss, but Cameron's not back on the coke is he? Of course not, Boss. No disrespect intended. Shouldn't the new Major Incidents Team be dealing with this? I see. Right. Fine. I'll be there as soon as I can."

"Do you need a car to bring you?" Hunter asked.

"No thanks, Boss, I'm in training for a marathon. I'm running in support of the charity Scottish Families Affected by Alcohol and Drugs, so I'm not drinking just now. I'll be fine to drive myself. I'll be there in twenty minutes."

"Are you always training for something, young Myerscough?"

Tim smiled. "I'll see you in twenty, Boss."

Tim Myerscough kissed his girlfriend and almost fell out of bed in his rush to make good on his time promise to DI Hunter Wilson.

"No idea how long I'll be. See you tonight, Gillian," he said quietly and kissed the green flash of hair on her forehead as he left the room.

***

As Hunter and Meera left his flat, Hunter had a feeling that they were being followed. He could sense it; it was almost a physical sensation. That, and the fact that the same red Volkswagen had been behind them all the way from Leith. He couldn't swear to it, but he thought he recognised the driver. He tried to make out the number plate, but in the early hours of the autumn morning, it was too dark.

"Slow down, Meera," he said.

The Volkswagen slowed down too.

"Speed up, dear," he said in a voice devoid of emotion.

The car behind them increased its speed.

"What is going on, Hunter? If I continue to drive this erratically I'll get picked up by the police," Meera joked.

"Just pull over to the side of the road," Hunter said.

The Volkswagen slowed down but then just drove on. Hunter told Meera to pull out into the stream of traffic and he did not see the red Volkswagen again. Maybe he had imagined it and the car was not following them at all.

Chapter Three

October can be one of the most beautiful months in Edinburgh, and the first two weeks of the month are often warm and sunny. This particular morning it was chilly, but the cloudless sky and slight breeze promised a typical 'Indian Summer'. Children back at school enjoy the challenges the academic year has to throw at them. College and university students, who invaded the city in August and September, find their feet and take full advantage of their freedom from parental restrictions. They have enthusiasm for studying their courses, but even more interest in studying each other.

Jamie Thomson pulled up outside HMP Edinburgh in Saughton. He had driven his pop's favourite old Range Rover to meet him. Pop was to be released from prison, at last, and would get out this morning. He was being let out very early in the morning to avoid a rush of journalists. Ian Thomson was one of the best-known inmates in the jail, and fame always comes at a price.

Jamie leant on the car and flicked through the Facebook messages on his phone as he waited. He was glad his pop would be back to run their car showroom, Thomson's Top Cars. Jamie and his cousin Frankie had done their best, but it would be good to have Pop back at the helm. Although goodness only knew how they were all going to fit into that three-bedroomed semi-detached house he shared with his cousin Frankie and Frankie's twin baby daughters. With Pop out, Frankie's brother Harry and his pal Gavin home on leave from Afghanistan, that would be seven of them squeezed in there. Jamie was sure it wasn't going to be him sleeping in the bath!

"That's a nice welcome, son! You with your eyes glued to that phone!"

"Pop! Good to see you. It's great to have you out of the big house." The men shook hands then hugged. Jamie had missed his pop.

"It is good to be free, that's for sure. Did you remember to bring me a hat?"

"Of course. Here you go."

"It didn't have to be an *Andy Capp* style like this, boy!" Ian Thomson doffed his cap and laughed with his son.

"I didn't think you wanted it as a fashion statement; just something to hide you from the journalists?"

"Well, it's certainly not a fashion statement, lad! Let's make tracks, before the paparazzi realise they've been conned. Oh, and I'll be driving, Jamie."

"Well, seeing you're back now, Pop," Jamie said as he handed over the keys with a grin.

"Aye. We'll go back to the house first and I'll get a proper shower and change into decent clothes before we go over to the showroom.

"You're certainly looking fit. Been working out in the gym inside, have you?"

"Not much else to do, really. But I have got a surprise for you. I did a wee deal inside, and we've got two new betting shops to add to our business empire."

"Betting shops? You mean you're a bookie now, Pop? That's mental! Whereabouts are they?"

"One in Frederick Street, one in Lothian Road."

"Wow! That's brilliant. Fine and central. They'll make good money."

"Aye, they do."

"So you kept that very quiet. Who's been minding them?" Jamie asked excitedly.

"Arjun Mansoor's wife," Ian said.

"What the fuck? You've got back into bed with old Argy Bargy. You're mad, Pop!"

"No, I'm not. With him and his brother-in-law inside his wife needed a job, and she's damn good at keeping the books straight."

"Well, I think you're insane. That old bastard Mansoor did

you over before, and I bet you'll find his wife's just as bad. But it's up to you."

"Yes, it is up to me. Now let's not fall out already, son. I know what faults the Mansoors have, but the wife doesn't ask any questions. Better the devil you know and all that, and, while Arjun Mansoor is still in the big house, he has nothing to do with this."

"You better hope not, Pop," Jamie said as he shook his head knowingly.

"Now, Jamie, let's change the subject. How's Harry?"

"Fine, as far as I can tell. As hyper as ever. Luckily he and his pal have hardly been in since they dumped their stuff. Just as well really; I've no idea where we're all going to sleep. The house is too wee."

"Don't worry about that, son. I've bought us a new place in Lauder Road. With twelve bedrooms, parking and a garden. There will be plenty of room for all of us, and a separate apartment for Frankie and his wee girls as they grow. They will have their own place within that fancy big house."

"Twelve bedrooms! You've got to be joking! Wow! I'll need to leave breadcrumbs to find my way around. Where is Lauder Road, then?"

"The Grange, son, the Grange."

"Lah-di-dah, won't the neighbours be glad to see the likes of us move in? How can we afford a place like that?"

"Ask no questions and I'll tell you no lies, my son. Safe to say, I didn't get done for robbing a bank for nothing, and the betting shops will pay the rest."

"Fuck, pop. The fuzz'll work that out."

"That's why it's not just in my name. But I hope you and Frankie, won't mind renting your old man a room or two."

"That's mental! How can me and our Frankie afford it, Pop?" Jamie shook his head and grinned.

"I'll explain it better when I get you and Frankie together. But not today, lad. Let's go home and enjoy being together, shall we?"

Ian started the car, and father and son drove off before any journalists arrived to witness the release.

Chapter Four

Only a few hours previously, Oleksander and Sergei Ponomarenko sat down to dinner. The names of these Ukrainian brothers struck fear into the hearts of those who opposed them. The brothers were known as the Priests. It was a pun on their surname meaning clergyman and the club or 'priest' used by anglers to dispatch their catch. Oleksander and Sergei had certainly caught and dispatched many people over the years.

Tucking into the tender fillet steaks and delicate dauphinoise potatoes before him, Oleksander poured himself another glass of the fine Bordeaux and handed the bottle to his younger brother.

"I am pleased with our new route into Scotland. It will serve us well, I think. Don't you, Sergei?"

"I hope so. We have not done business there before." Sergei emptied the bottle of wine and rang for the staff to bring another. "I will wait and see how it goes. You know I do not trust so easily as you, Oleksander. But time will tell if these local men you have found are as trustworthy as you say. I just hope you are right. It could cost us a lot of money if you are not."

"Don't be such a grouch, Sergei. The new business in Edinburgh is hungry for girls. It should be profitable for us. And with Xristina studying there, the new business will give me an excuse to visit her. "

"Like you need an excuse, Oleksander. Have you spoken to her?"

"Not recently, she seems to be too busy even to answer the phone to her beloved father."

"That's odd. Kids will be kids, I suppose. But she might

show you more respect," Sergei muttered. "Well. Just so you know, this business had better work out, as I have no plans to enter charitable works at my time of life."

"Nor me, brother," Oleksander smiled.

"I take it the next batch of girls from the orphanage are virgins?" Sergei asked.

Oleksander grimaced. "For the price we paid, they'd better be. They are certainly skinny enough: far skinnier than the last lot from the whore house. Far too skinny for my taste, that's for sure."

"The new fat woman we hired here cooks to my taste, though." Sergei chuckled at his own joke.

"Yes, thank goodness we do not have to eat your wife's dreadful cooking any more."

"At least I have a wife and she hasn't run away with the chauffeur," Sergei retorted.

Oleksander smiled. "I was glad to see her go. She saved me a fortune. Otherwise, I would have had to support her bastard son. Getting my wife out of my life has certainly simplified things, Sergei. You should think about it."

"You do know I am here, Oleksander, don't you?"

The third person at the table had eaten silently until now. The elegant, dark-haired Anya Sheptytsky Ponomarenko, had been a national beauty and noted socialite in her youth. She had ignored her family's warnings all those years ago about marrying beneath her into the ambitious Ponomarenko clan. There had been many times over the years when she had regretted her youthful stubbornness to proceed with the marriage. Perhaps she should have tried harder at school and travelled abroad like her cousin had done. Now, living and working in the West, he had a fine life there, her family told her.

Still, she could not fault the lifestyle Sergei provided for her and their children, but she was always careful never to enquire in detail about the sources of his wealth. The rumours were enough to curb her inquisitiveness: rumours of ruthlessness outside the home which spread about her husband and brother-in-law were amongst those she chose to ignore. That made life easier.

"Do you even know where your daughter is now, Oleksander? Do you even care?" Anya hissed. She was rarely this brave, but sometimes the brothers angered her so much.

"Of course I do! She studies in Edinburgh. Sergei, your wife is out of control. Will you permit her to speak to me like that?" Oleksander asked.

The woman's tears pricked the back of her eyes. There was no way she would allow Oleksander to see her cry. She excused herself and left the room quietly. Outside in the hallway, she wiped her tears before retiring to her room for the evening.

Oleksander scowled at his brother and then the men continued their meal in silence. Oleksander mused about their new venture and the additional wealth it promised, while he watched Sergei frowning. He knew his brother was considering the vast sums they would have to outlay to recoup a return. Oleksander had always seen things differently from Sergei. He was the older brother and thought of himself as charming and optimistic, whilst Sergei was much more introverted and cautious. But both of them had a ruthless and cruel streak.

Oleksander shared the second bottle of wine between them and rubbed his hands in expectation as they were served strong black coffee and slices of freshly baked sour cream poppyseed cake to finish their meal.

Chapter Five

"Why on earth would they chop off her fingers, Dad? And her poor face. It's gross!" Cameron stared in horror at the deformed body in front of him.

"Clearly somebody doesn't want us to know who this young lady is. Do you have any photos of her before this?" Hunter asked.

"No. She doesn't – didn't – like have her picture taken."

"Any of you girls got any pictures of Xristina?"

"No," Anichka said quickly.

"We didn't know her before," Symona said.

"She'd be pretty," Olena added.

Anichka shrugged. "If you don't know her how you know she pretty or no?"

Meera spoke. "Cameron, I know this is as horrible as it is fascinating, but can you gather all your friends and flatmates into the living room? I don't need this crime scene any more contaminated than it already is. Your dad will arrange for police officers to come over as soon as possible to take statements."

"No! No police! We cannot have with police," Anichka shouted.

"I don't want to get involved with the coppers," Gavin added.

"A bit late for that now," Hunter said sourly.

Just as Gavin was about to turn and make a dash for the door of the flat, he found the entrance blocked by the six-foot-four rugby-player frame of DC Tim Myerscough. Tim caught the young soldier around his shoulders with one arm, and held him still with the other. Tim knew that Gavin was in pain every time he moved as his left arm was pinned behind his back by Tim's vice-like grip. Gavin tried to kick Tim. This resulted in Tim moving swiftly to one side and yanking Gavin's arm further up his back.

"Who the hell are you? You're going to pull my arm off, ya big bastard," Gavin shouted.

"I'm DC Timothy Myerscough."

"You're a cop? You're a right big pig."

"Thanks, I think." said Tim. "Who are you, and where do you think you're going?"

"I'm nobody you know. Out of the way! I'm leaving."

"You're probably not, but I'll check," Tim said.

"Young Myerscough! Right time, right place. Well done," Hunter said.

"This guy seemed to think his time here was over, Boss. Is he right?"

"He knows he's not! I want him with the others in the living room. Then, Tim, you call and get a couple of uniforms over to take statements from the witnesses."

"Of course, Boss. Come on, you." Tim moved Gavin back down the hall.

"Get details of names and addresses of the witnesses while you wait for the constables. And I don't want any of them leaving until I have all I need from them," Hunter said.

"Shall I phone Dr Sharma?"

"No need for that, Tim. Good morning," called Meera's familiar voice from the kitchen.

"Good morning, Meera," Tim smiled at Hunter. Hunter looked at the tall, blond DC and blushed.

"Please could you call Samantha Hutchens, though, Tim?" Meera asked. "I need good photos of the victim, and I've just got my mobile here. That's not going to be clear enough."

"I'll do that. I'll call the CSI team too. And you want me to call the landlord as well, Boss? The tenants can't stay here tonight."

"No, you're right, they can't," Hunter said. "I think the lads will be all right. Cameron can come to mine and the young soldiers don't live here. I don't know about the girls. It might be best for you to call the landlord because you know him,

Tim."

"I do. I wouldn't call Lucky Buchanan a friend, but I know him well enough to phone him."

"Good. Carry on, Tim."

Gavin spoke again. "Could we decide what the fuck we're doing? My bloody arm's lost all its feeling being up my back for this long. You couldn't loosen your grip could you, big boy?"

"Correct. I couldn't," Tim said sharply as he marched Gavin the rest of the way along the hall to the living room. As they entered the room, Tim flicked the door shut behind him with his foot and let go his grip on Gavin. The living room was large and much better furnished than most rented places he had seen, but then it was in Frederick Street and the landlord was Lucky Buchanan. The monthly rent must be high. A lot higher than Tim imagined Cameron Wilson being able to afford.

A distinctive traditional red Afghan rug covered the middle of the floor, and red velvet curtains swept from floor to ceiling at the bay window. The tables were unfashionable dark wood, but antique, well-maintained and highly polished. The suite and chairs were not new, but had been re-covered in a camel-coloured tweed fabric designed to dissuade tenants from spending the night on the scratchy material. So far, that had worked. Cameron had not seen any merit in sleeping on the rough sofa when he had been supplied with a comfortable bed.

"When did the girls move in here, Cameron?" Tim asked.

"Only Xristina lives here. A big, huge guy who works for Lucky brought her here and gave me five hundred quid and told me she was moving in. We only met up with the others tonight."

"My goodness. Okay. Well, Cameron, can you close those curtains, please?" Tim asked.

Cameron got up without saying more and pulled the curtains shut.

Gavin complained to the girls about police harassment and how he had suffered because Tim had assaulted him.

Harry had taken a photo of the dead girl. He would send that to his brother. Frankie would freak: it would be a laugh.

20

***

"What the fuck are you doing phoning me at this time in the morning, Myerscough?" Lucky shouted. "In fact, what the fuck are you doing calling me at all?"

"You've not mellowed with age, Lucky. Just as charming as never."

"Why don't you just get used to the fact that Sophie is with me now, and neither of us care if we never hear from you again?"

"You are welcome to the lovely Lady Sophie Dalmore, Lucky," Tim sighed. "Believe me, I couldn't care less who she's with or what she does. However, this isn't about her. I understand you own a flat in Frederick Street. One of your tenants was found dead there in the early hours of this morning. I thought you might want to be kept informed."

"Good God! I've only the one property in Frederick Street. It's left over from my student days. Father bought it for me and I just kept it after I inherited his property and title. It must be Cameron Wilson who's dead. Poor guy. Good driver. Loyal bloke. What happened?"

"We don't know yet. But it's not Cameron who died. It's the young female tenant."

"I don't have any female tenants, Myerscough. I gave Cameron a driving job with me and the flat came with the position. He lives there alone."

"Not so, Lucky. At the last count there was definitely a female in the flat: the dead girl. Cameron says one of your employees brought her in," Tim replied, staring straight at Cameron.

"Tim, I'm coming over. It may take me just under an hour to get there, but this is not making any sense. I know nothing about any girl."

"See you then." Tim ended the call.

Tim glanced at Hunter as he entered the room. He noticed it was unusually quiet. All the witnesses were just sitting looking at him. The horror of what had occurred there that night was just sinking in. It had probably seemed unreal when they all

21

got back from the club, drunk and in high spirits. Now Tim could see in their faces that it was all too real.

"Tim, Samantha Hutchens has just arrived. I understand the CSI team will be here shortly, and PC Angus McKenzie and PC Scott Clark are setting up a cordon around the entrance to the building then they'll start going door-to-door to find out what anybody saw or heard. Sergeant Charlie Middleton and DC Neil Larkin will be up to start taking statements."

"That's great, Boss," Tim said quietly. "I've spoken to Lucky. He's on his way too."

"Good. He'll need to make arrangements for these young ladies to stay elsewhere."

"Yes. That's what I thought. But... Well, the thing is, Lucky says he doesn't have any female tenants. He says that Cameron got this place to stay in as part of the package for his job. When I told him one of his tenants had been found dead, Lucky immediately thought it was Cameron. Lucky's an arse, but I do believe him. He has no reason to lie about that."

"Cameron, come over here," Hunter called to his son. The three men stepped out of the living room into the hall. "Cameron, who are the young women? When did they move into the flat and who gave them the right to stay here?"

Cameron looked genuinely puzzled. "What do you mean, Dad?"

"I mean what I say. Who are they?"

"Only Xristina stays here in the other room. Well, I suppose Xristina doesn't stay here now she's dead," Cameron muttered.

"Lucky says only you were meant to live here. The flat comes with your job, Cameron," Tim said.

"No. Xristina was moved in by someone who came from the boss, but it's true the boys only picked up Olena and Symona at the club tonight, and I've never seen the other one. Don't even know what she's doing here."

"How would she get in?"

"I keep a key under the mat, for when I come home drunk and I've lost my keys," Cameron muttered. "But the lock on the door was broken when we got here and it just swung open."

"Really, son? When did Xristina move in?" Hunter asked, a little more gently.

"A few weeks ago. I've never seen the other red-headed one before. She must have come to visit Xristina when I was at the club, tonight."

"Who said Xristina was to stay here?"

"I don't know. Some big guy who works for Lord Buchanan."

"Or maybe not," Tim said.

"What do you mean? I'm not lying, Dad. He said he worked for my landlord and I was to keep her here. Dad, what's going on?"

"I wish I knew, Cameron. I don't think you're lying, son, but somebody is. Anyway, Lucky Buchanan is on his way now. Maybe he can shed some light on the subject."

Chapter Six

Frankie beamed as he shook his uncle's hand.

"Good to have you back, Uncle Ian," he said.

"It's good to be back, Frankie. My, how those wee girls are growing! Are you feeding them fertilizer, man?" Ian Thomson smiled at his great-nieces Kylie-Ann and Dannii-Ann. He bent down and picked them both up, one in each arm.

"Aren't they lovely? They take after their Mam, with that red hair." Frankie grinned proudly. When the twins' mother, Annie, died, Frankie had made a promise to himself, and to her, to do his very best for their girls. Although he was young, he had certainly made good on the promise.

"They are lovely and bright as little buttons. They get that from our side of the family. Do you ever see anything of Joe Johnson?"

"Annie's pop? Aye, sometimes. No' often."

Ian sat down on the large black leather sofa with a baby on either side of him.

"This is the life. Now which of you wasters is going to get me a decent cup of tea?"

Frankie turned on his heels and went through to the kitchen. "That'd be me, Uncle Ian. We've got Jaffa cakes, too."

Jamie laughed. "We've always got Jaffa cakes."

***

As the three men sat drinking tea, watching the babies playing with their toes, Ian told his son and nephew about the new property he had purchased for them.

"I knew we needed a bigger place," Ian said.

"Aye, but we don't need twelve bedrooms, Pop," Jamie laughed.

"Well, we're no' far off. One each for us, that's three. Harry will need a room when he's here. Then, it'll no' be too long before these wee mites each need a room."

"That takes us to six, Uncle Ian. Are we going to open a Bed & Breakfast joint in the rest?" Frankie grinned.

"No, lad. But a couple of guest rooms, an office out of the way of things for me, and a playroom for the girls, and we're all but there. Anyway, these houses don't come onto the market very often. They usually sell to friends of friends by word of mouth. So, when this one came up for sale, I just clinched the deal."

"It must be nearly a million smackers," Jamie said.

"And the rest," Ian laughed.

"So just how did you, me and Frankie manage to come up with the dosh for a twelve-bedroomed house in Lauder Road, Pop?" Jamie asked.

"Do you really want me to answer that, son?"

"Probably not."

"I'll just say that the new betting shops, Thomson's Bets, is apparently the source of most of the funds and, as you have been running the showroom, your off-shore business accounts will be seen to finance the small mortgage. The cash, of course, is clean as a whistle."

"Laundered to within an inch of its life, you mean," Jamie said.

"When did we ever have off-shore business accounts, Jamie?" Frankie wanted to know. "I have enough trouble giving folk the right change!"

"True enough! And Pop's bought these couple of betting shops when he was inside an' all!"

"You've been busy, Uncle Ian," Frankie laughed.

"But listen, Frankie," Jamie said. "You'll never guess who's managing them. Only Arjun Mansoor's Mrs."

"Mansoor? Old Argy Bargy? Are you mad, Uncle Ian? Why did you do that? You know that man's trouble."

"Maybe, Frankie, but it's his wife I've taken on. At least I know what he's like, and his wife is a bloody good book-keeper."

"Have it your way, but it'll all end in tears. Your tears. Wait till Harry hears about this," Frankie said.

"Where is Harry, anyway?" Ian asked, grasping at the change of subject before Jamie and Frankie decided to ask more about the money for their new home or Mrs Mansoor.

"He's not been back since he dumped his stuff. He's got a pal with him, Gavin, and they got showered and out to the pub faster than you would think possible," Frankie said.

"Can't blame the lad, can you? It must be heavy going in Afghanistan. Still, I suppose it's the life he chose. Any more tea going? Then we'll jump in the car and I'll show you our new home."

"Aye That would be great! We'd love to see it, wouldn't we, Frankie?"

"Yes, please."

"And then do you fancy going to the pub, Pop?"

"I'll make us a cuppa now," Frankie said as he gathered the mugs to make more tea, "but after we get back, I'll have to sort the girls with their meal. So youse two go. It'll be good for you to get out together."

Ian smiled. "That'd be good, Frankie. Then maybe, one time, I can sit in with the girls after they get used to having me around. It'd let you young ones out on the town."

"That'd be right good, Uncle Ian."

"So when do we move into the new place?" Jamie asked.

"Friday," said Ian.

"Friday? That's three days!" Jamie looked over at Frankie.

"We won't manage that..." Frankie began.

"We can and we will. The removers arrive at eight o'clock Friday morning to pack us all up and we'll be in our new place by dinner time," Ian smiled.

"Are you sure, Uncle Ian?" Frankie asked.

"Yes, I am. You two go to the showroom as usual, the girls will go to their child-minder and when you come home, you'll just come home to our new place and I'll show you round."

"It sounds like you mean our new palace, rather than place, if it's that big," Frankie said.

"Come on then, lads. Let's go and have a look at it."

26

***

"DI Hunter Wilson, may I introduce Lord Lachlan Buchanan, more commonly known as Lucky? He owns the flat here," Tim said.

"DI Wilson, I've heard good things about you. Call me Lucky. But there's nothing common about it, Timmy boy," The young man gritted his teeth as he held out his hand to shake Hunter's. "I'm sorry;, it took me longer to get here than I thought it would."

"No problem, Lucky. It's good of you to come and help us sort this out," Hunter said. "So you employ my son? What on earth does he do for you that makes him eligible for an elegant New Town apartment like this?"

"He's my driver, DI Hunter."

"How did he qualify for that job? He's got three points on his licence."

"Cameron and I went through rehab together. I want to give the boy a chance. I would have thought you might be pleased?"

"I don't understand why you chose Cameron for this position," Hunter said, "and when I don't understand something, I get suspicious. Always have done. It goes with the job."

Lucky frowned. "Well, I don't understand who broke the lock on my door. That makes me suspicious."

"Speaking of not understanding things, where is Cameron? Tim said something about there being a woman here, but as far as I am aware Cameron is the only tenant. So I want to know where this woman has come from."

Meera appeared at Hunter's side. "I don't know where this one came from, but I know where she's going. Hunter, I'm going to follow the victim back to mortuary. Sam is just taking a few final pictures and then she'll be leaving with me too."

"Okay, Meera. That's fine. Did you find the extra bits?" Hunter asked. He wanted to contain, as far as possible, the information about the removal of the fingertips.

"Unfortunately not. If CSI can't find them, I'll have to work with what we've got."

"Extra bits?" Lucky asked.

"She's missing her fingertips," Tim said.

Hunter glared at Tim. He noticed that Lucky looked as if he was going to be sick.

"If I leave the post mortem until this afternoon, will that give you time to attend?" Meera asked Hunter.

"Yes, indeed, that's fine. I'll be with you for a two o'clock start."

"As dates go, this one has to be very near the bottom of the heap." Meera smiled as she and Samantha left the flat.

"Boss, I need to get home and have a shower. Will that be alright now the uniforms are on their way?" Tim asked.

"Of course, young Myerscough."

"Briefing at ten?" Tim asked.

"Yes, Tim. Lucky and I are going to talk to Cameron and see what we can find out about the two red-haired young women. One is dead, the other Cameron has never seen before."

"I want to know who they are and why they are in my flat. And I certainly don't want to become responsible for finding homes for any squatters!" Lucky grumbled.

Hunter nodded at Lucky and followed him along the corridor.

Chapter Seven

Oleksander and Sergei always found it easy to contact their business associates in Scotland, so Oleksander was surprised that he was having such difficulty contacting his daughter. She had begged to study for her PhD at the University of Edinburgh. Apparently, the great Professor Sheptytsky had moved there. Sheptytsky was the cousin of his sister-in-law, but Oleksander was not impressed by the man. Still, he did see Xristina studying there as an excellent excuse to expand his business Edinburgh into the UK.

Now, however, he couldn't help thinking how rebellious young people were today. He knew his father would never have permitted him to travel or study in a foreign country, even if he had wanted to learn a foreign language. But he really couldn't understand why he had not managed to get hold of her. Anyway, it was for her to respect the father and contact him: not he who should chase after the daughter. After all, he had ensured she had the best mobile phone on the market – and he paid the bill.

He was quite pleased that he and Sergei had managed to make contact with Arjun Mansoor. The man had come highly recommended. Although he was in jail, the man was said to be a master manipulator and with fingers in more pies than Kiev had bakeries. Oleksander had found that to be true. He found that nothing was too much trouble for Arjun Mansoor, if it came to making money. It was through Mansoor that his wife had been appointed manager of two new betting shops, owned by an acquaintance of Mansoor's, Ian Thomson. Both shops were in the centre of Edinburgh. Both shops had large turnovers. Both shops were excellent for laundering the money the professional women would bring in for the business he and Sergei had established.

Although Mrs Mansoor managed both shops, Oleksander had already found her book-keeping to be exemplary. The woman had no difficulty keeping four sets of books. One for him, one for Ian Thomson, one for the tax man, and one showing the small premium he paid to Mansoor for facilitating the deal. Also, she was blessed with a singular lack of curiosity: that probably came from being married to a man like Arjun Mansoor.

**

Tim was pleased that Gillian had not left for work when he got home. He saw her wander out of the bathroom towelling her hair dry. Tim smiled at Gillian and pulled her to him. As her towel fell to the ground, he picked her up. She held his face in her hands and kissed him passionately. He loved hearing her giggle as he carried her across the room. He laid her softly onto the bed and undressed quickly before lying beside her and covering her body with delicate kisses as she moaned with pleasure and anticipation.

**

"I'm going to need another shower before I go into work at the University, DC Myerscough. Luckily I'm not giving my first lecture until eleven o'clock," Gillian teased as she ran her hands through Tim's thick, short, blond hair.

"Is that a complaint, Dr Pearson?" Tim grinned.

"Not at all! Just an observation."

"I need a shower too. But I need to be at my briefing by ten. Let's cut time and shower together."

"Only if we just shower, Tim. I do need to get to work."

"Me too, spoilsport."

"That's not what you were saying a minute ago!"

" No I was not!" Tim changed the subject as the water splashed around them and he washed Gillian's back. "Is your new boss easy to work with?"

"Professor Sheptytsky? Yes, he is a fascinating man, too. Comes from an aristocratic family in Ukraine. I'd love to visit Ukraine and Russia. I believe Georgia is beautiful too."

"Gillian, you would go to the opening of a paper bag, you love to travel so much!" Tim kissed the green flash at the front of Gillian's hair. It reflected the emerald green of her eyes. He smiled as he turned off the shower and led the way to the bedroom.

***

Tim entered the briefing room at two minutes to ten. He noticed the frown on Hunter's face when he saw him arrive.

"Nice of you to join us, young Myerscough," Hunter said.

"With respect, Sir, I'm not late."

"Only just. Let's move on."

"DI Wilson, will you lead us off?" DCI Allan Mackay turned to Hunter.

"Of course, Sir." Hunter looked around the room at his team. He was proud of them. Hunter noticed that Tim had gravitated to the back of the room and was standing beside DC Bear Zewedu. He knew the two men had been friends since school days and still played rugby together. At six feet two inches tall the Ethiopian DC was only two inches shorter than Tim, but his shoulders were equally broad. They made a good pair.

DC Mel Grant was sitting directly in front of the big men. Hunter couldn't remember how long she and Bear had been an item, but he thought it was about time the man made an honest woman of her and married her. Hunter smiled to himself. He knew he was being old-fashioned.

DC Nadia Chan and DS Colin Reid sat to Mel's right. The two of them had made an unexpectedly good partnership after Colin's previous partner, John Hamilton, had resigned from the force in disgrace. Hunter was pleased he had been able to keep Colin on his team after the younger man passed his sergeant's exams.

This had only become possible after DS Jane Renwick had been accepted for the Specialist Crime Division in Gartcosh, after the creation of Police Scotland in April 2013. Hunter was sorry to lose Jane from his team, but knew that she would be a tremendous asset to the new MIT. Jane's civil partner, DC Rachael Anderson, was the other member of his team in the room. Hunter was aware that she had applied to joint the Victim Support Unit, but was pleased that no decision had yet been made. The longer he had Rachael in his team, the happier Hunter would be.

"You all know PC Angus McKenzie. He has been seconded to us and will be working as a DC for the first time. Rachael, can you take Angus under your wing?"

"Yes, Boss," Rachael replied, although her words were almost drowned out by Bear's cheering and shouts for beer at the new DC's expense.

"Thank you people," Angus smiled. Angus had been born and raised on the western Isle of Harris and Hunter knew that he still found Edinburgh big, busy and noisy. Still, Hunter was sure that the quiet man would make a good addition to his team.

Hunter took a deep breath and began to explain what he had witnessed at his son's flat in Frederick Street.

"Do we know how the girl died?" Mel asked.

"Not yet. We don't know if she was beaten around the head before or after death. But it looks like her face was purposefully disfigured and her fingertips removed after death, as there was no sign that she had struggled and there was little blood from her hands. It looks as if she might have been surprised by her attacker."

"I don't like to say this, Sir, but is your son in the frame?" Angus asked.

"For your first question as a DC you haven't avoided the elephant in the room, DC McKenzie," Mackay said solemnly.

Hunter spoke again. "Until we know the time of death, theoretically he could have killed the girl. But this was such a frenzied attack, and quite outside Cameron's nature, that I would stake my career it wasn't him."

"What about the girl Cameron found there that he doesn't know?" Angus asked.

"Uniform are taking statements, but she seems to have stopped in to visit the dead woman," Hunter replied.

"Whoever did this, it's disgusting. Why would anybody do that?" Nadia looked at Colin.

"Whoever did it doesn't want us to know who the victim is. So who is she?" Allan Mackay asked softly.

"We don't know yet, nor do we have photos of the girl before the assault, Sir. All we know is her first name was Xristina," Hunter said.

"Or at least that's the name she used," Mackay said.

"Yes. Let me attend the post-mortem and find out what I can from that."

"Of course, Hunter. You do realise we are going to have to pass this on to MIT? They will expect to deal with this murder case now that we're all one happy family, don't you think?" Mackay said. "Major Incident Teams take the lead now on murders and other major crimes."

"Well, Sir, I wondered if I might speak to you about that. As the crime occurred in my son's home—"

"All the more reason for you to hand it over, Hunter," Mackay interrupted.

"Possibly, yes, Sir. However, my son's mental health is very delicate. It's no secret that he's only recently left rehab to get over a drug addiction."

"And so you are too close to this, Hunter," Mackay said firmly.

"I wondered if we might ask for someone to be assigned to us from Gartcosh for the duration of this investigation, Sir. Perhaps someone well-known to our team who might be able to assist us with their new expertise in the MIT?"

"DS Jane Renwick? Very clever, Hunter. But you can't expect MIT to accept that a murder investigation would be run by a DS, even one as able as Jane. Let me speak to her superior officer and see if we can work something out. In the meantime, do you want to take a second pair of eyes to the post-mortem?"

"Yes. Thanks, Sir. I appreciate this. I'll take Nadia with me this afternoon. The rest of them have too weak a stomach," Hunter looked at Bear and thought he had the good grace to blush.

"Nadia, you will accompany DI Wilson to the young woman's post-mortem starting at 2pm."

"Yes, Boss. That will be most interesting."

"In the meantime," Mackay continued, "we'll have to call a brief press conference to explain our, rather obvious, crime scene in Frederick Street. It's such a major artery of the city that we have no choice."

"Do you want me, and perhaps Nadia, to join you, Sir?"

"Yes, Nadia is a good choice. Get the press officer to arrange it for eleven-thirty, will you, Hunter? Bear, can you get us a dedicated phone number, with, say ten lines, by then so that we can give it out to the journalists?"

"Will do, Sir."

"Not that I expect anyone who knows anything useful to call us. However, we might get told, yet again, who Jack the Ripper was and who killed the dinosaurs," Mackay sighed and drew the briefing to a close.

"Sir, I'm going to have my son sit down with a sketch artist this afternoon and see if we can get an idea of what this man who brought the girl to his flat looked like."

"Good idea, Hunter. We're sure this Lucky Buchanan is telling the truth?"

"Fairly sure. When Tim told him about the murder victim in his flat, he immediately thought it was Cameron, because he believed Cameron lived there alone," Hunter explained.

"What does your son say?" Mackay asked.

"He says that a few weeks ago a big man wearing a cheap, two-piece suit and with a local accent, turned up with Xristina and five hundred pounds, and told Cameron she was to stay in there, his boss said so. Cameron thought he meant Lucky Buchanan, and as the flat has two bedrooms, he took the money and gave the girl his second bedroom. Instructions from the landlord, he thought. The money was to feed her, allegedly."

"How odd," Mackay said.

"Yes, Sir. He was told he wasn't to ask any questions, if he knew what was good for him."

"Hunter," Mackay said quiety, "I am sorry to ask you this, but can we trust your son?"

Chapter Eight

Frankie was sitting between the twins in the back of Ian's old car, staring at the most enormous house he had ever seen, when his phone sounded to let him know a text had arrived.

"Oh yuck!" Frankie said.

"What's the matter with you, Frankie? It's a beautiful house!" Ian said.

"Aye, it's great. But it's this here." Frankie said

"The girls puked or something?" Jamie asked.

"Nah. Harry's sent me a picture of a dead body he saw after the club last night. The coppers have been questioning him cos he's a witness."

"What?" Jamie asked.

"See!" Frankie handed the phone to Jamie.

"That's gross, man! Someone's nuked her face and it looks like they've cut off her fingers. That's mental!" Jamie showed the photo to Ian.

"What a fucking waste of a life," Ian Thomson said.

"When did this happen? Does he say?" Jamie asked.

"Nope. Just that he couldn't get home cos the cops are asking tons of questions and won't let any of them leave until they've spoken to everybody."

"Leave where? That doesn't look like a club. It looks like someone's kitchen. What the hell has that stupid sod been up to this time? Talk about overshadowing my big surprise."

"No, no, Pop, the house is great, isn't it Frankie?" Jamie said.

"Aye, it's great. And me and the twins get our wee bit of the place?"

"Yep," Ian said. "There's an annex, probably a granny flat once, with two living rooms, three bedrooms a kitchen and bathroom. I thought that would give you and the wee ones you own space."

"That's brilliant, isn't it, girls?" Frankie smiled at his daughters.

The twins played with their toes.

Ian Thomson turned on the ignition and put the car in gear. He wanted to find out what kind of trouble his older nephew had got himself into. The lad couldn't have been back in the city twenty-four hours before getting himself into a shitload of mess with the cops. Ian didn't like that at all.

"Frankie, call that numpty of a brother of yours and let's find out what's going on. I'll get you and the girls home, then Jamie and me can go and rescue him."

***

When the police officers let them leave, Harry and Gavin had walked the three miles from Frederick Street to West Mains Road and were draped over either end of the large black leather sofa when Ian's car pulled up outside the house. They did not stir when Ian and his passengers thundered into the living room.

"No surprise Harry didn't answer his phone," Ian said.

"I'll get the twins changed and fed and leave these guys in peace," Frankie said.

"Jamie and me are off to the pub. See you later, Frankie," Ian said.

Chapter Nine

Hunter answered the call from Sergeant Charlie Middleton. He listened quietly and agreed that they did not want to lose track of the three girls from Cameron's flat. But Hunter was not surprised that Lucky was unwilling to accommodate them. They were nothing to do with Lucky; Hunter wanted to know who they were and why they were here.

"And all three of them seemed remarkably reluctant to say anything, gov," Charlie said.

"Do they speak English?" Hunter asked.

"A bit. They say they didn't know the dead girl before they saw her dead, but who knows what to believe? I don't trust the Russians at all, that's for sure."

"What about the other witnesses?" Hunter asked.

"We've finished the witness interviews, and all the other witnesses have been released with a stern reminder to make themselves available as and when necessary. Should be fine – there's your boy, that Lord Lucky whatever, and a couple of soldier boys on leave from Afghanistan. However, gov, I'm just too long in the tooth to trust these three Russian girls to play the game properly. We're bringing them in."

"On what grounds?"

"They're Russian, they don't know our rules."

"But you bloody do. You better have a good reason for bringing them in by the time you arrive at the station!" Hunter ended the call, then looked up to see Bear standing at his door.

"That's the phone number all set up, Boss. Here it is." Bear handed him a sheet of paper.

"Thanks Bear."

"I wouldn't like you to think I'd been listening to your call with Charlie, Boss," he began.

"But..."

"But he does talk very loudly on the phone."

"He does. I think in his day they used two tin cans and a piece of string." Hunter smiled.

"It's just that I heard him referring to the female witnesses as Russian, but the names on the whiteboard sound more Ukrainian to me."

"And when did you become such an expert on the nuances of Eastern European and Russian girls' names, Bear?"

"What can I say, Boss?" The big man shrugged and smiled.

Tim stuck his head around the door. "And remember, Boss, he did his A-level History on Russia, or rather the old USSR. Mind you, he failed that."

"A 'D' at A-level isn't that bad," Bear said indignantly.

"If you're royal, big man – and you're not!" Tim grinned.

"Do you think we could draw this Punch & Judy show to a close, gentlemen?" Hunter said. "What are you doing here, anyway, Tim? Apart from teasing Bear, that is?"

"Well, I called Lucky, just to thank him for coming out so quickly."

"Good idea to keep him onside. I think he's put Cameron up in The Sheraton, the big fancy hotel in Lothian Road, while the Frederick Street flat is still a crime scene. All right for some. My boy seems to have really landed on his feet working for Lucky."

"I hope it lasts," Bear said. "I don't trust Lucky as far as I can throw him. He was an arse on the rugby field and he's still an arse now."

"I agree with you, Bear," Tim said. "But he did mention one thing that might be of interest."

"Always a first," Bear said.

"What did he say, Tim?" Hunter asked.

"Well, you know Cameron said the dead girl's name was Xristina?"

"A Ukrainian name," Bear nodded.

"Well, Lucky mentioned that one of the big Ukrainian gangster families, which has ties to the Russian Mafia, is led by the Ponomarenko brothers Oleksander and Sergei."

"Brilliant! That's what the meerkats in that advert are called. How can we take these fellows seriously?" Bear laughed.

"If they have their claws into the city we need to take it very seriously," Tim said.

"We do, but how does Lucky know so much about them?" Hunter asked.

"I didn't ask. He has some really dodgy contacts."

"What's this got to do with Xristina?" Hunter asked.

"Lucky says it's like this, Boss. The older brother, Oleksander, has a daughter named Xristina. And Gillian said they had a new PhD student in her department named Xristina Marenko, rather than Ponomarenko. I know it's not the same, but it's a bit of a coincidence, don't you think?" Tim's solemn blue eyes met Hunter's steely gaze.

"I don't believe in coincidences, as you well know, young Myerscough. You boys find a photo of this girl Xristina Marenko, her father and uncle on line. Get Colin and Mel to find out all they can about the brothers' 'business', and I'll attend the post-mortem with Nadia. I want Rachael to meet with the other three girls when they arrive. She and Charlie can play good cop/bad cop and young Angus can stand in. Good experience for him."

"No prizes for guessing who's going to play the good cop," Bear smiled.

"I'll stop in to DCI Mackay and get him to call a briefing for five o'clock this evening and we can all compare notes. Well, on you go! Don't just stand there looking at me." Hunter waved Tim and Bear away from his door and went to speak to Mackay, then left with Nadia to go to the mortuary.

Chapter Ten

"Miss Ailsa! How lovely to have you back. And Mister Timothy tells us you are back for good?" Kenneth said as he lifted Ailsa Myerscough's suitcases into the hall.

"Well, certainly for the foreseeable future. I have secured a job as a registrar at the Royal Infirmary of Edinburgh in their Accident and Emergency Department."

"That's wonderful! Your mother would be so proud of you. Of both of you. Such a pity." Kenneth shook his head.

Ailsa had only been twelve and her brother Tim fifteen when their mother died of cancer. Ailsa hugged the family butler, Kenneth, spontaneously. She doted on him, and his wife, Alice, who acted as cook and housekeeper. She treasured them as dearly as family. They were the only remaining permanent staff from those heady days before her mother died.

Ailsa became aware of another pair of eyes watching her from the end of the hallway.

"Miss Ailsa, I wasn't expecting you until dinner time. Let me give you a hug, young lady," the cook said, holding her arms out.

Ailsa moved towards the woman who had nursed her through those difficult teenage years, when forgiving her mother for leaving her had been such a challenge that neither her dad nor Tim had known what to say or do. She hugged Alice tightly.

"It's so good to be back, and I'll be able to help you both look after that big brother of mine."

"I'm counting on it," Kenneth smiled.

"Well, my new job doesn't start until the beginning of November, so I'll have a couple of weeks to settle back into the way of life in Edinburgh."

"Yes, you've been away a long time," Alice said. "You really haven't been back much since you left to go to Cambridge University."

"I'll take your cases up. We've put you in your old room, will that be suitable, Miss Ailsa?" Kenneth asked.

"Of course! I wouldn't have it any other way. I don't suppose you've made scones, Alice?"

"I have indeed; nice fresh, fruit scones. Come through to the kitchen and we'll have some with a cup of tea and Kenneth's home-made strawberry jam."

***

Nadia had only been to a mortuary once before: this mortuary, with DI Hunter Wilson. Still, the approach to the Edinburgh City Mortuary through the canyon of tall tenement buildings in The Cowgate made her shudder. No sun reached the ground, and the street reflected shadows of dark blues and purples like a fresh bruise.

The street was narrow: only one lane wide in each direction, and the pavements were tight too. She stared at the steep gradients leading off to either side. The Cowgate was close to the Grassmarket, and both derived their names from historic times when the streets were places of business on market days.

As they approached the mortuary, Nadia glanced at Hunter and noticed he was frowning. She saw there was nowhere obvious to park, so she gripped on to the handle of the car door as Hunter made a sudden, sharp turn and swung the car into the mortuary car park. He drew up at the rear beside the anonymous black 'private ambulances' outside the old Victorian building.

Hunter led the way into the building and found Meera waiting for them.

"Good afternoon, Meera. You remember DC Chan?" Hunter said formally.

"Of course. How nice to see you again, Nadia."

"And you, Doctor Sharma. But so sad about this young woman, isn't it?"

"Indeed."

"Another young life lost, I think you mean," Hunter muttered.

"Your gowns and covers are through there. Put them on and come in when you are ready," Meera said, pointing towards the cloak room.

"Good afternoon, Hunter," Dr David Murray said as they entered the room. "And DC Chan. I'm not surprised to see you, Nadia. You didn't faint or throw up last time. I think you will end up being DI Wilson's 'go to' girl for post-mortems." He grinned.

Nadia smiled. "I found the experience most interesting. Of course it is sad if you think of the person. But by the time the body comes to you, Doctor Murray, the spirit is long gone. You are just dealing with the container."

"Well, this container has certainly been chipped," Meera said.

Meera began her examination and spoke clearly into a microphone which was attached to a recorder in her pocket. When the formal description and measurements had been ascertained, Meera looked closely at the girl's face and head.

"Death seems to be the result of blunt force trauma to the back of the head. Can you see that, here?" she asked Hunter and Nadia. Her face has clearly been disfigured during the violent beating too, but it looks as if the attack on her fingers was post mortem, as there was no blood loss from these wounds. See?" Meera said to Nadia.

"I certainly think this blow here to the back of the skull won't have done her any good," Nadia grimaced.

"That's an understatement," Meera said quietly. Meera then scraped some skin from the girl's head and placed it in a container. "I'll send that for analysis in case the wound has the remnants of anything that can tell us what was used to hit her."

"Shocking," David commented.

"I presume nobody wanted us to be able to identify her, because they took her fingertips off too, removing the fingerprints," Hunter said.

"I'm sure you're right, Hunter," Meera said. "But although

43

she has been attacked around her face, it has not affected too much of her bone structure, and she still has her hair. I'm sure one of your sketch artists could get a pretty good likeness of her, despite the injuries."

"I wondered about that. If we needed it, where could we get the head reconstructed?" Hunter asked.

"I would never go past Dr Caroline Erolin at the Forensic Art Department at Dundee University," Meera said. "There is a woman who knows skulls! She and her department handle every skull with immense care. Her work is second to none, and when she's finished, every skull reveals the keys to the flesh that once sat on it."

"High praise indeed," Hunter said.

"Well deserved. She reconstructed the head of a murdered child for me a few years back. The likeness was uncanny."

"So if it wasn't the attack to her face that killed our victim, what was used to do that?" Nadia asked.

"I don't know yet, Nadia, but probably the same implement that was used on her skull," Meera said.

"Can you tell when she died, Meera?" Hunter asked.

"On the basis of what I saw and learned in Cameron's flat, and what I've seen now, I would put the time of death before three o'clock this morning."

"When Cameron left the club. It's some kind of a relief, that he was out, I suppose," Hunter said.

"To you, maybe, but not to this girl's family," Meera said. She held the victim's right hand and bent down to look at it closely. "This jewellery looks valuable, so robbery was not a motive."

"The removal of the fingertips would be terribly painful, but, again that wouldn't kill her, even if she had been alive when that was done," David said.

"But she wasn't, was she?" Hunter asked.

"No. Definitely not." David agreed. "But I wouldn't be surprised if this girl had been subdued with rohypnol or ketamine before the attack. They're both date rape drugs, but there's no sign of sexual interference. It's all very odd. I'll get a toxicology report ordered and find out."

Hunter and Nadia arrived back at the police station just a few minutes late for the briefing.

Mackay scowled at them as they walked in. He was sure he saw the other officers grinning. That did not surprise him; Hunter always made a biting comment if any of them were late.

"Good of you to make the time to join us, DI Wilson and DC Chan," Mackay said sarcastically.

Nadia went bright red and looked at the floor.

"Apologies, Sir, my fault," Hunter said. "The post mortem overran, and we got caught up in rush hour traffic trying to cross the city."

"Carry on, DS Anderson," Mackay said to Rachael.

"Well, as I was saying, Sir, when Charlie, I mean Sergeant Middleton, and I were interviewing the three females, we saw each of them them individually. None of them claims to have been familiar with the Xristina woman, prior to the visit to Cameron Wilson's flat after the night club."

"Cameron and the two soldiers did say that Symona and Olena were handing out vouchers for the massage parlour in Lothian Road where they work," Hunter said.

"Yes, Boss, and Symona, Olena and Anichka all work there and know one another. Apparently they are professional women, here to make their fortunes. Or that's what they were told back in Kiev when they paid all they had to get here."

"Which profession? Doctors?" Mackay asked.

"No, Sir." Rachael smiled. "They're prostitutes from Kiev."

Chapter Eleven

Oleksander Ponomarenko introduced himself as Mr Marenko when the University of Edinburgh switchboard answered his call, and he was swiftly connected with the Modern Languages Department. He smiled down the phone and his voice was dripping, sweet as honey, into the ear of the woman trying to help him. This Dr Gillian Pearson was most unusual, he thought. Her grasp of Ukrainian was excellent. Usually, he had to revert to the Russian language with foreigners. He explained to her that he was Xristina's father and that he had been unable to contact her for the last few days.

"I found her a second floor apartment in Frederick Street to live in. I am told it is central, and large. Perhaps you know that area, Doctor Pearson?"

"Indeed, I do. It is right in the middle of our historic New Town."

"I beg your pardon, Doctor Pearson, but how can a New Town be historic?"

"That is a good question, Mr Marenko," the woman laughed. "The centre of Edinburgh consists of two parts: the Old Town (or Royal Mile) and the New Town. The New Town is only new by comparison: it is 250 years old whereas the Old Town is nearer 500 years old."

"My goodness, I will look forward to exploring your city when I visit Xristina."

"I'm sure you will enjoy it. But as for putting you in touch with Xristina, I will be happy to ask her to call you when I see her, but I haven't seen her in the Department recently. Have you tried calling her at the flat?"

"Of course I have done that!" Oleksander's tone of voice changed sharply.

"Indeed," Gillian replied calmly. "Xristina is very diligent and usually in the library most days. I have never known her be absent before, Mr Marenko. Perhaps she is unwell and being cared for at the home of a friend?"

"So ill that she cannot phone her loving father or even take a call? I think that is unlikely, Doctor Pearson, don't you?"

"Perhaps she has run out of credit on her phone?" Gillian suggested.

"That is certainly not the case, my good woman," Oleksander snapped.

Gillian sighed. "May I take a message and ask her to call you when I see her?"

"Tell her to phone me!" Oleksander shouted and rang off abruptly.

"If I were Xristina, I don't think I'd be too bothered to take those calls either," Gillian muttered in Ukrainian, as she too rang off.

***

Sergeant Charlie Middleton was in an excellent mood. In three days he was off on holiday back to Antalya in Turkey with the wife. They were going on an all-inclusive package with a direct flight from Edinburgh. Magic! Five hours and a couple of beers on the plane, and then seven whole days of all the sunshine, beer, vodka and grub they could get through. Even a wee cocktail or two for the wife. No extra charge! Charlie did like an all-inclusive tariff and he was always determined to get the best of the deal.

Charlie knew that PC Neil Larkin had never experienced the cheerful Charlie before, and he was amused that Neil clearly found it rather unnerving. The sergeant had even made him a cup of tea. So what else could he want?

"And did you hear about that woman with her fingers cut off? CSI found them in the food recycling bin! I mean, that's nasty. Who would take a job where you have to rummage around in a bin, I ask you? Not a job I would want, would you Neil?"

Neil looked up from his desk and stared at Charlie in disbelief. "On balance, Sarge, I'd rather rummage through a bin than have my fingers cut off."

"Have you finished the paperwork for those three women DC Anderson and I were interrogating, Neil? They were in the same flat as the dead one, butr nothing bad happened to them. If you ask me, they did her over and then went out and got away with it that way."

"But nobody did ask you, Charlie. So please keep your lurid imagination under lock and key," Hunter said as he and Tim came down the final stair to the reception.

"Aye, Hunter, but you've got to admit it's odd," Charlie said.

"Neil, have you got the forms?" Hunter said, looking over Charlie's shoulder.

"Yes, Sir. Here they are."

"Fine, thanks. I want to get the women processed, and bailed, as soon as we can. We have neither room nor reason to keep them here."

"What are we charging them with, Boss?" Tim asked.

"Illegal entry, meantime. Not a brass farthing or a valid passport between them. But at least they speak some English," Charlie replied.

"It's a miracle," Hunter smiled. "Charlie is right!"

The sergeant scowled and went to make himself a cup of tea. This time, Neil could make his own.

***

Gillian got home just after Tim and found him sitting in the living room with Ailsa. She had never met Ailsa before, but felt as if she knew her.

"Hello, pet. Let me introduce you to my little sister, Ailsa," Tim said.

Ailsa smiled. "I've heard so much about you. I'm thrilled to meet you."

"Likewise. It's wonderful that you've managed to secure a job at the Royal Infirmary, Ailsa. Congratulations. You must have fought off a lot of competition."

"I am very lucky to have got the job,"Ailsa said modestly.

"A first class degree from Cambridge and a godfather who is the senior consultant in the department probably didn't hurt, though, Sis," Tim smiled.

Gillian raised her eyebrows. She looked over at Ailsa and smiled. She saw that Ailsa had long limbs and fair hair like Tim, but her intelligent eyes were more grey than the vivid blue of her brother's. Her long hair fell loose across her shoulders. Gillian smiled but could not help thinking that she had never seen anyone who looked less like an accident and emergency doctor than Ailsa Myerscough. The woman looked more like a model.

Ailsa smiled back but Gillian was aware Ailsa was observing her carefully. Gillian felt uncomfortable: was she assessing whether she was suitable for Tim, or was it just that she was Tim's type: leggy, blonde, pretty and intelligent? What business was it of Ailsa's? Gillian might not be rich like Ailsa and Tim, but he had chosen her as his girlfriend. She saw Ailsa stare at her hair: she did not look impressed by the flash of green hair in her fringe, but she thought it looked exciting and that it enhanced her emerald green eyes. And, after all, academics did live in a different world to doctors, didn't they? Gillian's thoughts were broken when Tim spoke.

"Shall we go and have some for dinner?" Tim asked.

"Yes, let's do that," Ailsa said.

"Good idea, but I must tell you about this phone call I had today. I had to speak Ukrainian. I don't get to use that too often." Gillian smiled up at Tim and took him by the hand.

Chapter Twelve

Ian Thomson relished his freedom. Three years of being confined within HMP Edinburgh had made doing business much more difficult than it ought to be. Nevertheless, he had managed to put the finance together to buy this fine house. Twelve bedrooms! Grand! Ian wandered from room to room admiring his purchase. He certainly didn't have enough furniture to fill it, but luckily the floor coverings were included, as were the fittings in both kitchens and all the bathrooms. Not that he planned to cook tonight. He would get a good Chinese take-away delivered for him and the boys to celebrate moving into their new home.

The doorbell rang to signal the arrival of the removers. He opened the door.

"Hello, Alfie. Just bring it all in, lads. The boxes are numbered as to which room they are to go to, and there are numbers on the doors of the rooms. All the living room furniture through there. When you get to the beds, give me a shout and I'll show you where each is to go."

"Aye, right Ian. We'll just get on," the man in charge said. He was Alfie Bonner: he and Ian had roomed together for a while courtesy of Her Majesty. Ian was pleased to be able to give him the business. He knew Alfie and his boys could be trusted; Alfie had only had a short sentence for shoplifting, after which he lost his job. Setting up the removal business and hiring ex-cons had been a stroke of genius on Alfie's part, Ian thought.

Suddenly his attention was diverted when his phone sounded to let him know he had a text. Mansoor's wife. What could she want? She held the title of manageress of his new betting shops, but all she had to do was take the card payments, pay out the winnings and put any cash bets into the old biscuit tin, to keep that away from the taxman. It wasn't rocket science. He let the call go to voicemail.

"Which bedroom, mister?" asked another man.

"Up these stairs, I'll show you." Ian led the way up the left hand stairs to what would be Frankie's and the girls' space.

His phone rang. It was her again. He answered the call. "What is it? You know I'm busy with the move today."

"I am busy too. Police are here, Fred's Street. You better come."

"Fuck's sake. Okay, I'll be there as soon as."

Ian went outside to find Alfie. "Alfie, my man, I've had a call. Fuckin' coppers at one of my new betting shops. I have to go and sort it."

"Aye, right Ian. What should we do with the rest of the beds?"

"Up the stairs on the right, Alfie. Do your best. It may be something and nothing."

"Hope so. Bloody menace those coppers are."

"Look, here's your cash anyway, in case I don't get back. There's a bit extra for a beer for you and the boys when you're done."

"Great! Thanks Ian."

"Just pull the door shut behind you, Alfie. I don't want to get robbed," Ian grinned. He got into his red Porsche and made his way to Frederick Street.

***

Sergeant Charlie Middleton didn't much like having to leave the station these days. He never knew what he would miss. However, today was different. Today, if he went out to help with door-to-door enquiries, he would get to see where Hunter's son was living, as well as having a chance to pick up his Turkish lira for his holidays. So, when the opportunity arose, he told PC Neil Larkin that they would be making the enquiries together.

Charlie led the way to his bank first. He had been with the

Bank of Scotland in George Street for years. He liked the fact it was central and all the staff knew Police Sergeant Charlie Middleton. On the way out a man coming in held the door for them.

"Good afternoon, officers," the man said.

"What a huge man! He must have been easily six feet nine," Neil commented.

"I don't fancy meeting him up a dark alley. No telling where he'd put my truncheon," Charlie joked.

When they got to Frederick Street there was no doubt which building they were heading for. PC Scott Clark was on duty outside, checking the identification of anybody entering the stairwell.

"Let's have a look at the flat first," Charlie said.

They climbed to the second floor and ducked under the police tape.

"Wow! Hunter's boy's living here? Swanky!" Charlie said. "I thought the kid was just a junkie. To live in a place like this he must be dealing."

"I thought it came with his job," Neil said sourly.

"I'm sure it does!" Charlie said sarcastically.

They made their way down the stairs and rang the bell of the first-floor flat, although there was no name on the door. There was no reply, and when Charlie looked through the letter box it certainly didn't seem as if anybody was home. "Look at all that junk mail behind the door. This place must have been empty for ages," Charlie remarked.

"You're right. There is a lot of letters behind the door, Sarge," Neil agreed.

Charlie led the way downstairs to see what they could find out from the betting shop on the ground floor.

"This is a new betting shop. I've never been in this bookie's before," Charlie said.

"I don't bet," Neil replied. "I'm saving for a deposit on a house."

Charlie asked the woman behind the counter if she had seen or heard anything unusual from the flats upstairs in the last week or so. She didn't seem to speak English, even when he spoke very slowly. Charlie shouted at her to get her boss.

While they were waiting, he put a few pound coins into one of the betting machines, but had no luck.

He was surprised when Ian Thomson came into the shop and introduced himself as the owner.

"Ian Bloody Thomson? How did you get a licence to run this place with your record?" Charlie asked.

"Oh, I'm not the licensee, I just own the business, Sergeant Middleton. Mrs Mansoor, here, is the manager and licensee."

"Her? She doesn't even speak English!"

"I speak English fine, when I feel like it." The little woman winked at Ian.

***

"Well, that was a waste of bloody time," Charlie said. "Ian Thomson and his manager saw and heard nothing. Even if they had, I doubt they would tell us."

"At least you got your holiday money, Sarge," Neil said as they walked back to their car. "Hey, isn't that the guy we saw going into the bank?" The PC pointed to the large, sandy-haired man who was going into the betting shop.

The officers watched as Ian Thomson frogmarched the man out of the place with the words, "I don't want you or any of your kind of arsehole in any of my places of business. Remember, Squires, you're not welcome!"

Chapter Thirteen

"I think we should have a party!" Tim said the next morning at breakfast.

"Good idea! What's the occasion?" Gillian asked.

"Ailsa coming back to Edinburgh. It'll be an easy way to let friends know she's back in town."

"Wouldn't a status change on Facebook be quicker?"

"Yes, but not nearly so much fun." Tim kissed the green flash in her fringe.

"We'll talk it over with Ailsa tonight and see what she says. Do you want me to drop you off at the University?"

"Yes, please. I wonder if Xristina will be back today," Gillian mused.

"Do you have a photo of this girl Xristina for University registration?" Tim asked.

"Of course."

"Could you e-mail it to me? I was thinking about what you were saying last night and there can't be so very many Xristinas living in Frederick Street in Edinburgh. I'm just worried that our girl might be your girl."

"No, Tim. It can't be."

"It could be, you mean, Gillian."

***

"Hunter, before we start the briefing, I have heard back from Gartcosh," DCI Allan Mackay said.

"What's the news?" Hunter asked flatly.

"You know our old Superintendent, Graham Miller MBE, is now heading up serious crime in Gartcosh?"

"Yes, Sir. What of it?"

"Well, he will be in charge of this case. We must clear

everything with him and keep him in the loop."

"Can't see a problem," Hunter said.

"His eyes and ears will be based in this station."

"Who?"

"DS Jane Renwick." Mackay smiled.

Hunter grinned. "Yes, Sir. It's the best we could hope for."

"Indeed. Now to the briefing?"

***

Mackay called the incident room to order. Although he did wonder whether it was worth the bother. The fact that DS Renwick was joining them as liaison from Gartcosh was greeted with cheers and a round of applause, and the noise in the room escalated fast.

"Calm down!" he shouted. "Good grief, you would think I had said the First Minister was coming to visit."

"I doubt that would get such a big cheer as my Janey." Rachael blushed.

"Maybe so, DC Anderson. Now, I think we are joined today by Sergeant Middleton and PC Larkin, who have made some interesting observations."

Charlie stepped forward to tell his story. He looked every bit as self-important as usual to Mackay.

"When me and Neil were coming down the stairs of the murder flat, we knocked at the first-floor flat. Nobody has been living there for ages, and there was lots of junk mail behind the door. I think those Russian girls could have easily killed the other one and nobody heard them."

"How very cosmopolitan of you to put it that way, Charlie," Colin smiled.

Hunter frowned at Charlie. "We have no reason to believe the other three young women were involved in any way. Two of them were at the club. The other one doesn't seem either tall enough nor strong enough to carry out such an attack."

"No motive, for any of them that I can see," Mackay said firmly.

"Aye well, just as we were leaving we saw Ian Thomson

throw a big man out of his shop. Thomson must have eaten his porridge in the big house, because that fellow is huge. Neil and I saw him coming out of the bank too."

"Could you hear what Thomson said?" Hunter asked.

"Aye, and he called the big lad 'Squires' and shouted something about him not being welcome."

"That must be Brian Squires," He's back in town, is he? Very interesting. He's always been the muscle never the brains, whatever he's doing. And he's definitely trouble," Hunter said. "And Cameron said a huge man brought Xristina to his flat and gave him five hundred pounds for her keep."

"That's useful, Charlie. You've included it in your report?" Mackay asked.

"Of course, Sir. And they're all done. I'm off for two weeks from tomorrow," Charlie replied.

Tim spoke for the first time. "Boss, this may not be relevant, but Doctor Gillian Pearson has a new head at the Foreign Languages Department of Edinburgh University: Professor Sheptytsky. He's a noted linguist from Ukraine."

"Too many bloody funny names in this for my liking," Charlie grumbled.

"Maybe, Charlie, but there's more. She also has a PhD student from Ukraine, Xristina Marenko. She was attracted to do her doctorate here because of Professor Sheptytsky."

"Understandable, if he's so well-respected," Hunter nodded.

"This student is normally very diligent, but she hasn't been around the department for a few days, and Gillian has now had a worried phone call from her father. He hasn't been able to reach his daughter for a while."

"Oh dear, I don't like the sound of that." Hunter frowned as Tim continued.

"I didn't like it either, Boss. I know you don't believe in coincidences, and how many Xristinas can there be in Frederick Street?"

"No, I don't like coincidences and I don't like this."

"I've asked Gillian to email me a copy of her Xristina's photo from the university records. I thought we could show it to Cameron and see if he recognised her as our Xristina."

"Inspired, Tim!" Hunter said.

"Boss, this might all tie in with what the girls told us," Rachael said.

"What did they tell you?"

"They said they paid a great deal to get here. None of them have travelled abroad before, and they were excited to come. But the journey was long. They seemed to think they had come through Poland, the Czech Republic and Germany to Belgium. They said it was very tiring. They came by train and bus; it took days. Olena said big a man kept them together. He was not kind to them."

"Who did they pay, Rachael?"

"Come on, Boss! They have no idea. Money passed up the line by gophers."

"Predictable." Hunter shook his head.

"Boss, they said they arrived in the UK through the Channel Tunnel. They thought they were going to sing and dance on the stages of London's West End, but the man put them on a Megabus and they arrived in Edinburgh," Rachael said. "The girls were met in Edinburgh by a tall man. He was not nice and would not reply when they asked where they were going. He bundled them into the back of a car, and the next thing they knew they were working in a massage parlour."

"Who was the man?" Mackay asked.

"They were told to call him Joe," Rachael said.

"Joe?"

"Yes, Boss. It could be anybody."

"Cameron said he had never seen Anichka until after they found Xristina's body," Tim said. "Do you remember, we were at the flat by then?"

**

Hunter decided to meet Cameron for lunch, while they discussed the picture of Xristina. Hunter made a quick call to his son.

"Yes, of course, Dad. But I'm meeting Lucky for lunch here at the Sheraton. Why don't you join us? He'd probably like to

57

know when he can get his flat back and stop paying hotel prices for me!" Cameron laughed.

"What time?" Hunter asked flatly. He was disappointed that he would not see his son alone.

"We're meeting at 12.30pm."

"Fine."

There was a pause before Cameron said, "I'm looking forward to seeing you, Dad."

Hunter smiled and said warmly, "Me too, son. See you later."

***

They had a window table at lunch. Of course, Lord Lucky Buchanan had a window table. Hunter almost wept when he saw the prices.

"This is my treat," said Lucky. "Not a bribe, Detective Inspector Wilson, just three friends out for lunch and it's my turn to pay."

"We'll be eating at the Persevere in Leith when it's my turn," Hunter smiled.

"We *always* eat in the Persevere in Leith when it's your turn, Dad," Cameron joked.

"Aye but it's never *your* turn. Is it son?" Hunter retorted. Then his face broke into a wide smile.

When the waitress came, Hunter ordered the beefburger, Cameron the fish and chips, but Lucky pushed the boat out, ordering the spring lamb with chive mash.

"Let me show you this photo," Hunter said to Cameron. "Do you recognise this young woman?"

"Yes that's Xristina!" Cameron exclaimed. "See her beautiful Titian red hair?"

"How did she and her pals come to be staying in my flat?" Lucky asked.

"That big giant guy who works for you brought her to the flat a while back and said it was your instructions Xristina was to stay there," Cameron said, nodding at Lucky.

"I don't have any big, giant guys who work for me. Not

especially big, anyway," Lucky said.

"No, this man was huge, even bigger than your sidekick, Dad."

"Tim Myerscough?" Hunter asked.

"Much bigger. At a guess, I'd say he was nearly seven foot tall."

"I wonder if that's anybody I know. Let me see if I can get a photo for you to look at, Cameron. If it's the man I think it might be, he's bad news." Hunter took out his phone and sent Tim a text requesting a photo of Brian Squires.

Hunter didn't have to wait long for his text from Tim. He showed the picture to Cameron and watched as his son nodded at the picture.

"That's him," Cameron said.

Lucky took the phone. "That's Brian Squires. I met him a few months back. But he certainly does not work for me."

Hunter texted the identifications to Tim, then they all tucked into lunch. It was very tasty.

When they were finished, Hunter laid his phone down and shook hands with Cameron and Lucky as he was leaving and made his way to the car park. Whatever Brian Squires was involved in, and wherever he was, there was trouble.

***

The red Volkswagen was parked behind Hunter's old Toyota. The Sheraton Hotel car park was not busy at that time of day; guests checking out had left and those checking in had not yet arrived. Lunch-time patrons were leaving, but loud music blared from the Volkswagen. Hunter could see chefs and servers smoking in the shadows. Hunter glanced over at the driver of the red car, and watched as the door opened quietly and a big man slid out.

Hunter squinted to see if he could recognise the man: he seemed familiar. His portly body was supported by a solid frame. His cold eyes glinted with hatred. He looked like a real-life version of Peter Griffin from the cartoon *Family Guy*, right down to the quizzical scowl.

During his many years on the force, Hunter had developed a sixth sense for trouble. It just happens when you work in the job long enough, but he didn't think he needed a sixth sense to recognise the threat emanating from this figure. The man walked towards Hunter: danger swept off him in waves like an exploding military device.

Then Hunter heard a voice he would know anywhere.

"Dad! Dad!" Cameron shouted.

Hunter turned and his son ran up to him.

"I'm glad I caught you, Dad," he said. "You forgot your phone. Here it is."

"Thanks, son. That would have been a nuisance."

"Don't I know it. I feel like my phone is an extension of my arm!" Cameron smiled. "Here you go. See you soon." Cameron slapped his father on the shoulder and turned to go back into the hotel.

Hunter turned back towards the red Volkswagen. Neither the angry man nor the car was anywhere to be seen. The sound of the car exiting the car park must have been muffled by the city traffic. "Shit!" Hunter swore softly under his breath and drove back to the station.

Chapter Fourteen

By the time Frankie and Jamie got back from the showroom at Thomson's Top Cars, Ian's face was almost as red as his Porsche.

As Frankie took the twins to show them around their new home, Jamie fetched two cans of beer from the fridge in the large kitchen and handed one to his pop.

"So what's wrong with you, Pop? The move seems to have gone well, but you've got a face like fizz."

"You will not fucking believe who came into my betting shop today."

"Then I won't try. Just tell me and give us both a break," Jamie grinned.

"Only that bloody brute Brian Squires," Ian bellowed.

"Squires? I thought he was keeping Arjun Mansoor company."

"Aye, but not for long enough. With time served and time off for good behaviour, he's out."

"That's a laugh. What was he after?" Jamie asked.

"A bet on the horses and to know if I knew what the coppers had found out in that place upstairs."

"What did you tell him, Pop?"

"I told him to fuck off and not come back."

"What happened?"

"When he realised who I was he started to explain that he's not working with Lenny The Lizard Pratt any more, and maybe we could scratch each other's backs a bit now,"

"Oh aye. And do you need your back scratched by Brian Squires, Pop?"

"I'll use a bloody fork first!" Ian growled. "Get us another beer, son, and one for Frankie. Then, shall we order a Chinese take-away for dinner?"

"Am I allowed to tell Gillian about Xristina, Boss?" Tim asked Hunter.

"You know the answer to that question, Tim. So why ask me?"

"More in hope than expectation, I suppose."

"DCI Mackay will have to run it past our representative from Gartcosh, anyway," Hunter said.

"It'll be good to have DS Renwick back," Tim said.

"Yes it will. Now I'm off to The Persevere and my darts match. You get off home, Tim."

***

By the time Tim got home, Gillian and Ailsa were curled up in the living room drinking ice-cold gin and tonic.

"Why don't you go and clean up while I pour you a large whisky?" Ailsa asked. She saw Gillian pull a face,and realised that the other woman felt she had over-stepped the mark. Ailsa blushed. It should be Tim's girlfriend who looked out for him, not his sister.

"Yes, go and make yourself comfortable, Tim, dear," Gillian said softly, as if to emphasise that point.

"Good idea. What's for dinner, anyway?" Tim asked.

"I think Alice has made us her steak and ale pie with mash and veg, with Black Forest gateau for pudding," Ailsa smiled.

"I love that woman's cooking more than anything!" Tim sighed as he left to take a quick shower and change his clothes.

"Thank you *very* much, Tim Myerscough," Gillian said with mock indignation to his back.

"He may love her cooking, but he needs to go running everyday and attend his rugby training to keep the weight off." Ailsa smiled at Gillian.

"I think Tim looks good on it," Gillian said defensively.

"Yes, but he has to stay active. Alice is a wonderful cook, but she has no idea of portion control. I think I'll enrol at Bannerman's Gym in Queen Street myself," Ailsa said.

"I'm lucky, we have a gym and exercise classes at the university," Gillian said.

The women then sat in silence until Tim came back followed by his beautiful Persian Blue cat, Lucy.

"Oh, dear. I forgot to take my anti-histamine!" Gillian jumped up.

"You're allergic to Lucy? Didn't Tim tell you – he and Lucy are an item?" Ailsa asked Gillian.

"No, but Lucy gave me that distinct impression! By the way, was that picture of Xristina useful to you, Tim?"

"Yes, thank you, Gillian. It was helpful to be able to show it to witnesses."

"Was it the same girl?"

"I can't tell you that, pet," Tim replied.

Gillian grimaced and left the room to get her allergy tablet. She shut the door firmly, but took longer to come back than should have been necessary. She was still angry when she came back into the room.

"Shall we have another drink before we eat?" Ailsa asked.

"Not for me, Sis. But Gillian and I were wondering if you would like to have a group around for a party to re-introduce you to the city?"

"Yes, that would be nice. Good idea. Thank you. But before that, remind me when we go to see Dad." Ailsa nodded at Tim and Gillian.

"We have a visit with Dad tomorrow, Ailsa. Gillian has not had that pleasure yet. When we get back, I'll make some calls, and arrange the gathering for Friday evening, if that suits you, Sis?"

"What's wrong with Saturday evening?"

"I've an appointment to meet with Ian Thomson on Saturday, to take a look at a new car."

"You've only had that huge BMW about nine months!" Ailsa laughed.

"I know, I'm keeping that, but I fancy something a bit more sporty and fun too for when Gillian and I go out," Tim smiled.

"Sounds good," Gillian said.

"Okay, big man, what gives?" Ailsa asked with a smile.

"I like the look of the Mercedes-Benz SLS AMG – good headroom and lots of va va vroom!" Tim grinned at his sister.

"You have always liked flash cars," she replied with a laugh.

***

Tim held the door open for Ailsa as they entered HMP Edinburgh. He hated the formalities they had to go through to see their father, but it was always worth it in the end just to have time with him.

"Do you ever get used to this?" Ailsa asked as the body search concluded.

"Not yet, but I'll keep you posted," Tim smiled.

Tim led the way to a table at the edge of the room furthest away from the vending machines.

"Why here?" Ailsa asked.

"It will be quietest and we can chat. Look, here comes Dad now."

Their father walked towards them. The index and middle fingers of his left hand were taped together.

"Ailsa, darling, how lovely to see you. Are you well settled in at home?"

"Yes, thank you Dad. But what has happened to your hand?"

"A dispute between a steel door and flesh is always going produce a negative result, my dear. It looks worse than it is. Don't worry. Tell her, Tim."

"He can be unbelievably clumsy," Tim said. "Shall I get us some coffees?"

"Yes, and don't forget Kit-kats." Sir Peter smiled at his son.

"So, I take it you are missing Ian Thomson's protection now he's out on parole?" Ailsa asked her Dad.

"I just have to get used to looking out for myself. But this was just a clumsy mistake and I broke my index finger, honestly." Sir Peter smiled. "When do you start your new job, Ailsa?"

"Beginning of next month. I'm looking forward to it. It was

kind of Uncle William to put in a good word for me."

"Yes, your mother chose all your Godparents very carefully."

Ailsa watched Tim approach with the coffees and waited while he unloaded the biscuits from his pockets.

"You do also have an excellent degree and good experience from London," Tim said.

"And when do I get to meet your new girlfriend, Tim?" Sir Peter smiled at his son.

"All in good time, Dad. It's early days. Give me a break," Tim said.

"Give me a Kit-kat," his father replied, finishing off the old advert for comic effect.

"Mansoor up to anything just now?" Tim asked.

"Not that I know of, but he and his brother-in-law are claiming religious privileges. What a joke! There's no religion known to man that would have them."

"Who is that visiting Mansoor today?" Tim asked.

"I have no idea, never seen him before. Looks rather serious and studious for one of Mansoor's types."

The bell rang to indicate the end of visiting hour, and Tim and Ailsa had to leave their father. They rose from their chairs and walked smartly towards the exit. Leaving their father behind in prison was always difficult. It was easier for all of them if they moved quickly and didn't look back.

"Prison visits are always tense, aren't they?" Tim said to Ailsa as they walked towards the car.

"I hope they'll get easier, as I get more used to them," she replied.

***

"It's good of your Pop to take care of the twins and let us go to the pub," Frankie said to Jamie.

"Aye, but somehow I had in mind we'd get out of an evening, not for a bite of lunch when we can't drink 'cos' we're going back to work!" Jamie said as they drove off.

"Harry and Gavin are going to join us. Harry suggested The

Shakespeare. Plenty of seats, and the food's good."

"Cheap too," Jamie said.

"Where will we be best to park?" Frankie asked.

"Not much parking on Lothian Road. We could look for somewhere around Tollcross?"

"Bit of a walk. What about sticking the car in the Sheraton car park? It's just opposite the pub."

"Oooh The Sheraton, lah di dah," Jamie laughed. "Blast, I swear we've hit every single red light. We're going to be helluva late. Phone Harry and tell him will you, Frankie?"

"He says he and Gavin have a date with a couple of tarts from The Edinburgh Massage Suite just further up Lothian Road, and if we're too late they'll be gone."

Jamie shrugged and turned right from the West Approach Road into The Sheraton car park. Parking was reserved for guests, but Jamie was not short of the gift of the gab. He began to explain his business to the attendant. Even he was surprised when the man eventually let the car in.

Chapter Fifteen

Hunter decided to go straight home rather than go back to the station. He had a darts match tonight. His team were now trailing their East Lothian rivals by four games, and that did not sit well with the competitive bunch.

He parked the car as near to his flat as he could get and made towards the front door of his tenement. Hunter had enjoyed lunch with Cameron and was surprised by the favourable impression Lucky had made on him, so he was in a good mood when he trotted up to the second floor. His good mood did not last long. His door had been skilfully opened. There was no damage to the structure, but somebody had left the door ajar and he knew that had not been him.

He caught the eye of his next-door neighbour, Mrs Lamb, watching him as he pushed the door further.

He shouted. "Who's there?"

His voice echoed around the flat. He walked in. He pushed open the bedroom doors and moved along the hallway to check the kitchen and bathroom. The place looked empty, but it did not feel empty. He shoved the living room door open with his foot and peered inside. He could sense another presence but did not see it.

"Who's there?" Hunter said.

Silence was the reply. He crept further into the room and a fast heavy blow to the back of the head laid him out on the floor.

"Oh, dear. Sorry, Hunter. Another mistake," a familiar voice said insincerely.

***

Hunter's phone rang. It went to voicemail. Cameron deduced his dad must be out with that bird of his. He just hung up.

***

Hunter's phone rang again, but went to voicemail when he did not pick up. Meera suddenly remembered about his darts match, left a message and rang off.

***

"Clouseau still not here?" Tom asked the rest of the darts team.

"No, not yet," they replied.

"He's not usually this late, and he's not answering his phone," Tom said.

"Must be busy on a case, I suppose. You better play again for the last leg, Tom," Jim commented.

***

"I'm going to switch this off. All these bloody calls are driving me mad," the voice said to Hunter's prone body.

***

Tim, Ailsa and Gillian were sitting relaxing after dinner. Tim and Gillian each had large mugs of coffee, but Ailsa stuck to decaffeinated Earl Grey tea.

"All that caffeine will keep you awake at night," she said.

"Believe me, Sis, the caffeine isn't the problem," Tim smiled at Gillian.

"Too much information." Ailsa raised her eyes heavenward. "Now who do we want to invite to this party? I thought we might have a wine tasting? David Robertson of Robertson's Wines on Comiston Road will do us a bespoke one."

"That is a great idea. A bit different and a lot of fun,"

Gillian said.

"If I remember rightly they provide guidance on unusual wines and whiskies and offer free glass loans. They'll even do alcohol -free wine for me," Tim added.

"Yes, but please let's stick to wine, Tim if we mix the grape and the grain Bear will be comatose by half past ten," Ailsa joked.

"True. Look, it's your do, you talk to them about the drinks. Will you and Gillian arrange the food? You are so much better at that sort of thing than I am."

"I'll be happy to help, if that's alright with you, Ailsa?" Gillian smiled.

"Excellent! Otherwise they all get the same old cheese board and veggies with dips that I remember Mum serving twenty years ago!" Ailsa paused and remembered how much her mother had enjoyed entertaining. Tim did too, but, like her Dad, she was much more reserved.

"Now that's decided, who do you want me to invite? Bear and Mel, because you mentioned the big man? Jane and Rachael?" Tim asked.

"Yes, they're a laugh," Ailsa smiled. "Can we invite Eric Samuels and Raaz Singh? I'll be working with them."

"Yep, no problem. Anybody you want to invite, Gillian?" Tim asked.

"May I include Professor Sheptytsky? He is new to the city."

"Of course, but do I need to worry about this brilliant, famous, young professor?"

"Don't be silly, Tim! He's my colleague," Gillian laughed.

"Good. Anybody else?"

"No, that makes ten of us. It's a good number for this room and for the wine tasting," Ailsa said. "I'll check tomorrow with Henderson's Wines if they can do Friday and let you know, Tim. Then you can invite everybody."

"You invite the professor, Gillian. By the way, what is his first name?"

"I will. And it's Zelay. Zelay Sheptytsky."

Chapter Sixteen

"Any sign of DI Wilson?" DCI Allan Mackay glanced around the room as he called the briefing to order.

"No, Sir. I know he was meeting his son for lunch yesterday and was playing in a darts match in the evening, but I don't remember him talking about anything that would keep him late," Tim said.

"It's not like him to be late. He's a stickler for punctuality," Nadia commented.

"Well, he can catch up. Let's get on," Mackay said. "I am delighted to welcome DS Jane Renwick."

A cheer went up round the room.

"Thanks," Jane said. "I will be your link to MIT. Superintendent Miller is in overall charge of this case, so keep me in the loop and let me know what you need from MIT by way of expertise or advice."

"That we will, DS Renwick. Thank you," Mackay said. "Now. Where are we with the corpse?"

"I may be able to help because I attended the post mortem with DI Wilson," Nadia offered.

"So what do we know?" Mackay asked.

"She was killed by a blow to the back of the head with a blunt object, but it seems immediately after death her face was knocked about a bit and then the tops of her fingers chopped off. CSIs found the fingertips in the food recycling bin," Nadia said.

"Yugh!" Mel grimaced.

"But how very green," Colin commented sarcastically.

"Dr Sharma thought the woman might have been subdued with a date rape drug, so we are waiting on toxicology for that," Nadia added. "Could you see if you can speed that up please, DS Renwick?"

Jane smiled and nodded.

"We know the girl's identity," Tim said. "She is Xristina Ponomarenko from the Ukraine. Cameron Wilson identified her from a photo taken by Edinburgh University. He also confirmed that it was Brian Squires who took her to his flat."

"Why?" Mackay asked.

"That we don't know, Sir. But Cameron identified him as the man who told him she was to stay there, because his boss said she was to stay in the second floor flat."

"I suppose Cameron thought that both he and Squires worked for Lucky Buchanan," Bear commented.

"Yes, he did," Tim said. "But DI Wilson told me that although Lucky knows who Squires is, he said he does not employ him and never has."

"You two know this Lucky fellow. Don't you?" Mackay looked at Tim and Bear. "Can we trust him?"

"No," Bear said.

"Not generally, Sir," Tim said. "He is a bit of a player. However, I believe him on this. He has no reason to lie."

"I agree," Bear nodded.

"Should we inform the University, Sir?" Tim asked Mackay.

"Yes. Now the identification is confirmed, I think we must. Tim, you have a university contact, will you do that?"

"Of course, Sir. What about the girl's parents?"

"They must be officially informed," Mackay said. "Get that translator woman in, the one that that Hunter knows, will you, DC Myerscough?"

"Doctor Gillian Pearson, Sir."

"Yes. Well, I'll draft a statement for her to read to them. They don't need to know all the gruesome details over the phone, but they must be informed about their child's death."

"Yes, Sir," Tim said.

"Where are the other young women?" Mackay asked.

"They are on bail and back at work at the massage parlour, Sir," Angus McKenzie said.

Mackay sighed and nodded. "I want to know who is behind this murder. Let's start with Brian Squires. Get him in here now. And find out what has happened to DI Hunter Wilson, DC Zewedu."

DCI Allan Mackay smacked his folder off the desk and marched back to his office. He picked up the receiver and dialled Hunter's mobile number, but the phone was clearly switched off as the call went straight to voicemail. He left an impatient message for Hunter to call him back as soon as he got the message.

Next Mackay dialled Hunter's home number, but the call rang out. Hunter must not have any kind of answering machine.

Mackay rocked back and forward on his chair. In the eight years he had worked with Hunter he had never known the man even be late for a briefing, apart from the slight delay due to the autopsy over-running yesterday, let alone miss it altogether. This was totally out of character. He debated his next move. Mackay did not want to intrude into Hunter's private life, but he wanted to know where the DI was, and what was so important as to detain him. Doctor Meera Sharma was his next port of call.

"Doctor Sharma, good morning. I am sorry to disturb you at work, but I wonder if you can help. DI Wilson has not yet arrived at the station and I wondered if you could shed any light on his plans this morning that might have detained him?"

"No, I'm sorry, DCI Mackay. I haven't seen Hunter. I know he was planning to have lunch with his son Cameron yesterday. He also had a darts match in the evening, but it is most unlike him to be late for work. Would you like me to call Cameron and see if he knows Hunter's whereabouts?"

"Yes, if you would, Doctor Sharma. And call me back."

Mackay was disappointed, but not surprised, when Meera phoned him back a few minutes later to say that Cameron had no helpful information.

"Where the hell is Hunter?" Mackay said to himself.

Chapter Seventeen

Ian Thomson found his purchases were fulfilling his needs nicely. The new house in Lauder Road was large enough that his son and his nephews did not disturb his days. They sometimes met at breakfast or when getting beers from the fridge, but for Harry and Gavin, he noticed, often breakfast *was* getting beers from the fridge. Ian overlooked this. The boys would not be home for much longer and they needed to relax in their own way.

He was also pleased with the profits coming in from the betting shops. He had arranged for Mrs Mansoor to give him both sets of books, one for him and one for the taxman, at the end of every week. Ian would have been less sanguine if he had known about the two additional sets: one for Oleksander and Sergei, and the other for her husband, Arjun Mansoor.

Ian noticed that even the business at Thomson's Top Cars was running well. The boys, Jamie and Frankie, had sold a Bentley to a German guy who worked for a hotel chain in the city. Apparently, he had had a big windfall by way of an inheritance and was able to indulge his love of cars. That young cop, Tim Myerscough, had also expressed an interest in a new motor. Ian knew he was not short of a bob or two, so was hopeful of getting the full asking price for the sporty Mecedes-Benz SLS AMG Myerscough wanted to test-drive.

The next thing on Ian's to-do list was to win back his wife Janice.

Ian's first stop was to the Turkish barber shop that he had used for years, before the incarceration that had interrupted so many of his pleasures. He was glad to be remembered as the owner showed him to a chair. They talked about the weather, holidays – no, it had been over three years since Ian had been on a holiday – and the lovely Janice. After his hair was as fashionably shaped as possible, Ian subjected himself to an open razor shave. He wanted to be sure there were no bristles to cause Janice any discomfort.

Pleased with the results, Ian made his way to the city centre. He wanted a new up-to-the-minute outfit that would meet with Janice's approval. He knew Janice liked her fashion, and he wanted her to know that he had made an effort and was a stylish catch.

He headed to Frasers at the West End of Princes Street. Many folk still called this 'Binns Corner', but it hadn't been Binns since before he was born. He knew that there were several different designers with concession areas in the big store and he would engage the help of a personal shopper to help him weave his way through the trends. Ian wanted to look stylish but not like a fashion victim. He had to get this right.

When Ian met his personal shopper he wondered, for a moment, whether it would be more fun to make a move on this pretty, young thing than to spend time with Janice. However, he realised that the 'young thing' must be spoken for, as she wore not only an engagement and wedding ring, but also an eternity ring. Back to Janice.

At the end of the trip around Frasers, Ian was surprised by how nervous he felt, even in his new clothes. He asked the 'young thing' to dispose of the old ones and tipped her handsomely before making his way to Ryan's Bar on the other side of the road. Ian did not want to arrive at lunch and meet Janice when he smelled of alcohol, but he did need to sit and gather his thoughts. He ordered a pint of orange squash and sat in the far corner of the room where he could watch everybody coming in and going out. Old habits die hard.

As he sat pondering over his drink, it occurred to him that he was close enough to the betting shop in Lothian Road to take a stroll up there and see how it was doing, but he decided against it. He was too tight for time. Lunch with Janice was booked at the Livingroom for one o'clock, and he didn't want to be late. He smiled as he thought about how good they had been together over the years. Then Ian remembered her tears as he had been taken down to the cells, convicted to a jail term of six years for bank robbery. He frowned. The job had not been a solo venture for him, but he was the only one caught, so the judge had thrown the book at him. But with time off for good behaviour, here he was.

Of course, he thought about that time Janice had come to visit him. The only time Janice had come to visit him. He could hear her voice now.

"You know me, Ian. I'm a woman with needs, and you just can't meet those needs from here. I've got no choice, babes, Lenny's offered me refuge at his home in Malaga. We fly to Spain tomorrow. No hard feelings, eh babes?"

Hard feelings, oh yes, Ian had had plenty hard feelings for Janice and for Lenny The Lizard Pratt. But now he smiled. The tables were turned. Lenny was inside for murder and Ian was outside, looking forward to tending to those 'needs' Janice had referred to all those years ago. He downed the rest of his pint and strolled across Charlotte Square, past the official residence of the First Minister of Scotland, along George Street and felt uncharacteristically relieved that there was no wind to spoil his hair.

He was shown to his table and ordered iced water. He was glad to be there first.

Ian stood as Janice walked towards him. He thought she looked beautiful. Her long, bottle-blonde hair was tied in a loose bun at the back of her neck. Very chic. He admired her earrings and she reminded him that they were the ones he had given her the day their son, Jamie, was born. Of course, Ian remembered. He was thrilled to see she still had them, and lifting them from Airdrie and Miles had been difficult. Their security had been so bloody tight. He decided against sharing that memory with her.

He gazed into her large hazel eyes and smiled. "It's been a while, darlin'."

"Too long, babes. Way too long. I've missed you."

"Really, Janice? Did you really miss me? It nearly broke me when you waltzed away with The Lizard to Spain."

"Biggest mistake of my life. babes. The Lizard is such a

reptile. I'm glad he's out of my life."

"Me too, darlin'."

They stood, still facing each other. Ian took Janice in his arms and it felt as though he had never been away.

The waiter came over with the iced water just as Janice moved backwards and the cold liquid splashed all over her blouse.

"Aaagh!" She screamed.

"Oh, darlin', do you want to stay for lunch, or shall I take you home and get you out of those wet things?"

"Let's go home, babes."

Chapter Eighteen

Gillian had a lecture and two seminars scheduled for that morning, so it was nearly lunchtime before she could head over to the station. She was glad that Tim came down to reception to meet her and showed her the way to DCI Mackay's office. Gillian had not had many dealing with Mackay, and found him intimidating. She preferred to deal with Hunter, and she was disappointed when Tim explained to her that Hunter had not yet arrived.

"Doctor Pearson, Thank you for coming to the station. Has DC Myerscough explained why we need your help?"

"No," Tim and Gillian said simultaneously.

"No, Sir," Tim said. "I thought it best that Doctor Pearson's briefing should come from you personally."

"Fine, fine. Sit down. Doctor Pearson, we have a most sensitive piece of information to give to the father of one of your students."

"Xristina!" Gillian exclaimed. "Is she dead?"

"How do you know that?"

"I supplied the photograph of her to DC Myerscough, and she hasn't been seen at the University for several days. Why would you need me if something awful had not happened to her?"

"Yes. Sadly it is the young Ukrainian woman. You speak good Ukrainian, I understand?"

"It's not as good as my Russian, but I get by."

"Good. Well. We believe her full name is Xristina Ponomarenko, not Marenko as she used for her studies."

"Why would she make such a change?"

"I would prefer not to discuss that, but she probably had good reason." Mackay looked at Gillian seriously. "We require you to speak to her father by telephone to advise of his daughter's death. I also need you to ask specifically for Mr Oleksander Ponomarenko at the beginning of the call, so that we can confirm his identity as well as his daughter's."

"I can do that," Gillian said. "What do you want me to say?"

"I have written it down. Perhaps you could translate it and then you can read it to her father, more or less."

"Of course. But he will be very shocked. He will have questions."

"Of that I have no doubt. Do not give additional information, but you may say what I have written in a different way. We also need to know whether he wants to come to identify his daughter or whether he would like a friend here or someone from the University to undertake that duty."

"How awful it would be to have to identify your dead child like that," Gillian sighed.

"Dreadful," Mackay agreed.

***

Gillian knocked on Mackay's door about an hour later. She could not see Tim anywhere, so she braved the intimidating DCI alone.

"Doctor Pearson, come in. I trust that wasn't too complicated a translation for you?"

"No, not at all. Do you want me to make the call from here?"

"Yes. Of course, it will be later into the evening in Ukraine as they are to the East of us," Mackay said. "Use my phone."

"I brought the number the father gave me when he called the University a few days ago."

"Good, good. Use that. On you go."

Gillian dialled the number and an unfamiliar voice replied. Gillian asked to speak to Mr Ponomarenko. She encountered some confusion as to whether she wished to speak to Oleksander or Sergei, and was embarrassed that she had not been more specfic, as she had been told to ask for Oleksander.

78

Eventually, Xristina's father came to the phone.

Gillian spoke quietly and firmly. She could see Mackay nodding at her, although she doubted he could understand anything but the names. When Gillian got to the bit where she had to tell the man his daughter had been killed, he yelled down the phone. Gillian took the receiver away from her ear and wiped a tear from her cheek. She watched Mackay frown and then make circles with his hands to tell her to get on with it.

When Gillian asked Mr Ponomarenko who he wanted to identify his daughter's body, he shouted at her that he would catch the first available flight and be with her tomorrow. Gillian explained that, if he informed her of the flight number, she and the police officer in charge of his daughter's case would meet him at the airport. She ended the call quietly and politely, but was not really ready for the immediate debrief Mackay expected.

"There are two Mr Ponomarenkos at that number: Oleksander and Sergei. They are brothers, but Oleksander is Xristina's father," she said.

"I am aware of that," Mackay said.

"Her father is understandably distraught by the news I gave him, and wanted to know all the details of her death. I could not give those to him because I did not have them."

"No. Those are not details for over the telephone," Mackay said.

"DCI Mackay, I must tell you, Xristina's father sounded not only distraught but angry. There was a steely tone to his voice that made my blood run cold."

"From what I know of the Ponomarenko brothers, that does not surprise me at all. They are dangerous men. I wonder who they pissed off to get the girl killed?"

"What? You really think that?" Gillian asked in a shocked tone of voice.

"I believe it to be a racing certainty, Doctor Pearson. The Ponomarenko brothers have fingers in many unsavoury pies all over Europe, I doubt Edinburgh is free from their influence, and the way they do business, they would not care if they ruffled any feathers."

"Until now," Gillian muttered.

Chapter Nineteen

Hunter rubbed his head before he opened his eyes.

"Oh, fuck!" he said.

A familiar throaty laugh at the other side of the room caused him to open his eyes and try to focus on the source.

"Back with me then, Hunter?" the voice said.

Hunter squinted without comment until his eyes had caught up with his brain. "John Hamilton! What the fuck are you doing in my flat, and what the fuck are you doing knocking six bells out of me?"

"Want a drink?" Hamilton asked.

"What is it?"

"Just water. I thought you might be thirsty."

Hunter took the proffered glass with a nod. "What's going on, John?"

"Just the beginning of getting my own back, Hunter."

"What the hell are you talking about? What did I ever do to you?" Hunter said, handing back the empty glass.

"You took away my career and my self-respect, and, because of you, most of my family won't speak to me any more."

"What the fuck? That's tosh. John, I need a couple of aspirin and another glass of water. Inside my mouth still feels like a sawmill has been emptied into it, and my head's full of little doors and they're all banging."

"I'd say that was too damn bad, Hunter my man. You're coming with me."

"I don't think so!"

But when Hunter tried to stand, he found his legs gave way beneath him. He heard John Hamilton laugh, but it sounded like a distant echo. The former Detective Constable dragged

Hunter to his feet. It was then Hunter noticed that his shoes and socks had been removed. He felt Hamilton shove him to the front door of his flat and then close the door quietly as they left. Hunter turned and noticed his neighbour, Mrs Lamb, as she watched them leave.

"Had one too many, Mr Wilson, have we? Lucky you've got your friend with you," she tutted as she wandered back into her flat. Hamilton smiled at the old woman. She watched as the two of them walked down the stairs, as if they were old friends.

When they reached the door of the close, the combination of early evening air and his surprise visitor were bringing Hunter back to his senses rapidly.

"How long was I out?" Hunter asked.

"Not long enough for my way of thinking," Hamilton growled. "Don't think about shouting or running. It won't help, and I will make sure your toe-rag of a son pays for your misdemeanours."

"Why? What has Cameron done?"

"Best way to hurt you is to hurt those you love," Hamilton said.

Hunter was shoved towards the red Volkswagen by Hamilton. The back door opened silently and a huge man stepped out. Hunter didn't like this.

"Squires!" Hunter exclaimed. Hunter could feel danger radiating from Hamilton and Squires like an exploding super-nova.

"You know my friend, Brian? Then you know what he's capable of. So you do as you're told Hunter. It will go better for you that way," Hamilton sneered.

Hunter watched Squires step to the side to allow him to get into the car, but Hunter didn't move.

"Get in," Hamilton said.

"No can do," Hunter replied. "I was always told not to get into cars with strangers, and there's nobody stranger than you and Squires, Hamilton."

"Hey, Clouseau!" Jim shouted as he ran towards the group. "Why did you duck the darts match last night? Not even a phone call to say you wouldn't manage it? It's not good enough, Hunter."

Hunter watched in horror as Squires took a step towards his darts team-mate and felled him with one punch. Jim landed hard on the pavement. He was out cold. Hunter dropped to one knee and looked up at Hamilton and Squires.

"Get in the car, or Brian here will jump on your friend's head."

Hunter cradled Jim's head and was satisfied that he was breathing. Hunter thought about making a move or a run for it, but he wouldn't get far or fast in bare feet, and the look in Hamilton's eyes told him that the threat regarding Jim had been more of a promise. And then Hunter saw Squires lift his foot.

"Alright, alright, I'm coming." Hunter eased himself into the back of the car. His head still throbbed and all his muscles ached from having lain on the floor of his living room for so long. The back seats had been cleared out of the car. Hunter watched as Squires lowered his body in the back beside him and Hamilton took the driver's seat. Hunter heard Tom, the darts team's captain, cry out.

"What the fuck, Jim?" He said as he ran towards their prostrate team-mate. "Was that Hunter getting into that car? Why would he leave you?"

If Hamilton or Squires were worried about someone spotting their registration number, Hunter noticed that they did not show it. Hamilton drove at a slow speed so that Hunter felt every bump on the tarmac and every muscle in his body jarred with pain. Hunter turned to Squires.

"Why the hell did you hit Jim like that?"

Squires just stared back at him with eyes that sent a chill through his heart. They were lifeless eyes with no thought or light behind them. Hunter thought it was as if he were looking into the eyes of an inanimate object. Hunter had always known that Squires was only ever the muscle of an operation, never the brains, but he had not realised, until now, just how vicious this man really was.

"Throw your wallet and phone into the front passenger

seat," Hamilton said.

Without any seats in the back of the car, Hunter found himself rolling from side to side to comply. He decided to try to reason with Hamilton. "John, What is all this about?"

"I had a nice cushy number as a detective, you know. Oh, I know that I'd never have made promotion. My face didn't fit."

"It had nothing to do with your face not fitting, John. You were a fat, lazy arse."

Squires kicked him sharply on the left shin.

"Bastard!" Hunter shouted.

"So I gets caught with a little bit of cocaine and I gets the shove."

"You resigned!"

"I had to, to keep my pension or you'd have done for me that way too."

"Oh *come on,* John. Your decisions, nobody's fault but yours!" Hunter said quietly. His head hurt too much to shout.

"But you kept on the pretty boy, didn't you?"

"Who on earth are you talking about?"

"Tim bloody Myerscough."

"Tim Myerscough didn't use cocaine. It was his father. That was a big difference, John."

Squires took another swipe at Hunter. Hunter was glad he missed that time.

"Well I've suffered enough. It's your turn now!" Hamilton sneered.

Hunter found his eyes were focussing better. He was getting used to the dim light and he looked around the back of the car but did not like what he saw. The carpeting had been ripped out revealing a metal floor. There was a rusty old toolbox at Squire's feet but Hunter had no idea what was in that. There was a bar soldered onto the far wall of the car opposite him. Then he swallowed hard. There was a pair of handcuffs attached to the bar. The other dangling handcuff loop was open. He feared that was waiting for his wrist.

When they reached the motorway, Hamilton seemed to relax. He began to drive with the palms of his hands and switched the radio on. Hunter did not need that, his head was still aching from that blow.

"Well Hamilton, where are we going?" Hunter asked.

"Shut him up, Brian. I am tired of his voice."

That was when Squires punched Hunter a deep liver punch into his core with full force. Hunter felt the air rush out of his lungs. He folded at the waist like a suitcase. He slipped over and his head dropped hard to the metal floor of the car. Hunter felt completely paralysed. He felt absolutely winded, as if all the air had been pushed out of his body and he was going to suffocate. All he could do was curl up into a ball and hope for the oxygen to return.

Chapter Twenty

"This is a great idea, Bro'," Bear said to Tim. He handed Tim a bag full of bottles of real ale and just shrugged at Tim's bemused expression. "Please just tell me Alice has been cooking."

"Not tonight, Bear. Gillian and Ailsa arranged the food."

"Oh God, then please tell me there is so much wine that I won't taste it!"

"Are you insulting my food before you've even tried it, big man? Come and give me a hug!" Ailsa said. Bear and Ailsa had known each other since they were kids. Bear had felt very protective of Ailsa, as well as Tim, since their mother's death.

"Not at all, Ailsa. I love boiled chicken and courgette pasta, or is it cauliflower rice today?"

Ailsa gave him a playful slap to his arm. "You should control this man, Mel," she laughed.

"It would take a better woman than me to manage that. How are you enjoying being back in Edinburgh?" Mel asked.

Just then the doorbell rang again, and Bear went with Tim to open the door. There were three men he did not know on his friend's doorstep.

"Gentlemen, you must be Raat, Zelay and Eric. Please help me out and tell me who is who. I am Tim, Ailsa's long-suffering brother, and this is my friend Bear Zewedu." Tim smiled.

After the introductions Bear and Tim led the way up to the living room. They had decided to have the wine tasting in there, with finger food available throughout the evening. Bear went over to stand beside Mel and watched as Tim made introductions and left the guests to help themselves to the fresh-tasting Prosecco that Robertson's had provided as the arrivals drinks. Tim went downstairs once more to greet their last guests, Jane and Rachael.

"We didn't know what to bring, so we brought a lump of Stilton cheese and a bunch of grapes. That way at least Bear won't go hungry."

"Seriously, Jane, have you ever known Bear to go hungry?" Tim asked with a grin. "But thank you, this is lovely. Come on up. I'll get you a glass of fizz and introduce you to the folk you don't know. I'm not sure where Gillian is, but I dare say she's not too far away."

Jane and Rachael were accosted by Ailsa. "Good to see you two," she said.

"And you, Ailsa. It is great you will be back in the city. Tim takes a lot of looking after!"

"Don't I know it!" Then she lowered her voice. "I am just not sure Gillian is the girl for the job."

"Why on earth not?" Rachael asked.

"I don't know. There is just something about her that I don't trust. And I certainly don't want Gillian to hurt Tim. He was badly affected when he split with Lady Sophie Dalmore: he might be a big powerful guy, but Tim wears his heart on his sleeve too obviously for my liking and I don't want Gillian taking advantage of him."

"Oh, come on, Ailsa. Tim is nobody's fool," Jane said.

"He is a grown man who can make his own decisions," Rachael said.

"I know, but at least I am here now to give him any advice or support he needs," Ailsa said.

Tim came over to hand the women glasses of Prosecco, and noticed Gillian had now joined the party. She came over to Tim and said, "I couldn't find my antihistamine tablets, so I ended up taking everything out of my make-up bag. I didn't want to be without them. I'm sure Lucy will join us sooner rather than later."

"Probably not, with this many people around. She'll hide in her basket, but I can understand the precaution," Tim said as he gave her a hug. "I'll get you a drink."

"Let me introduce you to the Prof, Zelay Sheptytsky, first."

"Lead the way. We met briefly on the doorstep, but I am looking forward to getting to know him better. Remember to protect him from Bear."

"Why?"

"He will bore the poor professor to death with all his A-level knowledge of the old USSR!"

Gillian giggled and took Tim by the hand to the other side of the room. "At last, the two most important men in my life get to meet!" she said.

"I doubt your father would agree," Zelay said as he and Tim shook hands.

"No comment." Gillian laughed awkwardly.

As Tim shook hands with the professor he had a feeling that he had seen him before, but he couldn't place the man. His attention was immediately diverted when David Robertson started to introduce himself and explain the first wine that the evening's tasting had to offer.

***

It really seemed silly, but Meera could not rest. She had been disturbed when DCI Mackay had called her to ask Hunter's whereabouts. She had no idea. She had not seen him at all yesterday, but she knew that it was not like him to be late for a briefing at work. It was unheard of for him to miss one altogether.

She had phoned Cameron, but he had not seen his father since their lunch together with Lucky Buchanan. She phoned Tim, but he told her that he had not heard from the boss. However, he did know Hunter was planning to go straight home after seeing Cameron because he had a darts match that evening, and wanted to shower and change before going to The Persevere Bar.

Still, whenever she called Hunter she was put through to voice mail. This was so out of character, Meera brooded. They had not fallen out. There was nothing left to be done, she would go over to his flat and find out what was wrong. It was probably something and nothing. Perhaps a few days off for peace and quiet that everybody had forgotten about. She would go over to see him just to put her own mind at ease.

It is always difficult to find a convenient place to park in Leith. Meera parked as close to the flat as she could get and noticed Hunter's old Toyota parked on the other side of the street. That gave her some relief. He must be at home, she thought.

Meera smiled and stepped out of her car and walked towards the stair door. She pushed the main door open and climbed the steps to the second floor. Meera rang the doorbell. There was no reply, but the door slipped open in front of her.

Meera frowned. This was not normal. Hunter never left his door unlocked, never mind open. Even taking the rubbish out to the communal bins, he locked the door behind him. She used to tease him that this was beyond what was necessary for a secure home. After all, his busy-body neighbour, Mrs Lamb, would notice anybody coming or going. But she had not been able to convince Hunter to change his ways.

She pushed the door a little further. "Hunter?" she called out.

"He's no' in, hen. Went out with his pal a while ago and hasny been back," Mrs Lamb said. The old woman next door, who acted as stair supervisor, had stuck her head out when she heard Meera's footsteps. "It takes me a wee while longer than it used to to get to the door, but I still likes to check who's in the building."

"Very sensible," Meera said. She was thinking of all the other terms that Hunter used to describe Mrs Lamb. "Did you notice which of his friends it was?" She asked.

"Not one I know, hen. A big fat fellow he was, with black hair. Certainly not one of the nice men in the darts team. They always get me a wee half of cider if I'm there to support them." Mrs Lamb smiled. Then her face fell. "One of the darts players got a right beating just outside near The Persevere yesterday. Just after Mr Wilson went out, it was. I wouldn't be surprised if Mr Wilson saw it even."

"Oh dear. I'm sorry to hear that, Mrs Lamb. I'll just have a quick look around and then go down to the pub and ask about the man to see he is alright. Thank you."

She went in. There was nothing out of place. Admittedly Hunter was not the most fastidious person in the world, but a used coffee mug in the living room was hardly out of the ordinary.

When Meera popped her head into The Persevere, Tracy was behind the bar.

"What the hell got into Hunter?" Tracy asked. "He didn't show up for the darts match. Then, when Jim went to speak to him about it, Hunter's giant of a friend thumps him good and proper and they get into the car with another bloke that Tom didn't see. It's not right, Meera. And to be fair it's no' like him, but what is Hunter playing at?" Tracy paused for breath and looked accusingly at Meera.

"I have no idea, Tracy, but I intend to find out," Meera said, sounding as worried as she looked.

Chapter Twenty-One

Oleksander took the first flight out of Kiev. It was with KLM, the Dutch airline. Oleksander remembered hearing that the country's King enjoyed flying so much that he worked as a pilot for the airline for many years. Oleksander was mildly amused to think of a King serving in such a capacity. But Why not? If Oleksander were King, he would make sure he could do as he liked. He smiled to himself. Maybe he was mixing up royalty with tyranny. His face fell back to a frown as he remembered the reason for his journey. Whoever had murdered his beautiful Xristina would wish he had never been born when Oleksander got hold of him.

Oleksander had to change planes in Schipol Airport in Amsterdam. From there he caught a flight to Edinburgh. He was sick to his stomach. Waves of nausea soured his mouth. It still felt unreal. Xristina dead? Who? Why? How? The frown deepened across Oleksander's forehead. Somebody would have to pay. At that exact moment he did not really care who, but somebody would suffer for the death of his darling daughter. He wanted to go to Xristina's home. The place where she died. The place he'd got to keep her safe.

"Oh God!" Oleksander moaned to a deity in whom he had never believed. "Please let her not have suffered."

The head policeman and the woman who spoke Ukrainian would meet him at the airport. They'd better have answers.

Oleksander spoke fluent, unaccented English. His service in the Security Service of Ukraine, *Sluzhba Bezpeky Ukrayiny* (SBU), had ensured that was the case. However, it suited Oleksander not to make the stupid Westerners as wise as himself. They had offered him a translator. They had never asked him if he spoke English. If they thought he did not understand their language, they would be more likely to let things slip: say things they did not want him to know or speak between themselves in an unguarded manner. Oleksander would hear, he would listen, and he would extract the appropriate revenge for Xristina's death.

***

Gillian knew that the wine tasting had been arranged before she had agreed to meet Mr Ponomarenko from the airport with DCI Mackay, but if she had thought about it more carefully, she would have been on the non-alcoholic wine with Tim. She had teased him last night for sticking to his guns and not drinking alcohol when he was in training for a marathon. This morning, the joke was certainly on her!

Mackay called Gillian at nine o'clock to tell her that Mr Ponomarenko's flight was arriving from Amsterdam at three in the afternoon. He wanted her at the airport no later than two o'clock. Gillian was still in bed but she was nodding her head in agreement with everything the senior officer said. She knew he couldn't see her down the phone but it was habit. She wished so much that she could break that habit. Her brain was begging her to keep her head still, keep her eyes shut and get the sandpaper out of her mouth.

She was amazed that Tim did not even once say 'I told you so.' She did love him.

He brought painkillers and a large glass of cold water to her. He helped her to sit up in bed and rubbed her back gently.

"Did you have good time last night?" Tim asked.

"Ssssh!" she whispered. "Not so loud."

Tim smiled. "Finish that water then go and take a shower. I'll go and make coffee."

She tried to smile, but wasn't sure that her brain was communicating with her face. Her head was just pleading for quiet, for water, for sleep.

Chapter Twenty-Two

Jamie and Frankie got home from Thomson's Top Cars a little later than usual. They had stopped off to buy nappies for the twins and beer for themselves before they picked Kylie-Ann and Dannii-Ann up from the childminder. Jamie helped Frankie manoeuvre the buggy over the threshold and watched his cousin take the twins into their part of the house.

"Joining us for a beer later, Frankie?" he asked.

"Aye, let me get the twins fed and bathed and we'll pop in to see you before their bedtime."

"No worries. Oh, Harry you're here. Gavin with you?" Jamie asked.

"That he is, young Jamie, and you wouldn't guess in a million years who else is here!" Harry grinned broadly at his younger cousin and stood with his arms stretched out to give Jamie a chance to list names of people he thought might be there.

"The Fuzz?"

"No."

"Strippers?"

"No."

"Arjun Mansoor's wife?"

"No. You really will never guess!"

At that point Jamie heard his father coming downstairs from the bedroom chatting and giggling with a very familiar voice.

"Oh no!" Jamie stared at Harry.

Harry nodded frantically.

"It's no' my fucking mam?" Jamie exclaimed.

"Aye it is! She had lunch with Uncle Ian today and now they're an item again."

"Jamie darlin', come and give you're mam a kiss, baby

boy!" Janice called from halfway down the stairs.

"Isn't this wonderful, Jamie?" Ian smiled at his son. "Your sweet mother and I met for lunch in town this afternoon and a lasting peace has been declared. We are re-united."

"What the fuck are you thinking, Pop?" Jamie scowled at his father. "Have you no' minded about her leaving us, me, when you went to the big house? I had to go and live at Frankie's, remember? She's a home-wrecker – a bloody liability! Please, Pop, no!"

Janice stared at Jamie and burst into tears. "Ian, are you going to let our boy speak to me like that?"

"I'm nobody's boy, Mam. I'm twenty-one next week, and I'll speak to you any way I like."

"Not in my house you won't!" Ian shouted. "Apologise to your mother, Jamie."

"Maybe no' in *your* house, Pop, but this place belongs to you, me and Frankie, if I remember rightly, and I'm not having her living in *my* house. So you can bloody lump it!"

"He owns this place?" Gavin whispered to Harry.

Harry shrugged.

"Why, you little brat!" Ian bellowed.

"What is he talking about, Ian?" Janice asked.

Ian drew a deep breath. He stared at Jamie, who stared defiantly back.

"Harry, could you and Gavin take your Auntie Janice and introduce her to the twins?" Ian asked.

"Aye, sure, come on with me, Auntie Janice. These girls are wee smashers."

Jamie saw his parents exchange glances.

"Come on, son," Ian said quietly to Jamie. "Let's get a beer and sort this out."

They chatted quietly, sitting in the kitchen at the breakfast bar. Jamie listened while his father explained how much he loved his mother and how much he had missed her. Jamie had to admit that he had missed Janice too. He was so hurt when she had taken off to Spain with Lenny The Lizard Pratt and left him behind. However, he agreed with his pop that she was worth another chance, and that it would be good to be a family again.

Ian and Jamie were sitting with another beer in the living room watching the News when Harry stuck his head around the door.

"Is it safe to come in now?" he asked with a smile.

"Of course it is. We're sorted, and Mam is staying, if she wants to," Jamie said.

"Thank you darlin' boy." Janice followed Harry into the room carrying Dannii-Ann. Kylie-Ann was in Frankie's arms. "Aren't these little girls just the sweetest things you could ever clap eyes on?"

"Of course they are," Frankie agreed.

"Frankie does a right good job with them too," Harry said.

"He certainly does. And I can even change a nappy," Jamie said proudly.

"We should celebrate tonight," Janice said. "I could make us one of my famous fish pies for us all?"

Ian and Jamie exchanged worried glances. The lack of fish pie had definitely been a plus since Janice left for Spain.

Ian smiled. "I thought I might order us all pizza. So that you don't waste any of your energy cooking for us hungry lumps, Janice."

"Well just for tonight. Back to my fresh home cooking tomorrow."

Jamie could not help but wonder if the profits from his father's new betting shops would run to the hiring of a cook.

Chapter Twenty-Three

Hunter was still hurting in the back of the car. His breath was gone. He tried to stay calm because he remembered that, if he didn't struggle with it, his breath would come back. Still, he felt as if somebody was holding his head under water.

"Hunter?" John's voice came from the front of the car.

Hunter could not reply. He had no breath, and Squires kicked him again, this time hard in the side of the head. He rolled onto his back and saw stars. His chest started hitching and his breaths finally started coming in small grateful sips. Squires kicked his head again. Hunter felt blackness seep into the edges of his vision. His eyes rolled back. His stomach clenched and he thought that he might be sick. Hunter was so confused that he actually thought the missing carpet was a good thing. The metal floor would be easier to clean if he vomited.

"How do you like my brand of punishment?" John asked. "I had to leave the force because of you, and you're lost to the force because of me. Neat, isn't it?"

Scuttling to the far side of the car, Hunter said, "John, this is madness! We can sort this out and nobody needs to know, I swear!"

Hunter pressed his back against the car wall. The bar with the handcuff was above his left shoulder. Squires kept staring at him. Hunter didn't move. He was trying to buy time. Catch his breath. Think straight. His head was still sore, making everything hazy, but he found the pain was an efficient way to bring clarity back to his life: the present.

He pulled his knees to his chest. Squires never stopped looking at him. Hunter felt something small and jagged against his foot. Bare feet can be useful. He thought it was probably a shard of glass or a rough pebble, but with mounting dread he saw it was neither. It was a tooth.

His breath caught in his throat. He glanced over at Squires, who continued to stare at him. Then Hunter watched as Squires opened the box he had seen in the corner of the car. Hunter felt sick again when he realised the contents were old rusty tools. He saw a set of pliers, a hacksaw, a hammer, and then he stopped looking. He didn't like to think about how the tooth came out or who it had belonged to.

"Are we having fun yet, Hunter?" John asked.

"We need to talk this through, John," Hunter said. "This is crazy."

"That is a very disappointing attitude," John said, shaking his head.

Hunter watched Squires. The huge man remained impassive, waiting for his instructions. But now the box was open, his attention was distracted from Hunter to the tools.

"Squires, cuff him now. He is getting on my nerves," John commanded.

"What!" Hunter exclaimed.

"Brian is going to cuff you now, Don't do anything stupid, he could crush you to death just by sitting on you. Understand? Stay still."

Hunter felt the car move into the right lane. They were still on a main road, possibly a motorway, but Hunter had no idea where they were.

"Go ahead, Squires, cuff him."

Hunter didn't have much time. Once the handcuff was in place, he would be fastened to the wall of the car – and then, he believed, he was finished. He stared down at the tooth. It made him think about what might be to come.

Squires moved towards Hunter from the rear of the car. Hunter thought about rushing him but decided against that. Squires would be expecting that, and the weight advantage was all with the man-mountain that was Squires. Then he thought about trying to open one of the doors and rolling out. He could take his chances, but with the car moving at least seventy miles an hour those odds weren't good. Anyway, he noticed the locks were secured. He didn't think he would get a door open before Squires grabbed him.

Finally Squires broke his silence and spoke. "Grab the bar next to the cuff with your left hand. Use all your fingers to hold on."

Hunter understood why. That would mean that he had one hand occupied and Squires only had one to watch. Not that it would matter. It wouldn't take Squires more than a second or two to snap the cuff into place and then it would be game over for Hunter. He gripped the bar, then he had an idea. It was a very long shot, probably impossible, but Hunter did not like to think about what would happen if he were cuffed to the wall of the car and Squires got to work on him with his tool box. Hunter had no choice. He could see that Squires was prepared for Hunter to rush him, but he was not prepared for Hunter to go in the other direction.

Hunter tried to be calm. Timing was all. He was tall enough – without that he didn't stand a chance – so when Squires moved towards the cuff, Hunter made his move. He only had a fraction of a second. Using his hand gripping the bar for leverage, he used all his force and swung his legs up. Not to kick Squires; they would have been expecting that. Instead, he pushed off making his body horizontal. He snapped his legs around like a whip, and aimed one heel for the side of John's head.

Hunter knew Squires would react fast, but luckily it was not quite fast enough. The kick had landed on John's head with great force, jerking it to the side. John's hands instinctively lifted from the steering wheel and the car veered sharply, sending Squires and Hunter into a rolling heap. Squires had his arm around Hunter's neck. Both men were experienced fighters and Squires had the weight advantage, but his extreme height made it difficult for him to manoeuvre in the back of the car.

Hunter smashed Squires' head against the back of the car and felt his grip around Hunter's neck loosen. Hunter smashed Squires again. Squires let go his grip of Hunter's neck as the car continued to veer right and left. John struggled to regain control of the vehicle.

Hunter scrambled forward on his hands and feet, but overbalanced and landed heavily on his knees. The sharp pain stopped him short and Squires grabbed him by the leg to pull him back. They had a brief tug-of-war then Hunter tried to kick Squires in the head, but missed. Then Squires lowered his head and bit Hunter's bare ankle hard. Hunter let out a howl of pain then kicked out harder. Squires held on. The pain was making Hunter's vision grow cloudy again. Luckily for him, the car swerved. Squires was thrown to the left. Hunter rolled to the right. Squires landed near the tool chest. His fingers disappeared inside it.

From the front of the car John Hamilton's voice said, "Give up now, Hunter, and I might stop and let you out."

The feeble possibility didn't even meet Hunter's consciousness. He knew John planned to take revenge for all the Police Force's alleged wrongs on him. He looked left and right, then saw Squires' hand come back into view. It was holding the hammer.

Squires moved towards him. Hunter was cornered and trapped. He had no chance of jumping Squires without getting badly beaten. That left him with only one choice.

Hunter made a half turn and punched John Hamilton in the head. Again, the car swerved sharply, sending Hunter and Squires airborne and causing Squires to drop the hammer. When Hunter landed he saw an opening: he dived at Squires and grabbed him. He could feel John struggling to control the car. Hunter and Squires started rolling around but the big man's extreme height was against him. He could not move as dexterously as Hunter. Hunter jammed his arm around Squires neck.

Something must have happened up front because Hamilton jammed on the brakes. Hunter's hold and the velocity of the car knocked Squires out cold. Hamilton was unconscious and his head was bleeding, but Hunter could not stop to check on him. He wriggled to reach into the front of the passenger seat and grabbed his wallet and phone. Then he looked at Hamilton's feet and spotted his shoes. They looked about the right size for Hunter. He felt guilty thinking about them, but Hunter needed shoes. He couldn't go far in bare feet. He struggled briefly with his conscience and decided he had no choice. Hunter took the shoes from the unconscious man with a muttered apology.

He crawled back into the rear of the car and escaped from a back door just as he could hear Squires beginning to stir.

Chapter Twenty-Four

Gillian was grateful to Tim for driving her to the airport. She liked his big, hybrid BMW; it was like riding on a large, comfortable sofa, but she did think it was a bit stuffy for them as a young couple. She was glad he was going to look at something a bit more sporty. He could afford it. She knew that now.

She tried with all her powers of persuasion to get Tim to come into the terminal with her. DCI Mackay was scary, but Tim was having none of it.

"It's not my fault that your head feel like it is full of candy floss rather than brain matter," he chided her. "I am off to look at cars. Anyway, Mackay won't eat you. Of course, Ponomarenko might, if he really is the dangerous man we think he is!"

Gillian scowled at Tim and climbed wearily out of the car. She turned back to see him leaning over into the passenger side of the vehicle waiting for a kiss. She was angry with him and considered whether she should award him such a favour before bending down and giving him a peck on the cheek.

"No. No lips when you are sending me into the lions' den all alone!"

She heard Tim laugh as she slammed the car door and headed off to find Mackay.

DCI Mackay was not difficult to find. He was wearing a smart suit and had DC Angus McKenzie, looking equally smart, as his driver. Gillian felt distinctly under-dressed in an Arran sweater, skinny black jeans and her favourite short walking boots. She could tell by looking at Mackay that he was not impressed with her choice of attire. Well, she could speak bloody Ukrainian and he couldn't, so it was just too bad.

"Good afternoon, Doctor Pearson. Thank you for joining

me," Mackay looked her up and down.

"Hello, I'm DC Angus McKenzie." The younger man stretched out his hand to shake.

She could feel his arm trembling, and was glad that at least one of them was more nervous than she was.

"How do you want me to play this?" Gillian asked Mackay.

"A rather unfortunate turn of phrase, Doctor Pearson. I doubt Mr Ponomarenko will think of this meeting as any kind of game."

"I understand that DCI Mackay," Gillian said. Her head was beginning to throb again. She needed another painkiller. Why had she not accepted Tim's suggestion to bring some with her? "But I, for one, would like to know why Xristina enrolled at the University under the name Marenko."

"Her father may not know the answer to that. I think, as the man is grieving, we may let that pass just now."

"The first time her father spoke to me, he introduced himself as 'Oleksander Marenko, Xristina Marenko's father'. So I am sure he was quite well aware of it."

"Interesting," Mackay looked thoughtful. "Let's take him to the mortuary first. He will want to see his daughter. Then, if my experience is anything to go by, he will want to see where her death occurred. I have Lord Buchanan (the landlord) and young Cameron Wilson (the tenant) on standby to meet us at the flat. After that, I plan to bring Mr Ponomarenko to the station so that he can ask any additional questions of me. And, it would appear, I may make necessary enquiries of him."

"Thank you, it is good to know your plan of action. Do I have time for a quick coffee before the plane lands? I have some tablets to take."

"If you must, but don't be long."

Gillian felt Mackay watch her make her way, first to the pharmacists for those painkillers, then to the cafe for a flat white coffee and a small bottle of still water to take away. She was back at Mackay's side in under ten minutes, sipping the hot coffee to take away the taste of the tablets.

Gillian had no difficulty spotting Oleksander Ponomarenko as he strode towards them wheeling a small case and carrying an old brown leather briefcase. She stepped forward to make the introductions and to express the condolences of all three of them personally and the University in general.

Oleksander nodded. "Unfortunately the sorrow of the institution will not bring my daughter back to life, and it is a pity that the University does not take better care of its students," he said sourly.

Gillian reddened, but thought better of mentioning to the man that the murder occurred in the accommodation he had found for his daughter, not on University grounds. She glanced at Mackay.

"He is not happy," she said.

"Good God, woman! Did you except him to be? What a stupid thing to say. Ask him if he would like a coffee and something to eat just now," Mackay said.

Oleksander wanted nothing but his daughter.

"Ask him if he wants to go to the mortuary to see Xristina," Mackay said to Gillian.

She listened respectfully while Oleksander agreed that it might be best to get that done and then he wanted to see where the crime had been committed. Gillian translated what he had said.

"Go and bring the car round then, and while we are in the mortuary, confirm with Cameron Wilson and Lord Buchanan that they will be there to meet us at the crime scene, will you DC McKenzie?" Mackay said quietly.

"Yes, Sir." Angus left to fetch the car.

The four people sat in the car as Angus drove to the mortuary. The rush-hour had started and traffic was heavy. Gillian found the silence too much.

"The mortuary is in an old part of the city known as The Cowgate," she said to Oleksander. "It is part of the lower level of the Old Town of Edinburgh that I told you about on the phone. It is also very narrow, and consequently The Cowgate can appear quite gloomy and dark in sections."

"That seems fitting," Oleksander replied and turned his head to look out of the window.

Aiden Fraser was the pathologist on duty. Gillian had not

met him before, but Mackay introduced them and she, in turn, introduced Mr Ponomarenko. She listened quietly as Aiden explained that Xristina had been killed by a blow to the head with a heavy object."

Gillian translated.

"Oh, my poor girl, what pain!" Oleksander cried.

Gillian asked Aiden if Xristina would have felt much pain.

"She probably did not feel much pain as she had been drugged with rohypnol. She also would have felt nothing when her fingertips were cut off. That happened after her death."

Oleksander let out a shout before Gillian translated this. She stared at him in bemusement.

"Yes, Doctor Pearson, I should have been honest with you. My English is not too bad. I feel for my poor, dear Xristina and I am going to see whoever murdered her is suitably punished."

"We are working on finding the culprit, Mr Ponomarenko," Mackay said sternly.

"Doctor Fraser, please may I see my daughter now?"

Aiden unveiled the corpse in silence.

"Her poor head! Her pretty face! Perhaps I can have a little while with my daughter alone, DCI Mackay? I will join you back at the car."

"Well, that's a turn-up for the books, Doctor Pearson," Mackay said, when they were out of earshot.

"It makes you wonder what else he hasn't told us, doesn't it?" Gillian said. "Do you still need me?" she asked, hoping to be released.

"I think you had better stick around. I think the visit to the flat could be difficult." Mackay offered her his first smile of the day.

Chapter Twenty-Five

Janice was very impressed by the new house.

"Imagine us living in the Grange!" she said. "It is a right fancy piece of property this, Ian, and I like how you've got that wee separate bit for Frankie and his girls. Nice, that."

"It's not bad, is it? Enough space for all of us, even when Harry is home."

"It's funny right now, the place is half empty! We've no' got nearly enough furniture for a house as big as this. You're lucky the last folk left the carpets and curtains or the neighbours would've got an eye full when I went for my shower." Janice laughed.

"I know. It'll be nice 'cos' we can choose stuff together, I just haven't had time to get round to it yet," Ian said.

"Just as well. I like what I like and I've got taste. I don't want your choice in every room," Janice smiled and tried to make her comment sound like a joke.

"Thanks," Ian said sarcastically.

"There is one thing that I'm curious about?"

"What's that, darlin'?" Ian asked.

He knew what she was going to ask, but she hesitated before she put her hands on her hips and spoke. "How did we afford a huge big gaff like this, Ian? And how come Jamie thinks it belongs to him and Frankie?"

"Do you really want all the ins and outs of it, Janice? You know your eyes'll glaze over as soon as I get technical."

"That's probably true. But I'll tell you what I do want to do."

"Oh dear, how much is this going to cost me?"

"About a grand. But it will be money well spent."

"I'll be the judge of that," Ian smiled.

Ian heard the door open and smiled at Janice giggling as she saw Frankie enter carrying the twins. The girls clung on to their dad's neck and fiddled with each other's fingers.

"Those are such beautiful little girls," Janice smiled. "You can tell they've got their Mam's red hair."

"Aye, Annie had lovely hair," Frankie smiled.

She watched as he put the girls gently onto the big black leather sofa that had come with them from the previous house in West Mains Road. It was amazing to see her young nephew cope so well with the little ones. He deserved something good to happen, and she would make sure it did.

"Your Uncle Ian and I were just talking about you, Frankie."

"We were?" Ian asked.

"Oh aye? Anything good?" Frankie grinned.

"Yes, very good. I've been noticing that your acne is still bad. Not as bad as it was, but bad."

"I know. Thanks for mentioning it. I don't like to talk about it. I don't even like to think about it," Frankie picked a pimple and brushed the pus onto his jeans. "I've tried everything. Steam, cream from the chemist, antibiotics from the doctor. Nothing seems to work."

"Well, I know what will work. We're going to go to the doctor and I am coming with you." Janice tapped him on the shoulder.

"Really, Auntie Janice? I don't think so."

"I am not asking, I am telling you what is going to happen," Janice smiled. "We will get a prescription for isotretinoin capsules. They work."

Janice watched in amusement as Frankie looked at her gloomily. "I've heard about things that work before," he said. "It's never been true."

"And your Uncle Ian has just been saying how he would like to be able to help, so he will pay for you to have a course of treatment at the skin clinic in Lothian Road, just near his new bookmaker's shop. We'll get you light therapy there. In three months you won't recognise yourself." Janice paused for breath and smiled at Frankie. "Have I ever lied to you?"

"Don't answer that, Frankie," Ian laughed.

Chapter Twenty-Six

Hunter saw cars coming towards him. He ran to the side of the road, keen to get out of the way. He was dancing slightly with the shoes still in his hands and the roughness of tarmac and grit hurting his feet.

He should have looked where he was going, because a car passed very close to him and its tyres screeched. Horns began to blare and he heard a driver curse out of a window at him. He felt the dirt from the road fly towards his face. It stung in his eyes and tasted nasty when it got into his mouth.

Hamilton's car began to move forward. Hunter couldn't see why Hamilton had braked so sharply, but he couldn't help smiling in relief. He thought the disgraced cop would just drive away and Hunter sat down on the verge to pull on the shoes he had taken.

But Hamilton did not drive away. The car was on the hard shoulder about twenty yards from where Hunter was sitting. He watched as Hamilton jumped out of the driver's-side door and Hunter couldn't help grinning as Hamilton swore violently when he felt the sharp pieces of grit on the road through his socks.

Hunter was exhausted, he didn't think he could move, but with Hamilton heading towards him, the pain and exhaustion became very secondary. He had only one choice open to him – get away from Hamilton – and fast.

He climbed as quickly as he could up the steep verge to the side of the road. He had the advantage of the shoes, so at least the twigs and brambles did not tear his feet. Hunter could hear Hamilton's curses becoming less distinct as he moved upwards, and when he got to the top, he saw farm land. Hunter didn't look closely: he didn't think for long: he just leapt down the steep slope towards the fields. He had not realised quite how sharp an incline there was, so he stumbled, then gravity took over and he tumbled the rest of the way down.

It seemed to take a long time to reach the bottom, but at least he was rolling further away from the road and further away from Hamilton and Squires.

As he rolled, his legs hit a tree: he hit his head against a rock and he didn't even like to think what his ribs hit as his eyes began to close and the world turned black again and everything felt still.

Hunter had no idea how long he had been lying there, when he was woken by a man leaning over him.

"Sir? Are you all right, sir?"

Hunter opened his eyes and squinted up into the light. "Where am I?" he asked.

"You're on my farm, Landsmuir. Did you come from that motor that went out of control? I saw it from my tractor. That field there is a bit higher and I could see the road."

"Yes, I think I did. It's a wee bit of a blank exactly how I got here." Hunter shook his head. That didn't help.

"You looked like you were running for help, but you didn't get very far, I'm afraid." The young farmer reached down with his left hand to help Hunter up. When Hunter got his balance the farmer held out his right hand and said, "Simon Land, at your service, sir."

"DI Hunter Wilson of Police Scotland," Hunter said as they shook hands.

"My guess is, by now, some of your boys will be down at your car. Want a lift round?"

"Yes please. I'd rather not go back the way I came!"

"We'll have to get back to the farmhouse for the Land Rover, but I can give you a lift on the tractor. You won't have to walk far."

"Thank you, that's very good of you. I'd appreciate that," Hunter said.

"I hope you won't think I'm being rude, but you don't look too clever."

"I don't feel too clever."

"Do you want me to see if my mother can fix you up a bit?"

"No, I'll manage. I don't want to waste time on that right now. Let's get back to the car," Hunter said. "Lead the way, will you, Simon?"

Hunter peered through the windscreen of the Land Rover. This was clearly a working vehicle, and it was not clear when, or if, it had been washed. He could see that the red Volkswagen had veered into the hard shoulder. John Hamilton stood in stocking feet in front of a bemused traffic cop. Hunter could see that Squires was already in an ambulance.

"Do you need me to stick around, DI Wilson?" Simon asked as Hunter climbed gingerly out of the car.

"No, son, but let me put your name and contact details into my phone, in case I need you to remind me of anything later."

"It wouldn't surprise me a bit if you needed that," Simon laughed. "You may know a couple of old school mates of mine too, Tim Myerscough and Bear Zewedu?"

"I do, they make a good team," Hunter said.

"Always did," Simon smiled.

Hunter walked over towards the police car. He leaned against it heavily.

"Sorry, sir, you'll need to move along. This isn't a public spectacle," an officious PC commanded.

"And I am not the public. I am DI Hunter Wilson from Edinburgh and these men kidnapped me and assaulted me. Arrest them, officer."

"I can't do that on any old say-so, sir. Have you got ID?"

"No I bloody haven't they kidnapped me! I can give you my FIN if you like, and you can check it."

"You want me to run around looking for what may be a non-existent Force Identification Number? Do I look like a man with time on my hands, sir?"

Hunter took out his phone and dialled DCI Mackay's number. The phone was switched off. Hunter stared at his phone and swore.

"Nobody believe you're a big bad policeman, Hunter? I'm not surprised. Look at yourself! You're a mess - and those are my bloody shoes!" John Hamilton said.

"So much for Police Scotland being one big inclusive police force," Hunter sighed at the traffic constable and shook his head. He looked thoroughly frustrated. Then he smiled. He had an idea. Hunter dialled Tim Myerscough's number.

"Good afternoon, Boss. Where the hell have you been?" Tim asked anxiously. "Meera's been terribly worried about you."

"I'm glad somebody has. You won't believe me when I tell you, but the short version is John Hamilton fucking kidnapped me and now I'm trying to prove to this traffic cop from Glasgow that I'm a DI but I've got no ID."

"Fuck! Really? We did think it wasn't like you to miss a briefing," Tim said.

"I have never missed one in my bloody life – until yesterday," Hunter replied.

"So, has that numpty Hamilton not got something worthwhile to do? A job, perhaps? Rather than beating up former colleagues and making life more difficult for himself?"

"Your guess is as good as mine, Tim. Can you come and get me, please?"

"Look, Boss, I'm on a day off today and I'm in the middle of something, otherwise I would come, you know that. But I'll call PC Neil Larkin and get him to come and pick you up. Where exactly are you?"

"On the motorway just near Landsmuir Farm. I believe you know the owner?" Hunter said.

"I'll get it sorted, Boss," Tim said.

***

It was as Tim rang off from speaking to Neil that he suddenly remembered where he had seen Professor Zelay Sheptytsky before meeting him at the wine tasting.

Chapter Twenty-Seven

Lucky and Cameron were in the flat when Mackay, Gillian and Angus arrived in Frederick Street with Oleksander. They climbed out of the car and Oleksander looked up at the building first.

"This is where she died, my girl," he muttered. He walked around in a full circle and stopped when he got to the view to the North. "What is that across the sea?" he asked Gillian in Ukrainian.

"It's not really the sea. It's a river. The mouth of the River Forth that leads into the North Sea. The land you can see over there is another part of Scotland, known as the Kingdom of Fife. It's a beautiful view in the summer."

"It is quite lovely now. So they have their own king there, you say?"

"No, but I'm sure they would have if they could have. They are proud of their home county."

Oleksander smiled and turned back towards the door. "I don't suppose I can postpone going up any longer. Let's go in. The place I got for her is on the second floor."

He pushed open the stair door from the street and led the others up the old stone steps. He reached the door with no name on the first floor and stopped. He stood looking at it.

"I thought you said there would be somebody here to let us in?" he asked Mackay.

"Yes, Mr Ponomarenko, they are at the second floor," Mackay replied.

"This is the second floor. The shop is on the first floor and this is the second. The floor above is the third floor, I think. Why is my daughter's name not on this door?"

"I don't think she told anybody her real name, did she?" Gillian asked. "And anyway, this is the first floor, not the second, Mr Ponomarenko."

"I know what flat I got! Shops first, this second. I got my contact to fetch her here when she arrived in the country and gave him one thousand pounds to give her to settle in."

DC Angus McKenzie cleared his throat. Oleksander glared at him, Mackay glanced in his direction.

"DC McKenzie?" Mackay prompted.

"Sir, I think I understand what has happened."

"Yes?" Mackay asked.

"Mr Ponomarenko, were you taught English by a British person or an American?" Angus asked.

"By a Ukrainian!"

"Where did he learn English?"

"Ukraine. But the workshops were run by agents, I mean officials, who had worked in the USA. Why?"

"That is what has caused the confusion. In America the shops would be on the first floor, this would be the second, and the flat above the third, and so on. However, here, Mr Ponomarenko, we say that the shops are on the ground floor, this is the first floor and the flat your daughter was delivered to was the second floor."

"Ridiculous! So my daughter was not even in the right place. She shouldn't have been in that flat when she died?"

"That's what I think," Angus said quietly.

"Angus, you are brilliant!" Gillian said. "That is exactly right. Your daughter was not living in the flat you got for her, Mr Ponomarenko, but in the flat on the floor above. It was a British person that you asked to get her to her flat?"

"Yes, a Scottish man."

"Then that is why there was the confusion," Gillian said. "Shall we go up and see the place?"

Oleksander slowly followed Gillian up the stairs to Lucky's flat. The ghastly realisation of the mistake and its outcome sank into his mind. The door was standing open and they walked in followed by Mackay and Angus.

"Lord Buchanan?" Mackay called out.

"DCI Mackay, I presume. And I remember you, you're Myerscough's woman, aren't you? We met a while back at the rugby." He shook hands with Mackay and Gillian and offered his condolences to Oleksander after they were introduced.

"My daughter should never have been here," Oleksander said miserably.

"I'm well aware of that. Have we discovered what your daughter was doing in my flat in the first place?" Lucky asked gruffly.

"A huge man dropped her off. He had keys, but didn't need to use them as I was in when he arrived with Xristina," Cameron Wilson said as he walked into the hall. "He said the boss had told him to drop her off here at the flat on the second floor and he gave me five hundred pounds for her keep. I just thought the boss he was talking about was you, Lucky."

"No, that boss would be me, and if he had tried to use the keys this whole wicked murder of my daughter should not have happened," Oleksander said. "He should have brought her to the flat below."

"It's empty, right enough," said Cameron. "But it's on the first floor, not the second."

"I have worked out what caused that confusion," Angus said from the back of the group. Everybody else stopped talking. They seemed to have forgotten that he was there. Angus explained his theory again.

"Yes, yes, I can see how that would happen," Lucky said. "Cleverly worked out."

"So who was the man that brought her? I gave him a thousand pounds for Xristina, to get her settled. Why did he not just give it to her?" Oleksander asked gruffly.

"I didn't know who he was at the time. A man mountain. A really huge, tall guy with light-coloured hair. But you know him, don't you, Lucky?" Cameron asked.

"I've met him a couple of times a while back. His name is Brian Squires. When he referred to the boss, he did mean you rather than me, Mr Ponomarenko, and didn't realise Cameron misunderstood. Don't you think?"

"I don't know what he meant. I did make arrangements for other women to be brought into the city. But they were employees: that requirement certainly didn't extend to my daughter. She was just to be shown the way to the place I got for her. It seems that should have been the flat below yours," Oleksander said to Lucky.

"If you want my opinion, Brian Squires is not the sharpest knife in the drawer," Lucky said.

"This man is dangerous and carries a knife?" Oleksander asked anxiously.

"No, I'm sorry. I mean he is not very intelligent."

"Well, that will be true if, as it seems, he caused my daughter to be here to be killed. And it seems that he owes me five hundred pounds," Oleksander said angrily.

***

Tim was having a much happier day than Gillian. After dropping her at Edinburgh Airport, he drove over to Thomson's Top Cars. He had considered carefully whether to give his business to this place, but decided that, as Jamie and Frankie had stayed out of trouble for several months and Ian Thomson was out of prison on parole, the best way to keep the hapless trio on the straight and narrow was to support their legitimate business.

"Hello, Blondie, what can I do for you today?" Jamie called as Tim wandered into the showroom.

Tim smiled. "I wanted to speak to your dad about getting a new car."

"You'll no' get Pop right now. In fact you may not get him at all today."

"Really? What's up?"

"You won't guess."

"Try me."

"He and my Mam got back together yesterday."

"No, you're right. I'd never have guessed that in a million years."

"I'm not right pleased. I think Pop is being taken for a mug, but there's nought I can do about it. You'd have thought he'd have learned by now, wouldn't you?"

"Well I hope it works out for them this time."

114

"It won't."

"Frankie not in?"

"No he's having a day off with the twins, so you're stuck with me. What you after, anyway? I thought you'd not long got that big flashy BMW. Hybrid, isn't it?"

"Yes, I did, and I love it, but I want something a bit more sporty too. You know, when I'm out and about with my girlfriend."

"Knowing you, you'll have your eye on something right particular, so spill, Blondie. Let's see the damage."

Tim sat down beside Jamie at his computer.

"You want a coffee?" Jamie asked.

"No thanks, Jamie. Now, I like the look of the Mecedes-Benz SLS AMG."

"Aye, with your height you might need that; it's got decent headroom," Jamie said.

"And it's got some power," Tim agreed.

"Aye, but you can hardly drive more than twenty mph in the city, so does that matter?"

"It does to me!"

"You want it new?"

"Why not? Yes," Tim grinned.

"Any special colour?"

"Probably black, Jamie."

"That's not very flash! Why not let us get it body-wrapped to your own design? That would look right flash. See!" Jamie turned his computer towards Tim showing him cars in various gaudy designs.

"My goodness, Jamie! Those are certainly quite different from the plain old black I had seen in my head." Tim smiled. He wasn't sure a body-wrapped car was quite up his street, but he couldn't fault Jamie's enthusiasm. "Can you get hold of a black Mecedes-Benz SLS AMG for me and I'll think about the design? I take it that it won't matter what the base colour of the car is before it gets body-wrapped?"

"You take it correctly, Blondie. Now what specs do you want? And I'll order it up for you. I'll need to ask you for a deposit, mind." Jamie grinned.

Chapter Twenty-Eight

DCI Allan Mackay called the room to order. He saw that Bear, Mel and Angus were still tucking into bacon rolls, while Colin Reid was in the middle of peeling a tangerine.

"I don't suppose any of you could find the time to eat at home before you get here, could you?" he grumbled.

"Only Jane and I manage that, Sir," Rachael said.

"I hope you're not feeling too virtuous, DC Anderson. You both seem to be armed with mugs of tea."

Before Mackay could comment further, he saw Hunter come into the briefing room. He was carrying a large mug of coffee from the coffee maker in his office. Mackay smiled as a round of applause met Hunter's entry.

"I can tell you are all as pleased as I am to witness the return of DI Hunter Wilson," he said. "I read your statement and you have identified former DC John Hamilton as having broken into your home and then driven you away against your will. Can you tell us what on earth happened, DI Wilson? And why? And then you can tell me why you are not still in the hospital!"

Hunter shrugged. "I can't tell you everything, to be honest. I was out cold for a great deal of the time that I was with John Hamilton, and struggling with Brian Squires for the rest of it. The brute force of Squires is not to be sneezed at."

"Why does Hamilton feel so violently towards you, Boss?" Tim asked. "That was a nasty attack."

"He seems to blame the team in general, and me in particular, for the fact that he left the police force."

"But he resigned, rather than being disciplined for taking cocaine," Colin said. "Everything that went wrong for him was his own fault."

"It makes no sense. He made his own choices. Bad ones, but they were his choices," Jane said.

"Yes they were. Nice to see you back, by the way, DS Renwick, in your new official capacity," Hunter smiled. "But if the going gets tough, it is always easier to blame someone else than to accept your own faults."

"True enough," Mackay nodded. "So he bundled you into a red Volkswagen car to punish you because he resigned from the force?"

"More or less. He said that he wanted me to suffer as much he had," Hunter said.

"And did he see this ending well?" Bear asked.

"There were times when I didn't see it ending at all, Bear. Brian Squires was in the back with me and he is a big beast of a man." Hunter grimaced. "When I saw Hamilton had teamed up with Brian Squires, my heart sank, because Squires is never good news."

"But to be fair, Boss, Squires doesn't have the brains he was born with. He is just the muscle any time he's involved," Mel said.

"True, but as far a sheer force goes, you won't get much stronger," Hunter said.

"Brian Squires? We heard that name yesterday, didn't we Sir?" Angus said to Mackay.

"We did, but let's get to the end of DI Hunter's attack first, shall we, DC McKenzie?"

"There's not much more to say, Sir," Hunter said. "Both Hamilton and Squires were taken to hospital as a result of the injuries they sustained. I was cautioned because Hamilton told the traffic boys that I had come with them willingly but that I injured both him and Squires. Luckily DC Myerscough answered his phone and arranged for PC Neil Larkin to come and pick me up."

"We will get that cautioned against you squared away, don't worry, Hunter," Mackay said.

"Where were you, Boss?" Nadia asked.

"I was found by a farmer, Simon Land of Landsmuir Farm off the M8."

"Land? That'll be the farm boy who was at school with us, won't it Tim?" Bear asked.

"The very same. He's a decent man, Boss," Tim said.

"Some farm boy if he went to Merchiston Castle School!" Hunter smiled.

"That was how I got someone to you so quickly. I know the area and that farm. After Mum died, Ailsa and I spent many a weekend with the Lands when Dad was working. Ailsa had quite a crush on Simon's horse, Jonty. That's where she learned to ride."

"I thought you were going to say she had a crush on him or maybe a brother. It never occurred to me you were going to say 'horse'." Jane laughed.

"He certainly did the right thing by me. I am very grateful to him," Hunter said. "Neil took me back to Meera's but she insisted on taking me to hospital because I had been unconscious. I had to stay in overnight, but I persuaded them to let me out first thing this morning. That's why I'm able to be here, Sir."

"What injuries did you sustain, DI Wilson?" Mackay asked.

"Multiple bruises, a couple of cracked ribs and a cut to my head here," Hunter pointed to the back of his skull. "The hospital also found rohypnol in my bloodstream. Hamilton must have got it into me: he gave me a glass of water to drink when I woke up."

"They found rohypnol in Xristina's body too, didn't they, Sir?" Nadia asked.

"Can forensics tell if it is the same batch?" Angus asked.

"I have no idea, Angus, but we can ask," Hunter said.

"So Squires has teamed up with an angry John Hamilton? I don't like the sound of that," Colin said.

"Are they in custody or did they get bailed, Sir?" Rachael asked.

"I have no idea. DS Renwick, could you find out for us?" Mackay asked.

"With respect, MIT doesn't usually have information on traffic cases," she replied.

"I'll see what I can find out, if that would be useful, Sir,"

Angus said. "I can make the enquiries so we get a proper handle on Hamilton and Squire's whereabouts."

"Yes, that will be helpful, DC McKenzie," Mackay nodded. "Now perhaps DC McKenzie and I can report back as to our meeting with Oleksander Ponomarenko?"

"Yes, sir," Angus said.

"Why did he and his daughter use Marenko instead of Ponomarenko?" Tim asked.

"No good reason given, DC Myerscough. When he was asked by Doctor Pearson he just let it drop," Mackay replied.

"They are, apparently, a very famous family in Ukraine, and maybe he did not want that to influence the grades the University awarded his daughter," Angus said.

"Famous? Notorious more like," Bear said.

"What do you mean, Bear?" Colin asked.

"There are two Ponomarenko brothers. They officially run an import/export business, buying and selling all over the world, but when I was doing my A Level on the old USSR the name often crept in with a mention to the Russian Mafia. I don't doubt the daughter wanted to avoid being associated with that, if she's a decent girl. Sorry, was a decent girl."

"Could that be why she was murdered?"Hunter asked.

"That might make sense," Bear said. "One of the Ponomarenko brothers married into a very well-respected family, the Sheptytsky family. I doubt the woman's family were too thrilled with her marrying a local gangster."

"I may have something to add here," Tim said.

"Well spit it out, young Myerscough," Hunter said.

"We had a wine tasting at the house on Friday, because I was going to see about a new car on Saturday."

"I don't really want to hear about your social calendar, Tim," Hunter said flatly.

"No, Boss. But one of the guests that Gillian invited was her new professor, Professor Zelay Sheptytsky."

"Really? Now where does he fit it? I wonder if there's a connection?" Hunter asked.

"Well, I couldn't place him at first, but then I did. Ailsa and I had been to see Dad, and in the visiting room, I saw the

119

professor talking to Arjun Mansoor. He is certainly not Mansoor's usual type of visitor. Sheptytsky is very academic in look and in the way he holds himself."

"He is well respected in his field, too," Bear added.

"Could Mansoor be involved in Xristina's death?"Angus asked.

"I never underestimate that bloody man Mansoor," Hunter said. "How did Xristina end up renting a room in my son's flat, anyway?"

"Now that was really interesting, and it was young DC McKenzie who worked that one out," Mackay said.

"It was simple, really. Mr Ponomarenko had secured the second floor flat for his daughter to use, or so he thought. In fact there was a mix-up between the floor numbering. The flat which was empty, and which Xristina should have been living in, was on the first floor, the way we count things: ground, first, second."

"Yes, I remember Sergeant Charlie Middleton saying the first floor flat was empty before he went on holiday," Hunter commented.

"Yes, Sir. But as English is not Mr Ponomarenko's first language, he got confused and counted the floors the way they do in America. He told Squires to drop Xristina off and see she got settled in the second floor flat," Angus said.

"Squires? What does Brian Squires have to do with this?" Hunter asked.

"Your son identified him, and Lucky Buchanan confirmed his name, don't you remember, Hunter?" Mackay said. "He admitted that he is acquainted with Squires. Met him socially a while back, apparently. But he was able also to confirm that Squires does not work for him and never has."

"Oh yes, I do remember, now. With that bump on the head, I had forgotten. So when Squires said to Cameron the about the boss saying Xristina was to stay there, Cameron thought he meant Lucky, but Squires was actually talking about *his* boss, Ponomarenko?"

"Probably." Angus shrugged.

"Squires is too damn thick to ask what Cameron was doing

in Xristina's flat!" Hunter said.

"And perhaps Cameron is too naïve to question an order he thinks comes from Lucky," Tim said quietly.

Hunter nodded. "Sadly, yes."

Chapter Twenty-Nine

If Frankie had thought about it, it should not have come as any surprise that his Auntie Janice had already arranged his series of appointments at the skin clinic. He knew she was not a patient person, and once she got an idea in her head it was very hard to dislodge it. Frankie had certainly never managed.

When Janice had offered to come with him to the clinic or to look after the twins, he chose the lesser of two evils. He kissed his girls, and headed into town alone.

He stood outside the salon for several minutes, girding up his courage to enter. The windows were floor-to-ceiling and he could see the interior clearly. There were only women inside. He couldn't see the clients. That was a good thing. However, the staff all wore white overalls, trousers and white crocs. They were all so beautiful, even if their old-fashioned footwear did leave a bit to be desired. Frankie hoped that whoever treated him would not be too unnervingly pretty. He had always got tongue-tied if girls were pretty. Except with Annie.

Eventually, Frankie pushed open the door of the skin clinic. He was smiling: he always did when he thought about Annie. The door was surprisingly heavy, and he noticed that there was a door closer, so he guessed its resistance added to the weight he was feeling.

"How can I help you?" one of the pretty members of staff called from the counter.

Frankie walked over to her and as he approached, he realised she was no older than he was. Nevertheless, she was attractive enough to be intimidating to him.

"I'm Frankie, Frankie Hope. I have an appointment."

"Yes, it was Mrs Thomson who phoned wasn't it? She's one

of our regulars. Lovely lady, Mrs Thomson. Now, let me see."

Frankie watched as the young woman read the notes beside his name. He could feel his heart-rate rising and his cheeks colouring. His hands felt clammy. The smell in the salon was unfamiliar, and he thought he was going to pass out. Why on earth had he let Auntie Janice talk him into this?

"Yes, this all looks fine. Your series of treatments is all pre-paid, Mr Hope. Just have a seat behind the alcove there, and Donna will be right with you. I'll tell her you've arrived."

Frankie tried to thank the girl, but he was so nervous that no words came out. He turned and walked in the direction the girl had indicated. He had hardly had time to sit down and look at the other patients (the old man with the hairy nose, the girl with even more spots than he had, and the woman with the worst case of rosacea Frankie had ever seen) when he heard his name called. He turned to look at Donna. Frankie blushed. She was the most beautiful girl he had seen since Annie died.

"Just follow me," she said, and led the way to a treatment room.

***

As she closed the door, she asked Frankie to sit down on the only chair in the room. She noticed how shy Frankie was and realised that he was embarrassed by his acne. Donna also knew that she could assist him. She knew that the light treatment would help.

"Now, Frankie, may I call you Frankie?"

"Yes, it's my name," Frankie whispered.

"I mean, would you rather I used 'Mr Hope'?"

"No. Frankie's fine."

"That's grand, I'm Donna," she said in a lilting Irish accent.

"Nice to meet you," Frankie said shyly.

"Do you know much about light treatment?" Donna asked.

"Nothing really. Will it help? My aunt told me I should go to the doctor and get isotretinoin prescribed as well."

"No, not while you're undergoing light treatment, Frankie. There can be nasty effects if you use both at once."

"Oh, right, thanks, so just the lights," Frankie said.

Donna explained to Frankie that although, for centuries, people who had acne had been told to sit out in the sun to 'dry out' their skin, that advice was only partly right. Dryness and sun can harm the skin, but visible blue light can kill acne.

"Throughout this treatment you must be gentle with your skin. Keep it moisturised and no picking!" Donna could tell by the scabs around his face that Frankie was a picker.

"Right, let's get started!" Frankie grinned.

"Not so fast, Frankie," Donna smiled pushing him back down into the chair.

She went on to explain that if she also added red light as well as blue light into the skin treatment mix, pores deeper down in the skin would get treated because red light can travel further than blue light. In addition, if the red light was used in the right amounts, it could shrink the glands and reduce the production of oil in the skin.

Donna saw the blank look on Frankie's face. "Have I baffled you with science?" She laughed.

"Just a bit. What do you think I should get?"

"Well that was a long way round for a short cut to tell you that I need to do skin treatment samples today and get you to come back in a few days so I can see the results. I need to take photos of your skin as it is first. Is that all right?"

"Do you have to?"

"I do, but I'm not going to take pictures like you would take on the beach, I want to take one of each area of skin we are going to sample today, so that I can compare them as they are now with what I see when we meet next time."

"That sounds fine then, Donna. Go ahead."

Donna asked Frankie a few additional questions and then cleaned his skin with a soft wet wipe before handing him goggles to protect his eyes. She helped him to fit them and then carried out fifteen seconds of different treatments on each of the three areas she had chosen.

"I've just put blue light on your left cheek: red light on your right cheek and I've pulsed red and blue light onto your forehead. Can you make an appointment to come back in a few days, and we'll see the difference?"

"Will there be a difference that quickly?" Frankie asked.

"Gosh, I would hope so!" Donna smiled.

"How often will I have to come?" Frankie asked.

"I'll know better when I see the results or the tests, but probably once a week for six months and then regular maintenance after that. Your aunt has paid for a year's worth of treatment. You are a lucky guy, this isn't cheap. So, I'll see you next week?"

"I'll look forward to it," Frankie smiled.

"So will I. You do have beautiful brown eyes, you know, Frankie," Donna said as he walked away.

Even with his back turned towards her she knew he had blushed. Donna giggled.

Chapter Thirty

Frankie was leaving the clinic when he saw his brother Harry with Gavin. They were just coming out of The Edinburgh Massage Suite a little further up the street on Lothian Road. Frankie waved to them and Harry waved back.

"Where you been, Bro'?" Harry shouted across to Frankie.

No chance in hell I'm telling you that, Frankie thought, as he called back, "Just a wee wander round the town. Auntie Janice offered to have the girls and give me some time off." He ran across the road and a car blared its horn at him.

"That red Volkswagen was going far too fast in the city," Gavin said, as they gathered on the pavement outside The Edinburgh Massage Suite.

"We were just going to The Shakespeare for a pint, you want to join us?" Harry asked.

"Aye, go on then. I'll only stop for one, like, because I'll have to get back to the twins. I don't want to leave them with Auntie Janice for too long." Frankie fell into step with the others. "You been to see Olena and Symona again?"

"Right on!" Harry laughed.

"Why don't you take them out, you bloody tight wads, instead of always popping into see them at work?" Frankie frowned.

"They don't seem to get much time off, and they're not meant to date the clients."

"So what do you get at a massage, then?" Frankie asked.

"Wouldn't you like to know, Bro'?" Harry said, and Gavin laughed.

Frankie was pleased to have time out with the lads. It wasn't as if he didn't love the twins. He did, and with all his heart. Still, every now and again it was nice not to have to play

'*Round and Round the Garden*' or '*This Little Piggy*' to get a laugh out of someone. He also guessed that if his uncle and aunt were back together, the twins should get to know Janice.

"You're a million miles away, Frankie, lad," Harry said. "What do you want to drink?"

"Sorry, Harry. Corona, no lime. That'd be great."

"Fancy!" Gavin smiled.

As Harry went to get the round in, Frankie turned to Gavin and said, "So really, do you just get a back-rub at the massage place?"

Gavin leaned close to Frankie and whispered, "That's what most folk get, but me and Harry pay for a long session and we gets the works cause we're their boyfriends." Gavin made a sign with his hands indicating what 'the works' meant.

"So they don't fuck anybody but you?" Frankie asked incredulously.

"Course not! They're our special girls!" Gavin replied with a certainty that surprised Frankie.

Frankie was about to get up and leave the other lads to their second pint when he saw his Uncle Ian storm into the bar.

"Barry, set me up a pint and a large whisky chaser, will you?"

"Of course, Mr Thomson. You had bad news?"

"I'm not sure what I've just found, Barry. But there's a name that spells trouble every time I hear it." Ian downed the whisky in one slug and indicated to Barry that he should fill the glass up again.

Frankie went over to Ian.

"What's up? Is there something I can help with, Uncle Ian?"

Harry and Gavin brought their glasses to the bar and stood on either side of Frankie and Ian.

"You need someone fixed, Uncle Ian? Me and Gavin can do that for you, you know," Harry said.

"Aye. No probs." Gavin nodded. "Just say the word, Mr T. You've been right good to me, letting me stay an' all."

"I've just come from the betting shop up the road. I'm not sure what's going on. Let's get a table," Ian said. He placed a fifty-pound note on the bar. "Another round for me and the lads, Barry. Bring it over will you? And just keep the change."

Barry smiled. "Thank you, Mr Thomson. That's right nice of you."

Frankie followed Ian, Harry and Gavin to a table in the corner. He noticed that there was nobody within hearing distance.

"What's up, Uncle Ian?" Frankie asked.

"You are only going to say 'I told you so', and Jamie will say it even louder."

Frankie frowned. "Then it has to be something about Argy Bargy Mansoor and his wife."

"Got it in one, lad!"

"The guy that used to manage Thomson's Top Cars? I never really took to him," Harry said.

"You were right not to," Frankie said.

"Well, more fool me. I think the devil you know is better than the one you don't know. So I took the wife on as manager of the new betting shops. She's been doing a fine job, I thought, keeping two sets of books: one for me and one for the taxman. But I goes in to Lothian Road today when she's in Frederick Street, just to have a look at the accounts because she didn't get them to me for last week. What do I see?" Ian grimaced.

"Here's the drinks, Mr Thomson," Barry said before lifting each in turn off the tray, and walking back to the bar to serve two very young ladies wearing incredibly skimpy tops.

"You girls should take care. You'll catch pneumonia dressed like that in Edinburgh in October!" Barry laughed as he walked towards them. The girls looked at each other and giggled as they ordered double vodkas with Redbull.

"No problem, two vod-bombs coming up ladies," Barry grinned. "Don't talk too loud, will you? I'm trying to earwig those boys chat over there." He nodded towards Ian's table.

The girls giggled and shrugged.

"So what did you find? Has she been skimming?" Harry asked.

"God, I wish that was all!" Ian exclaimed. "You really won't believe it, boys."

"If it's bad and it's a Mansoor, I bet we will," Frankie said.

" Aye, well, I found the taxman's accounts, titled 'HMRC', and my set of accounts, titled 'Thomson' – and, of course, a healthy difference between the two."

"Well that's fine, it's what you expected, wasn't it?" Harry asked.

"Aye, lad. What I didny expect was another set of accounts titled 'Ponomarenko' and another one titled 'Mansoor' – each showing money getting creamed off. In fact, the last two have money coming in that doesn't show in either my accounts or the taxman's." Ian swallowed another whisky in one and held up his glass for Barry to see.

"That doesn't make any sense!" Frankie said angrily.

"It does if this Ponomarenko, whoever he is, is laundering money through my fucking business and Mansoor is taking a cut," Ian growled.

"Ponomarenko? I've heard that name," Gavin said. "Harry, isn't it the proper last name of that lassie we found after the club? The dead one? It's been in the papers that her dad came over to identify the body. Rotten job that would be, to come all this way to see your dead wean."

"It's no just a dead wean he'll be having if he's trying to scam me," Ian Thomson said softly. "I'll go down after closing tonight and see if it's the same in the other shop, then I'll work it all out tomorrow."

"You can't drive like that, Uncle Ian. I've only had the one bottle and this wee sip, do you want me to drive you there and home?"

"You passed your test then, Frankie?"

"No' quite," Frankie grinned.

"That'll be a no then, lad. The last thing I bloody need is to get stopped by the boys in blue with you at the wheel and me comatose beside you!"

"Have it your way, Uncle Ian."

"I will, thanks. I'll call Jamie and leave my Porsche at the Sheraton. Thanks anyway, Frankie!" Ian laughed.

Chapter Thirty-One

Jane couldn't help feeling like a bit of a spare part in Xristina's murder case. She wasn't part of the team and she was out of her office at Gartcosh. Sitting in the middle did not suit her. She wanted to get right into the mix and find out who had killed Xristina and why.

"You look a bit down, Janey," Rachael said. "Do you want a camomile tea? It might help."

"Yes please, Rache. It won't help, but it'll taste good," Jane said. Just then her phone rang showing Superintendent Miller's name. "Boss? Yes, it's good to be back, but I'm missing the new challenges we have in MIT. I'm just writing up my notes from this morning's briefing, but it appears that one of the professors at Edinburgh University is known to Arjun Mansoor and went to visit him in prison."

Jane listened carefully and noted down the instructions Miller gave her.

"Yes, Sir. I'll inform DI Wilson that you want him to take DC Myerscough to question the professor. But, it's just a thought, Sir, DC Myerscough's girlfriend works with the professor. Wouldn't it be better for somebody else to attend?"

Jane scored out something on the note pad in front of her and amended her notes.

"Yes, Sir. I am certainly free to attend with DI Wilson, if you think that's best?" Jane punched the air and grinned. She was back in the game! Then she stopped and listened to the rest of what Superintendent Miller had to say.

"What, both of them, Sir?" she exclaimed. "And nobody stopped them? That's insane! Where are they now?"

Jane blushed.

"No, of course you don't know, Sir. Yes, I'll go and inform

DCI Mackay at once." Jane ended the call and stared miserably at the desk in front of her.

"Janey? Your tea?" Rachael said. "What on earth's wrong? You look even more miserable than when I left you!"

"Hamilton and Squires got up, got dressed and left the hospital without being challenged, and now nobody knows where Dumb and Dumber are or what they have planned next."

"Shit!"

"Yup. You got that right, Rache."

Jane went to find Mackay to give him the bad news.

Chapter Thirty-Two

When visiting other places, Oleksander normally made a point of socialising with the local people. His charm and natural exuberance for life made it easy to strike up a conversation, usually with a pretty lady, but sometimes he would talk with a local businessman and find out how he could extend his trading interests. However, Edinburgh people were not so given to talking with foreign strangers. They would give him a polite nod, or exchange pleasantries about the weather, but that was all.

Then it occurred to Oleksander that this time it might not be the locals who were different. It might be him. Since seeing where his dear Xristina died, he'd felt empty and miserable. Death had never fazed him before, but he had never seen the body of his own murdered child before. Maybe it was him. Wait till he got hold of that idiot Squires. He didn't care how huge a man he was.

The tenant at the flat where Xristina had lived, had recommended The Sheraton Hotel to Oleksander. It was central, he said, and had a fitness centre, a spa and a good business centre. He had said he thought Oleksander might need that. The young man was right.

Oleksander sat in the restaurant after a lonely dinner, sipping a large cognac and gazing out of the window. The light was fading outside, but even the brightness inside failed to raise his spirits. He debated whether another brandy would do the trick, but decided against it. He wanted to stay sharp, and it was a nuisance that he was not permitted to smoke his cigar indoors here. He wondered why not. Everybody enjoyed the smell of cigar smoke.

Oleksander signalled to a waiter and signed the meal to his

room. He would take his cigar outside.

He wandered out of the hotel and down the steps, and lit a large fat cigar. The taste and the smell comforted him. He walked at a leisurely pace across Festival Square. From here he could see the famous Castle up on its rocky precipice, a plain old-fashioned clock tower outside a concert hall, and the glass frontage of The Royal Lyceum Theatre. Oleksander liked a good play. Front row of the stalls, so you could see the whites of the actors' eyes. But not today.

Then, up the street, he noticed the neon lights that announced the existence of The Edinburgh Massage Suite. He was sure that was where he and Sergei had sent the last lot of whores from Ukraine. He smiled for the first time that day, and wondered whether that little minx Olena was there.

***

Olena hadn't looked pleased to see him, but Anichka and Symona looked relieved when he didn't ask for them. They all probably thought they would never see him again, now that they had left Kiev.

Oleksander told Olena of his requirements. The girl nodded, but didn't look too pleased. She had no choice. She clearly didn't enjoy it very much. That was obvious to Oleksander from the look on her face, not that he cared. He was not interested in whether she enjoyed the things he had done to her or made her do; he wasn't stupid enough to think the whores ever did. The way he saw it, that was part of her job, to pay back the cost of sneaking her to the West. They all paid something, but a life-time of savings from such a poor family was not enough. There was still much to be repaid.

In truth, Oleksander got even more from the experience when the whore showed she hadn't enjoyed it. He liked the fact that she couldn't even pretend.

Still, he had given her a tip of fifty pounds. That would be enough to buy the bitch some mouthwash to take away the taste, and arnica gel to get rid of the bruises. He walked back to the hotel feeling much more relaxed than he had felt all day.

Oleksander went back to his room in the hotel and poured himself a whisky from the mini-bar. He placed it on the table beside his bed and got undressed, then he walked into the bathroom and spread his legs to clean himself up. The girl had been keen to see him go, and he wondered lazily if she had bothered to wash before seeing to the needs of her next punter. It amused him to think about some other poor sod getting his sloppy seconds.

He walked back to his room and flung himself onto the bed. He fell asleep to the unmistakeable sounds of girl-on-girl action in a poor blue movie.

Chapter Thirty-Three

Frankie had bathed his girls and read them a bedtime story. They both liked their *Spot the Dog* books with bright colours and the puppy's wagging tail. Frankie had invested in an intercom that allowed him to hear the little ones sleeping and also to react if they woke. So he made coffee, handed one to Janice and sat down to watch *Corrie*.

"How long has that Ken Barlow been in this?" he asked her.

"Forever. I wonder if he ever forgets that's not his real name?" his aunt mused.

"Uncle Ian was calling Mansoor every name under the sun this afternoon," Frankie said.

"How come? He can't be getting up to much; he's in the big house, isn't he?"

"Aye, but Uncle Ian's got his wife working for him in the two new bookies he got, and he's found out she was trying to play a fast one."

"More fool Ian," Janice said patiently. "How many times does he need to be fooled by that family?"

***

The front door closed quietly and Ian walked into the living room, followed by Jamie, who had driven him home.

"Nice to hear I've got such great support from my nearest and dearest," Ian said sarcastically.

"You're blootered," Janice said pushing him away.

"Aye, true." Ian admitted. "I've got the four sets of books from the Frederick Street and Lothian Road shops, But I'm much too tired—"

"... and blootered?"

"... and blootered to work out what she was up to tonight. I'll put them all in my office and work on it tomorrow."

"Probably a good idea, darlin'.'" Janice smiled.

"Could you make me a coffee, Frankie?" Ian asked.

"And a tea for me please, Frankie. With Jaffa cakes," Jamie said.

Frankie smiled wearily and went to make the drinks.

***

Several hours later, when Janice and Ian had turned in, Frankie and Jamie had been left to their own devices and were chuckling their way through a boxed set of *The Big Bang Theory*, when Harry and Gavin rolled in.

"Shut it, you two, you'll wake the twins," Frankie complained.

"Not in a place this size we won't, they're half way to Glasgow," Harry giggled. "We went back to see Symona and Olena, tonight, eh Gavin?"

"Aye, Olena was that pleased to see me. One of her punters had been a bit rough, so she got right wet as soon as she saw me!"

Frankie pulled a face. "Too much information, Gavin."

"Those girls always seem to be at that place working," Jamie said.

"They don't get out much, right enough," Harry said.

"Hey, there's three of them, you could have Anichka, Jamie!" Gavin said.

Jamie shook his head. "I don't think so, Gavin, but thanks."

"Gavin and I have decided to take a little bit of rest and recuperation on Ibiza because the girls are always busy. There'll be loads of lassies up for it there," Harry said.

"Great idea, isn't it, Frankie? Can me and Frankie come?" Jamie asked.

"Why not! The more the merrier. You up for it, Bro'?" Harry asked his younger brother.

"When would you be going?" Frankie asked.

"ASAP, Bro'. Soon as we can get it fixed up."

"Let's get the iPad and we can see what's cheap." Jamie got up from the chair.

Frankie hesitated. "I really can't. I've got the girls."

"Oh come on, Frankie, you could leave them with my mam," Jamie suggested.

"They don't know her so well, Jamie. And I've never been away from them overnight, never mind a week or however long you're going for."

"A just a few days, maybe. I don't think our livers'll take much more than that." Harry grinned.

"You go, Jamie, but I can't. I'm staying home. The twins are my responsibility," Frankie said. He had to go and see Donna too, of course, but he'd no intention of telling the others about that.

He left the other three men quarrelling over control of the iPad. He couldn't help smiling as he heard Jamie shouting, "Let go, you big oaf, it's mine!"

"Oooh, it's his, Harry, get off," Gavin teased.

***

Jamie got sick of his cousin and his pal making fun of him. He handed over the iPad with a growl.

"Right, if you're so smart, you find something."

He sat and watched over Harry's shoulder, late into the night. He got tired of the bickering about where they should go, should they go all-inclusive or self-catering, four nights, a week or ten days, and how many girls they could 'bag'.

"Really, guys, can we just decide on something?" Jamie groaned.

Harry got up to go to the loo and he handed the iPad back to Jamie. "Here you go, you do better," he said dismissively.

While Harry was away, Jamie and Gavin found a place that they thought would suit perfectly. A self-catering apartment, but the resort was near the beach and not far from the town centre. It was in Can Joan Yern. "I've not heard of it, but it sounds great," Gavin said.

"And it says it's good for families, and me and Harry are

family! And if it's central we can walk back from the clubs with our birds," Jamie joked.

"Harry! Me and Jamie have found the very dab. See!" Gavin said, as Harry returned.

Jamie turned the pictures toward Harry. "Let's book up before we miss out."

Chapter Thirty-Four

"It's good to be back out with you, Jane. I haven't seen much of you since we became the one big happy force that is Police Scotland," Hunter said. "How are you finding life at MIT?"

"I love it, Boss," Jane replied. "I've bought myself a motor bike to get to and from Gartcosh, and that in itself is fun."

"You know how surgeons refer to motor cyclists in wet weather?" Hunter asked.

"No. Do they have a special name for them?"

"Yes: donors!"

"Ha ha! Very funny. I admit Rache isn't too pleased about my choice of vehicle, but it gets me there and back faster than a car would."

"My point exactly," Hunter replied. "Anyway, what do we know about Professor Zelay Sheptytsky?"

"Born in Kiev, Ukraine, in 1981. Cousin of Oleksander Ponomarenko's sister-in-law, Anya. Gifted linguist, highly academic, no blots on his copybook that we have been able to find, here or in Ukraine."

"So where does Mansoor fall into his social circle? They make unlikely bed-fellows, by the sounds of it."

"I agree with you, Boss. It doesn't seem to make sense."

"Do we know what his relationship with his cousin and her family is like?"

"No record of them being either very close nor estranged. They follow each other on social media, but the Professor rarely uses it and Anya seems to use it largely to keep tabs on her children and arrange coffee with friends."

"Nothing there that's going to set the heather alight, then."

***

"Thank you for seeing us, Professor Sheptytsky," Hunter said as they shook hands.

"In my country, it is rarely wise not to assist the authorities." Sheptytsky smiled.

"I am DI Hunter Wilson, and this is my colleague DS Jane Renwick. She will take notes of our meeting today."

Sheptytsky nodded. "How can I help?"

"I hope you can," Hunter said. "There may be a very simple answer to this, but due to the death of one of your students..."

"Xristina Ponomarenko?"

"Exactly. We just need to ask a few questions," Hunter said.

"Please go ahead, I will do what I can to help. Very sad, a bright young life cut so short," Sheptytsky said.

"Yes indeed, it is. Right now, you immediately identified the student by her correct name, but she registered with the University under a different surname. Did you know her previously?"

"I have known her since she was born. I was at the family party to celebrate her birth. Her aunt is my cousin, Anya Sheptytsky Ponomarenko."

"Do you see much of your cousin and her husband's family?" Hunter asked.

"Not really. I live abroad because of my work. I have done for some years. Anyway, the families are not close. Our family did not approve of Anya's choice of husband."

"Why not?"

"If you were Ukrainian you would not have to ask. The Ponomarenko brothers are not highly thought of. Not well respected. They are considered, what would you say, wide boys? Or maybe worse. My cousin could have married into any family in the country. It was a huge disappointment to my aunt and uncle when she chose that one."

"I see. And where has your job taken you to live, Professor?" Hunter asked.

"I lived in Hartford, Connecticut when I was studying for my Masters degree. I taught seminars at Harvard. Then I moved to Baghdad to complete my doctorate on the origins of language. Unfortunately it became a little too dangerous, and I

completed my work at Islamabad University, in Pakistan."
Professor Sheptytsky smiled.

"Very impressive," Hunter nodded. "And what is your
connection with Arjun Mansoor, Professor?"

"I don't have one."

"Evidence seems to suggest otherwise, sir," Hunter said
softly.

"I beg your pardon, Inspector. What do you mean by that?"

"An informant saw you meeting with Mr Mansoor during
visiting hour at Saughton Prison in Edinburgh last week. The
two of you seemed deep in conversation. What did you have to
talk about?" Hunter asked.

"An informant? It must have been Tim Myerscough. I
recognised him as soon as he opened the door on the night of
his wine tasting evening. I attended his party."

"I am not really interested in your social life, Professor.
Please just answer the question," Hunter sighed.

"Tim's girlfriend is Dr Gillian Pearson. We work together in
this department and she included me in the evening." He
nodded at Jane. "You were there."

"Yes, I was, but that doesn't explain to DI Wilson why you
were visiting Mansoor in prison," Jane said dryly.

"It is really very simple, let me get us some coffee and I
will explain." Professor Sheptytsky rose from his chair and
walked out of the room. He didn't come back.

***

Janice came wandering into Ian's office wearing little but
her pink silk dressing gown and a smile.

"The boys up yet?" She asked.

"Don't you think you should get dressed?" Ian smiled.
"Frankie's had breakfast and got the girls ready. Now they're
away for a walk. God knows when we'll see Jamie, Harry or
Gavin. It must have been back of three in the morning before
they went to bed, and they were all well-oiled."

"That's the pot calling the kettle black! What were you like
last night?"

"Aye, well, I think there's something nasty going on with the books that Mansoor's wife is keeping at the betting shops."

"Really, Ian. You need your head examined taking on a bloody Mansoor again. It's as if you have a great big Mansoor-shaped blind spot, and sooner or later the black heart of that family scoops you up with a big black spider's legs into their web. It has never ended well yet, and I know it won't again." Janice frowned at Ian.

"I really don't want to hear that!"

"It doesn't make it any less true. You want another coffee?"

"Aye, I think I'll take a break. This is making my head spin. Let's get some breakfast." Ian lifted his mug and followed her back to the kitchen.

***

Oleksander saw the young man from Xristina's flat come down to breakfast. He sat near the window. Oleksander had already taken a table in the far corner, away from the window, facing the door. This allowed him to watch the comings and goings of everybody else, without it being obvious.

He could not understand how these people could indulge in large amounts of fried meat this early in the day. He preferred a little brown bread with some cold ham and cheese. Then maybe a little light pastry to sweeten the deal.

Oleksander poured himself more coffee from the large pot the waiter had left on his table. The young man from the flat was just tucking into what he remembered they called a 'Full English' with toast and a pot of tea. Not interesting. Then Oleksander did a double -take.

A huge man with light hair and broad shoulders walked in. He was wearing designer jeans, a pale blue shirt and a Barbour tweed jacket. He smiled all around him and took in the room, but he did not seem interested in Oleksander. After all, they had never met. He pointed out the young man from Xristina's flat to the waiter.

Oleksander could not hear what was being said, but he saw the huge man take a chair at the young man's table. They obviously knew each other and were on friendly terms. There was a bad smell in this, Oleksander knew. The young man had said that the person who had brought Xristina to his door was huge with light hair but that he did not know him. It must be a lie. Oleksander could not remember many more details, although he knew the landlord had identified the man as Squires. There was no doubt in his mind this was the man he was looking at.

Oleksander signed for his breakfast and slid out of the restaurant without going past the two men. He went back to his room and made sure his gun was loaded. Fuck with him, would they? They would be sorry.

He then checked his suit and made sure he was smart for his visit to the University before he met with the police again.

"Thank you for making the time to meet with us, Mr Ponomarenko," Hunter said as he and Jane sat down in a quiet corner of the bar in The Sheraton.

"In my country, it is rarely advisable to ignore a request to help the police," Oleksander replied with a smile.

"I've heard that said before," Hunter said.

"I am sorry to be slightly late. I went to the University to see where Xristina studied and spoke to her teachers. I am told she was a good student."

"I have no doubt that she was," Hunter said. "We just want to ask you a few questions about your wife's cousin, Professor Zelay Sheptytsky."

"You are mistaken, Inspector. Anya Sheptytsky married my younger brother, Sergei. Sadly my wife and I separated a few years ago."

"So Anya Sheptytsky is your sister-in-law?"

"That's right. And the professor is nothing to me at all."

"I see," Hunter said. "But you've met him?"

"Yes, I know who he is. We have attended occasional family gatherings together: to mark the birth of children, weddings, funerals, that kind of thing. But I do not know him well."

"Did you know he is working at Edinburgh University?"

"Of course. It was because of his reputation that Xristina

wanted to come here, to study under the great Professor Sheptytsky." Oleksander's voice had an edge to it that Hunter did not understand.

"You did not approve?"

"If she had not been here she would not have died. I find him partly responsible for my daughter's death."

"If you'll excuse me for saying so, that seems a little harsh, Mr Ponomarenko," Hunter said.

"No, I will not excuse you. Now, if you will excuse me, I have a meeting with my consul in just ten minutes."

"Of course, may I ask what the meeting is about?" Hunter asked.

"It is none of your business, DI Wilson. However, there is no harm in telling you, I suppose. The consulate requires to strengthen its import/export department. As I am here, and have such expertise, I have been appointed attaché to that department. The consul will confer my official status and diplomatic passport this afternoon. It is a great honour to be appointed to assist my country in this official capacity. I never thought I would ever reach such great heights."

"Congratulations, Mr Ponomarenko. Your expertise in that field certainly precedes you." Hunter and Oleksander shook hands.

"Good bye. Good wishes. I must immediately go to prepare." Oleksander rose and strode towards the elevators.

Hunter watched the Ukrainian leave and turned to Jane. "What did you make of that?" Hhe asked her softly. "He certainly had no plans to hang around with us any longer than was absolutely necessary, did he?"

"He did not. That is one scary man. I wouldn't want to get on his bad side. Lord help us if he finds out who killed Xristina before we do. And now he'll have diplomatic immunity."

"God help us! He will, won't he? We must get back to work and get some results. Let's get back to the ranch, Jane."

Chapter Thirty-Five

"Let's make this short, can we, people? It's late in the day and we all want to get home, but there are a couple of important things we all need to be aware of so we can get off to a flying start tomorrow." Mackay rapped his knuckles on the desk to get everybody's attention.

He saw Tim and Bear continuing to talk at the back of the room. "If DCs Myerscough and Zewedu could please just pretend to pay attention, we can start?"

"They've got rugby training tonight, Sir, and Bear wants a lift," Mel said.

"Thank you, DC Grant, but this is not the face of a man who cares. Now, DS Renwick got some important news today from MIT."

"Thank you, Sir, yes." Jane stood up and faced the rest of the room. "I got a call from Superintendent Miller. He had received worrying news from the hospital where Hamilton and Squires were being treated."

"Please tell me their condition has worsened and they are near to death," Colin grumbled.

"Exactly the opposite, Colin," Jane said. "They got up, got dressed and walked out."

"Without anybody challenging them?"

"The copper outside their doors had gone for a pee and they took their chance."

"Oh for fuck's sake! How do you miss a man the size of Squires? He's huge!" Colin exclaimed.

"He is, and he and Hamilton must be holed up somewhere. We have no idea where," Mackay said.

"Well, when Hamilton and I were working together he always said that if he wanted to escape from Scotland, he

145

would take the ferry across to Belfast and drive South. He said getting a plane to anywhere you wanted from Dublin would be a piece of piss," Colin said.

"Jane, can you get MIT to cover ferries to Belfast?" Hunter asked.

"Yes Sir. May I be excused to do that? I think you've got our meetings with Sheptytsky and Ponomarenko covered."

"Thanks Jane, of course," Hunter said.

"Hamilton's family come from Tranent, in East Lothian, I think," Colin said.

"Right, good, Colin, you contact the local stations and tell them to be on the lookout," Hunter said.

"I will, Boss, and I'll send a copy of a photo from his file. It'll be old, but it might help."

"Good idea, Colin," Hunter said.

"Can you tell us about those interviews, now, DI Wilson?" Mackay asked.

"Jane and I went up to Edinburgh University to meet with Professor Zelay Sheptytsky," Hunter began. "Tim had seen him talking to Mansoor last time he went to visit his father at Saughton."

"Not Mansoor's usual calibre of visitor. This one could read," Tim joked.

"In several languages, Tim. Sheptytsky speaks Russian, Ukrainian, Arabic and English fluently, that I am aware of," Hunter said. "He was just about to explain why he was meeting with Mansoor when he offered to make Jane and me coffee. He left the room to get it, and never came back."

"That's very odd," Tim said.

"It was. There was no tension in his body language. Everything seemed to be going fine and he was very courteous," Hunter said.

"He was nice enough at the party. Good company for the wine tasting, Tim," Bear said.

"Yes, and Gillian rates him," Tim added.

"Well, we waited about half an hour then went to look for him, but we couldn't find him. I left a note on his desk asking him to call me, but I haven't heard from him yet."

"Could you ask Gillian if she's seen him since this morning, Tim?"

"Do you want me to phone her now, Boss?" Tim stood up.

"Wait till after the briefing. There is something else I need to make you all aware of," Hunter said.

"Right Boss," Tim sat down again.

"Jane and I couldn't wait any longer because we had arranged a meeting with Oleksander Ponomarenko to find out how well he admits to knowing Sheptytsky."

"What did he say?" Mackay asked.

"Both Sheptytsky and Ponomarenko agreed that they know each other, and had met at extended family gatherings, but they do not know each other well," Hunter said. "Ponomarenko is certainly an angry man and looking for someone to blame over his daughter's death. He seemed to believe that Sheptytsky bore some responsibility, just for teaching at the University."

"Yes, when I spoke to him, he was blaming Squires for delivering her to the wrong flat," Mackay commented.

"Yes, Sir, but he apologised to us for being late because he had been to see where Xristina studied at the University. So, he must have been there around the same time we were, but we didn't see him," Hunter said.

"It is quite a big place, even within the department, Boss," Tim said.

"True, but he also ended our meeting quite abruptly, by saying that he had a meeting with the Ukrainian Consul. Ponomarenko said that he had been made an attaché for trade, and was going to get his diplomatic passport conferred on him. He was very pleased with himself," Hunter said.

"Oh shit! That will give him diplomatic immunity," Nadia said.

"I didn't think of that at first, but it is exactly the point Jane picked up as well, Nadia," Hunter said.

"I don't like the sound of that," Mackay said.

"What do you need us to do, Boss?" Nadia asked.

"Tim will contact Gillian about Professor Sheptytsky. Mel, can you find out what you can about him?" Hunter asked.

"Of course."

"Bear, I want you to find out as much as you can about Oleksander Ponomarenko. Rachael, find out all you can about Xristina."

"Yes, Boss," Bear and Rachael said.

"Nadia and Colin, I want to know anything you can find on those other three girls that were in Cameron's flat the night Xristina was found murdered," Hunter said. "McKenzie, you are with me. We are going to interview Lucky Buchanan"

"That just leaves your son, DI Wilson," Mackay said. "When DS Renwick and DC Myerscough are finished their phone calls, I suggest they interview him. Just at his hotel, nothing heavy, but we must keep his part in this above board."

"Good idea, Sir," Hunter replied, through gritted teeth.

Chapter Thirty-Six

"Hello, are you missing me already?" Gillian joked to Tim.

"Of course, but that's not why I'm calling."

"I didn't think it was. What's up?"

"No big deal, but have you seen Professor Sheptytsky since this morning?"

"Come to think of it, I haven't," Gillian said thoughtfully. "And one of the students was complaining that she was meant to have a one-to-one with him, but he never showed. That's very unlike him."

"Okay, but if you see him could you ask him to phone DI Wilson?"

"Yes. No problem. Well actually there is a problem, I can't get one of the cupboards in our wee kitchen opened and I've dropped a packet of sugar. I want to sweep it up before we get mice or I get cursed by the cleaners. The sweeping brush is in there."

"Jane and I have to stop by the Sheraton to take a quick statement from Cameron Hunter, then I'm going to pick up my new car. Why don't I stop by and get you, when Jane and I are finished? I can open your cupboard and then we'll pick up the car together and I could take you for dinner?"

"Now you're talking. That'll be lovely, Tim."

***

"Nothing is ever simple, Jane," Superintendent Miller said.

"That's certainly true, Sir," Jane replied.

"I'm already watching airports but I'll also ensure that we have officers watching the ferries sailing out from Troon and Cairnryan to Belfast. We have good photos of both Hamilton and Squires."

"To be honest, Sir, Squires is so huge that I can't see him being difficult to miss," Jane said.

"And yet all the staff at the hospital managed it. Wait till I get hold of the PC who left his post," Miller said.

"Sir, he had been in post for over four hours and his relief was over half an hour late," Jane said quietly.

"So he went to relieve himself and Hamilton and Squires just walked out! You couldn't make it up, could you?"

"No Sir," Jane said quietly.

"Anyway, the other thing I have to make you aware of is that we have had wind of money-laundering out of two bookies. One is in Frederick Street, the other in Lothian Road. The licensee is a Mrs Mansoor. The money guys here believe she may be Arjun Mansoor's wife."

"He is certainly married, Sir. I have met Mrs Mansoor, I would recognise her if I saw her," Jane said.

"That may be very useful. I'll get back to you, DS Renwick."

When Tim found Jane she was just ending her call. "We are tasked with interviewing young Cameron Wilson," he said.

"Hasn't Cameron told us all he can already?"

"Probably, but Mackay wants to make sure we are seen to treat him just like everybody else," Tim said.

"That'll be DCI Mackay to you, DC Myerscough." Mackay's voice travelled down the corridor.

Jane smiled. "You drive, Tim."

Chapter Thirty-Seven

"Just as well it's a late flight, isn't it lads?" Jamie grinned at Harry and Gavin as they all sat in the bar at Edinburgh Airport washing down the all-day English Breakfast with pints of lager.

"Aye, it's even better that your pop has a decent washer and dryer in the new place, or we'd be out of clothes within two days!" Gavin grinned.

"This is the life, eh boys? Off whenever we like for sun, sea and lots of sex," Harry laughed. "We're what the girls in Ibiza have been waiting for. They just don't know it yet!"

Jamie was glad they were near the front of the queue when their flight was called. He wanted to sit with Harry and Gavin but none of them wanted to pay the extra to book seats on the budget airline. Jamie was just glad there wasn't a charge for using the cludge.

"You got a couple of quid for a beer on the plane?" Gavin asked Jamie.

"Aye, you?"

"He's always got money for beer: not always for food or the bus home, but he's always got money for drink." Harry glanced at Gavin and they both laughed.

Jamie nudged Harry. "See over there, cuz? A hen party!"

"That's what we like to see!" Harry said. He wandered back down the queue to speak to the girls.

Gavin watched him and shook his head. "What's he like?" he said to Jamie.

Jamie watched Harry's moves. He heard him talking to the girls.

"Looks like we're all going to Ibiza, ladies. What are the chances? The best-looking guys and the prettiest girls!"

Jamie heard the girls laugh. He couldn't help cringing. That chat-up line was worse than his pop's. He listened while Harry introduced himself and pointed back to Gavin and Jamie. Jamie thought he made out that all three of them were soldiers. Good! That wouldn't do him any harm.

"So, girls, what place you staying at?" Harry asked.

"San Antonio! San Antonio here we come!" The bride-to-be waved a garter in the air.

"Hooray!" cheered the hens.

"Oh aye? Good there is it?" Harry asked.

The girls giggled. The bride-to-be said, "It's the best! There's sunset strip with cafés and bars, and at night we can party till dawn in the clubs! Where you staying?"

"Not far from you. Can Joan Yern it's called, and it's no' just Joan longing to get a load of this." Harry pointed up and down his body.

The girls giggled. One of them said, "My gran went there with her pal. They liked it fine." Then she laughed and turned back to her friends. Jamie watched as Harry wandered, a little less sure-footedly, back to him and Gavin at the front of the queue.

"What they like?" Jamie asked.

"Not our type, I don't think," Harry said.

"Well they're female and breathing, they've got to be in with a chance," Gavin joked.

"Come on, that's us boarding," Jamie said. He nudged Harry and they shuffled forward to present their passports and boarding passes.

Jamie was pleased enough that they sat together. He didn't mind sitting in the middle and when Gavin said he wanted the window, because he always sat at the window, Harry agreed to sit at the aisle. Harry grumbled that they were too far back and it would take the drinks trolley too long to get to them.

"Cuz, just shut up, will you? We're on our hols and I don't want to have to listen to you whinge all the way across the ocean," Jamie said.

"Hear hear!" Gavin agreed. "Where are the hens sitting anyway?"

"Way at the front," Harry muttered.

"Want a sucky sweetie?" Jamie took a bag out of his pocket.

"Oh, good idea. Can I have two?" Gavin said, digging in and not really waiting for an answer.

"You, Harry? It's to help your ears my mam says."

"Go on then," Harry smiled. "We really are on our holidays, boys! And how do we get to the hotel?"

"We've booked transfers, mind?" Gavin reminded him. "It was an extra thirty quid, but how else were we going to find it?"

Harry nodded. "I do remember, now you mention it."

***

It was a two-beer flight. No movie. No meal. When Harry got out of the plane the hens were long gone but the warmth and smell of the air hit him. It wasn't the searing heat of Afghanistan's days nor the freezing temperatures of its nights. This was a balmy evening and the air smelt of flowers: he didn't need his jacket. Lovely.

"Who would have believed it? Our luggage off first. That's never happened to me before," Jamie said.

Harry wandered over to the hens who were still waiting for half their suitcases to arrive.

"You girls know where we catch the coach?" he asked.

"There's a desk over there," one of them said. "Fiona has gone to find out for us while we wait for the rest of our stuff."

"Thanks," Harry said. "We've got all our luggage, so me and the boys'll just go over and find out what's happening. See you on the bus, girls!"

"I doubt it'll be the same coach." The bride-to-be glanced over to him.

Harry felt himself going red. He hoped she hadn't noticed.

He led Gavin and Jamie to the desk and they were told their coach was out of the exit and along the left-hand side of the walkway. They wandered away, looking out for coach A5.

"Well at least it shouldn't be rocket science to find the coach. The ones on the left are A and over there they're all B,"

Gavin said.

"Yep and they're numbered from the door here, one, two, but they're all different sizes," Jamie added.

Harry stopped at the coach numbered four. He couldn't see anything beyond it. He could hear the hens giggling and loading their luggage onto a big bus numbered B3. Then he heard Gavin laugh out loud. He watched Jamie take a step forward and join in the joke.

"What is it?" Harry asked.

"You are not going to believe this, cuz," Jamie laughed.

Harry looked at coach A5. It wasn't a coach at all, it was an estate car with room for the three of them in the back seat and their luggage in the rear. An elderly woman was already ensconced in the front seat.

"Evening, lads," she said. "Have you ever been to Can Joan Yern before?"

"No, no we haven't, first time in Ibiza," Jamie said.

"Well, it's lovely. Quiet, nice walks and little shops and cafes. None of those noisy drunken clubs that they have in some parts of the island."

Harry sighed, but the woman's opinion of the resort just kept coming.

"And our hotel is lovely; the owners have had it for years. Very nice and away from everything, you know? My Harold and I used to come here before he died. But they still make me feel so welcome. I just take a walk along the prom in the morning, and in the afternoon, I sit and watch the sea. Sometimes, I have an ice cream." She giggled.

Harry stopped listening and looked across at Gavin and Jamie. They seemed just as confused as he felt.

Chapter Thirty-Eight

"I don't suppose you just want me to pull the door off, do you?" Tim asked Gillian.

"Not really, but there is a funny noise coming from in there now," she replied.

"What kind of noise? Do you think it's a mouse?" Tim said.

"If it is, it's making a weird noise. No, if the cupboard were bigger, I'd say there was somebody locked in there."

Tim thumped the door hard. It vibrated, and he distinctly heard a muffled yelp from inside the cupboard.

"Good Lord, Tim," Gillian said frantically. "It's quite a small cupboard. I'm surprised whoever is in there hasn't suffocated,"

"Stand back, pet. This door is coming off." Tim took off his jacket and unbuttoned his cuffs. He put one hand on the handle of the cupboard and his feet were parted to take the strain. He pulled with all his strength, which was far more than was needed for the flimsy unit. His free arm took Gillian with him and they both went flying into the wall behind them, but the handle of the door was still firmly within Tim's grasp.

"Zelay!" Gillian shouted.

"Professor Sheptytsky, what on earth happened?" Tim dropped the handle and started to untie the gag around the professor's mouth.

"I came through to get coffee for your colleagues who came to speak to me. Someone was waiting for me and I was hit of the head," the professor said.

"Do you know who it was?" Tim asked.

"Oh yes. I only caught a glimpse of him, but I'd know Oleksander Ponomarenko anywhere." Zelay shook his head and groaned.

Tim looked at Gillian. "I'll call an ambulance. But Jane and I have another interview to conduct."

Gillian smiled. "You go, Tim. I'll wait with Zelay and go with him to the hospital."

"I'll log the assault, professor, and I'll take a statement tomorrow, when you feel up to it. But have you any idea why Ponomarenko attacked you?"

The professor groaned. "He seems to think that I could have prevented Xristina's death. But I wasn't even there."

***

"Can you hang on a minute, Jane? I just want to log this," Tim said.

"Log what? A lost cupboard key? I can't see that going down very well. Come on, Tim. We only stopped here as a favour to Gillian."

"It's just as well we did. Ponomarenko seems to have a beef with Professor Sheptytsky. He attacked him, knocked him out cold, gagged him and locked him in that tiny wee cupboard."

"You're joking! Why didn't he just kill him?"

"Oh, that's very nice, DS Renwick!"

"No, but really, now the professor can identify him," Jane said.

"He wouldn't have been able to identify Ponomarenko if he'd been in there much longer. Zelay would have suffocated, but Ponomarenko could have fooled himself that he wasn't responsible for the death."

"Aaah, yes, I see. That makes sense with there being a family connection. Anyway, you call the station and log it, and I'll drive us to the Sheraton to see Cameron."

***

"You again, big man? What is it this time?" Cameron rose to greet Tim and Jane.

Jane looked curiously at Tim.

"I'm collecting my new car today," Tim explained to her,

156

"so I popped in here earlier to speak to Cameron and see whether he would go to Thomson's Top Cars, if I gave him money for a taxi, and drive the BMW back."

"Oh, I see. Where's Kenneth?" Jane asked.

"He's sprained his ankle. Can't drive at the moment, so Cameron has said he's willing to come to my rescue. I can tell you, Jane, it cost far more to put him on my insurance than Kenneth ever did!"

***

Oleksander sat in the far corner of the hotel bar, apparently reading a paper. How interesting, he thought. The huge man was meeting with the young man from Xristina's flat again. They must both be involved.

Chapter Thirty-Nine

"I honestly don't think Cameron knows any more than he's telling us," Jane said to Tim, as the two of them walked slowly back through the hotel towards the car park.

"I agree. He seems to have been genuinely fond of Xristina; she was a pretty girl. My guess is that Squires turned up on his doorstep saying the boss wanted this good-looking lady to stay in his flat, and Cameron probably couldn't believe his luck."

"He certainly doesn't seem to have asked too many questions," Jane remarked.

"He didn't ask any, not that he mentioned. I believe him when he said he didn't want to jeopardize his job with Lucky by asking him directly or seeming to make a fuss."

"Yes, and let's face it, Squires' big ugly mug doesn't invite questions, does it?"

"I wonder why Xristina didn't tell her dad about Cameron?"Tim asked.

"From what Bear's told me about the Ponomarenko brothers, they are not the type of people who take kindly to getting questioned," Jane said.

"No, but you'd think she'd have said something about there being a young man living there – and then the fact that she was in the wrong flat would all have come out."

"Maybe she was just enjoying the freedom? Not sharing every detail with her dad? aAnd Cameron isn't bad looking, if you like that sort of thing."

"You're probably right, Jane. None of us tells our folks everything," Tim said.

"Assuming you have folks to tell," Jane muttered. "So you plan to get your new car today? You'll be looking forward to that."

"Yes, I am. My idea is that I'll drop you off at the station and then drive over to Thomson's Top Cars to pick it up. Cameron will take a taxi out there then drive my BMW back to my place and Kenneth can call him another taxi to get him back to the Sheraton."

"Lucky Cameron. You've never let me have a shot of driving your BMW. That is *such* a great car." Jane smiled.

"It is. It's a big improvement on that tiny car Sophie used to make me fold myself into, but I just wanted something a bit sportier as well. I was going to take Gillian for a drive and then maybe find a country pub for a bite of dinner."

"That sounds nice., tThere are lots of lovely little places out in East Lothian."

"There are, but, of course, she's gone to the hospital with the professor, so that plan is somewhat overtaken by events," Tim said. Then he noticed that Jane had stopped walking and was hovering in front of the door to the Ladies. "Shall I wait over there?" He pointed towards another group of comfortable-looking chairs.

Jane smiled and nodded.

***

Tim did not see the older man come behind him. The hotel carpets were soft and luxurious, so he did not hear him approach either. The first thing he knew about the man was the gun poking into the small of his back, centrally situated at his spine. Tim could feel the cold steel through his shirt.

"You will do what I say, when I say and you will not ask questions," the man whispered. "Walk."

Tim looked around. He caught a glimpse of the man, but he did not know him. He saw Jane come out of the Ladies. He shook his head to warn her to keep away. The gun was jammed into his back too tightly for him to lunge and grab it, but he was younger and faster than his assailant. There must be a way he could stop this, without harm to himself or anybody else.

"Face forward! And you won't get hurt – yet." the man

159

hissed.

Tim could tell that Jane had taken in his situation. He watched as she disappeared back into the Ladies, knowing that she would call for back-up.

The gun at Tim's back was largely hidden by the man's jacket, so people did not notice it or panic. The man's English was excellent, but the slight transatlantic accent gave him away as a foreigner. Tim guessed he was Xristina's father, but had no idea what beef Mr Ponomarenko thought he had with him.

Tim knew his reflexes were second to none, but he couldn't out-run a bullet. He lowered his voice and took a chance. "Just put your gun down, Mr Ponomarenko, and I'll let you go."

"It is not for you to let me go. I am in control. I told you I would not hurt you here., dDo not make me go back on my word."

"Oh? I don't think you will," Tim said softly.

"Move!"

Tim started to walk towards the exit, as instructed. He saw Jane re-appear from the rest room and nod at him just very slightly. She kept her distance, about twenty feet away from Tim. He wondered whether there were any patrol cars nearby. Maybe Jane had spotted the gun and there were armed officers waiting outside to take Ponomarenko with a single shot.

Tim stopped surmising and thought about the situation as it was, not as he wanted it to be. He did not want any member of the public, nor any of his colleagues, to be harmed.

"Think you can just drop my daughter anywhere and take half my money, do you?" Oleksander hissed. "They all say you are not so clever. And you are not clever. You are an idiot to try it on with me. My daughter is dead because of you."

"I think you are mistaking me for somebody else," Tim said quietly.

"I am mistaking you for somebody who is going to rot in hell looking heavenward and begging for the forgiveness of my darling Xristina."

Hearing the man sob, Tim took his chance. He spun around and grabbed the gun with his left hand, twisting the man's wrist so that it pointed to the ceiling. In the struggle, the gun fired once. Tim heard the loud crack echo around the fine lounge of the hotel.

Not a car backfiring.

Not fireworks.

Anybody who has heard a gun fired never mistakes the sound of a gunshot for anything else. Tim held the man's arm high above his head. The hotel guests were clearly shocked.

Somebody squealed. Another woman fainted. Tim smacked the man's hand off a table and the gun flew towards Jane. She picked it up carefully in a paper tissue, and Tim grabbed the man's other hand with his right hand.

The man struggled and kicked at Tim, but Tim was far too strong and his arms too long for any of those blows to reach their target.

"You think I am Brian Squires, don't you?" Tim said calmly. "Well, that big ugly mug is not me. I am DC Timothy Myerscough of Police Scotland. May I introduce my colleague, DS Jane Renwick."

Tim held Oleksander securely as Jane put handcuffs on him and explained his rights to him, then stood quietly with Oleksander and watched while Jane walked away to find the hotel manager. She explained what had happened and the damage caused to his hotel. Shortly after she got back to Tim and Oleksander, PCs Scott Clark and Neil Larkin bounded up the escalator from the car park.

"Neil, you got an evidence bag for this?" Jane held up the gun.

"Of course, Sarge. Now, if you'll just come this way, sir." Neil marched Oleksander Ponomarenko out of the hotel.

"Good job you still go to rugby training and keep your reflexes and strength up to par," Jane said to Tim. "Do you want me to drive you to the hospital for a check-up?"

"No, I'm fine."

"You should get checked. You were threatened at gunpoint."

"I know, I know, But I really am fine," Tim said. "Tell you what, you drive me back to the station. If I don't have any nervous twitches from your driving, I must be fine."

161

"You cheeky thing," she said taking a playful swipe at his arm.

"Help! Help! Assault by a senior officer!" Tim said grinning.

"Come on, let's go. We'll have to write this up."

"And then I'm going to get my new car," Tim smiled.

"You certainly know how to fill a day, Tim," Jane teased.

"I do, don't I? I suppose I'd better phone Ian Thomson and Cameron Wilson to tell them I'll be running a bit late."

Chapter Forty

By the time Harry, Gavin and Jamie arrived at the hotel, they were tired, hung over and more dishevelled and dehydrated than they probably realised. At reception, their elderly travelling companion was greeted by the owners as a long-lost friend. They took her over to the chairs that passed themselves off as the hotel lounge, and a little girl with long dark hair and big brown eyes was sent away to the kitchen. She came back quickly with a plate of bread, olives, cold meats and cheese and a large glass of red wine. It was only then the boys realised that they were hungry too. This meal on arrival would suit them very well.

The old woman was clearly hungry too. She polished off the plateful, and the wine in jig time. As the boys watched, the little girl danced between the reception desk and the old lady, ferrying her passport to be copied, taking her booking form to be signed, and delivering her key. When all that was done the boys saw the owner ring a bell, and a teenage boy came out from another room. He grinned at the woman in recognition and picked up her case as he led her to the room assigned to her.

Then the boys turned back to the reception desk. The owner smiled and asked for their passports. He took copies of these and handed them back. The boys looked around, but the little girl had disappeared and made no return with something for them to eat. The teenage boy wandered past them and out of the front door with a dog on a lead.

"You have the self-catering apartment?" the owner behind the desk asked.

"Yes, that's right," Harry said.

"Here is your key. If you go out of this door, go to the left and past the garage, the stairs to the apartment are there. You are just above the garage. Enjoy your stay."

"Thanks," Harry hesitated. "Any chance we could get a wee bite to eat and a drink like the lady did?"

"We're right hungry," Jamie agreed.

"You provide your own food. The apartment is self-catering, you see. Anyway, Mrs Macnab has been coming to us for years. She eats with the family, now she is alone. You do not get food from us. You are cheaper - self-catering," the owner explained.

"Please?" Gavin said. He had realised how really hungry he was, and he knew none of them could be bothered to find somewhere to go out and eat tonight. Beer, lack of sleep and excitement were catching up with them.

The owner relented. "Food like Mrs Macnab and a beer each?"

"That'd be grand."

"Ten euros each," he smiled.

"That's a bit steep," Harry complained.

The owner shrugged and turned away.

"We'll take it," Gavin sighed, taking the money out of his wallet. They needed to eat.

***

Harry agreed with Gavin that he felt better after the food, and the three adventurers wandered past the garage and up the stairs on the far side of the building.

"It's dark here," Jamie commented. "I wonder where the clubs are? Shall we have a look when we've dumped our cases?"

"No' me tonight," Gavin said. "I need to sleep, lads. Probably one too many beers on the plane."

"Just one?" Jamie grinned. "Aye, right!"

When Harry opened the door to their apartment, the boys were all favourably impressed. They walked directly into the living room/kitchen and were pleased to see the large bottle of water and little container of milk in the fridge. There were sachets of tea, coffee and sugar in a basket by the kettle.

"This isn't too shabby," Harry grinned. "I think we'll be okay here, lads."

He watched as Jamie walked across the room and switched on the light in the bathroom.

"There's wee packets of soap and shampoo in here, and loads of toilet paper if we gets the runs." Jamie pulled a face.

"There's two single beds in here," Gavin called through from the only other doorway in the apartment.

"So one of us'll be on the sofabed in here. I bags this!" Harry sat down on the sofabed. "It's a double. Youse two'll just have to make do with your lassies."

"Ah, Harry!" Jamie complained.

"If yer no' fast yer last, cuz!" Harry grinned.

"There's no telly," Gavin noticed.

"We don't speak Spanish, ya chump. Who cares?" Harry said. "We'll be out dancin' and chancin' with the lassies! I wonder if we'll catch up with that hen-party? They were fit."

Chapter Forty-One

"You want me to come and pick you up and we can go to get the new car together, Gillian?" Tim asked.

"I'd love that," Gillian replied.

"Perhaps we can go for a spin and find somewhere nice for dinner."

"Yes please! Zelay is being kept in hospital at least overnight. I'll call tomorrow and see how he is then."

"As soon as he's well enough, the Boss will want to interview him. He'll need to tell us exactly what happened between him and Ponomarenko."

***

As they were driving towards Thomson's Top Cars, Tim recounted to Gillian the events at The Sheraton Hotel. He explained that, although the interview with Cameron Wilson hadn't lasted very long, the subsequent attack by Oleksander Ponomarenko resulted in an unexpected delay.

"That's a calm way of putting it! What on earth was Xristina's dad thinking?" Gillian said.

"I'm not sure the man is terribly stable right now," Tim replied as he continued to tell her of his earlier experience.

"He mistook me for the man who took Xristina to Cameron's flat instead of the one he had arranged for her. He seems to blame this fellow, at least partially, for Xristina's murder, and so he formed this half-baked plan to punish him."

"My God! Tim, you could have been killed," Gillian exclaimed.

"Not a chance, it never came close to that. I did thank God for strength and fast reflexes, though." Tim smiled.

"Forgive me, DC Myerscough, but having a loaded gun pointed at you is very dangerous. Shouldn't you get checked by a doctor after an experience like that?"

"It is protocol, but I want to relax with you and get my new car. That is all the therapy I need, Gillian, honestly. I thought I might take you for a drive through East Lothian and we could have dinner at the Longniddry Inn?"

Gillian smiled. "East Lothian is a beautiful county, and dinner would be lovely, Tim. Mr Ponomarenko seems determined to find somebody to blame for Xristina's murder, though. First Zelay, now you. The man is a maniac."

"Family is important to me too, Gillian. If it were my daughter, I'd probably be just as desperate as he is," Tim said softly.

"I understand," she said.

But Tim knew she did not. She could not, because he had never told her about the child he had looked forward to having with Sophie: the child Sophie had so brutally aborted because it would have interfered with her career. Tears welled up in his eyes. He shook his head as Gillian reached her hand towards him.

***

"Thanks for staying open for me, Ian," Tim said, as he and Ian Thomson shook hands. "I'm amazed you managed to get the car so quickly."

"Ways and means and contacts in the trade, Tim. And who is this lovely lady?" Ian smiled.

"This is my girlfriend, Doctor Gillian Pearson."

"You can examine me any time, Doctor." Ian smiled as he shook hands with Gillian.

"Not that kind of doctor," she said.

"Pity," Ian said. "It wasn't entirely out of the goodness of my heart that I stayed open, DC Myerscough. I need your advice on something, privately."

"Don't worry about me," Gillian said. "I'll have a look at the cars. I've never had a chance to sit in a Ferrari or a Rolls

Royce before. Which one are you buying?"

"That one, the Mercedes-Benz SLS AMG Black. I can't wait to get behind the wheel. It has a Bang and Olufsen stereo."

"Oh come on! If we're going to talk cars let's talk about getting from nought to sixty miles an hour in three point seven seconds, the seven speed, dual clutch gear-box and a top speed of two hundred miles an hour," Ian said enthusiastically.

"You're right. It is a fabulous car, Ian," Tim said. "Gillian, if Cameron Wilson arrives for the BMW while I'm in with Ian, will you just give him the keys for me? He's taking it home for me."

"Of course, no problem." Gillian accepted the keys to the big car from Tim, then wandered away to lust over Tim's new car as Ian led Tim to his office.

"This doesn't really put me in a great light, but let me tell you what I have found out."

"Go on, Ian. We've been through too much together not to be able speak frankly to each other."

"I got hold of two betting shops, Frederick Street and Lothian Road," Ian began. "I needed someone without a criminal record to be licensee."

"So far so good. You found someone suitable willing to do that?" Tim asked. "I'm amazed you knew anybody that fitted the bill." He smiled.

"Very funny and I don't think," Ian said. "Looking back on it, perhaps they were a bit too willing. It got round the big house that I had this problem, and blow me down did Arjun Mansoor not send me a note through wee Mick on the cleaning team that he wants a word with me after chapel."

"Mansoor is never good news. At least he has certainly never been good news for you."

"Maybe I should have thought about that."

"What's happened?"

Ian took a deep breath. "He said his wife was looking for a job, because of him being inside, and they had business acquaintances who had an interest in girls at The Edinburgh Massage Suite in Lothian Road. It was through these acquaintances that he'd learned that I'd bought the bookies down the road from them."

"Please don't tell me you did what I think you're going to say you did, Ian," Tim groaned.

"I probably did. After a fair bit of soul-searching, I agreed to take on Mansoor's wife as my book-keeper."

"Why in the name of God would you do that? How many times has that man shafted you now? What made you think this was going to turn out well?"

Ian looked at his desk and shook his head. "I have no idea. Looking back on it, this was about the daftest thing I could have done."

"Well, we can agree on that, and I don't even know what the problem is, yet!"

"The problem is this, and this is where I don't look too good. A lot of the cross-counter betting is done in cash, so I asked Mrs Mansoor to keep two sets of books: one for me and one for the taxman."

"I can't say you've shocked me yet," Tim said quietly. "Did she do that?"

"Oh, she did way more than that. What do you call it? She 'exceeded her authority'. When I went to get the books to check on how I was doing, I found she was keeping four sets, not two."

"Four sets of books? That seems excessive," Tim said. "Why did she keep four sets of books?"

"Well, I've not quite got to the bottom of that, but they were all labelled: HMRC, Thomson, Ponomarenko and Mansoor."

"Ponomarenko? I know that name well enough. Where do they come in?" Tim asked.

"I have no idea. She's the girl that was killed, right?"

"Right."

"Well, her family has put sixty thousand pounds into my business and taken forty-eight thousand pounds out, with the Mansoor account getting the remaining twelve thousand. And I've been open less than a month."

"Wow!"

"Yes, wow, but that's not really very helpful. What do I do

now? I don't want all that money going through my business with me getting nothing out of it!"

"Meaning you would have no objection if there was something in it for you?" Tim asked.

"Meaning I don't like being taken for a fool," Ian said. "Can I turn these books over to you and you can do your detective bit?"

"I'll need to take all four sets for each betting shop, Ian," Tim frowned. "And I'll need to report it properly. You know that?"

"I don't suppose you could leave out the ones labelled HMRC, could you?" Ian asked.

"No, Ian, I can't. I could if I didn't know about them, but you've told me and I do know about them. It's all or nothing, I'm afraid," Tim said solemnly.

"Do what you have to do, Tim. Just sort it for me."

"I'll do what I can, but I can't make any promises."

Ian nodded. "Right, fair enough. Now how do you want to pay for this new car of yours?"

Chapter Forty-Two

"Tim, this is an absolutely beautiful car," Gillian smiled. "I have never been in such a fantastic vehicle, and it has that lovely new car leather smell too. But it must have cost a fortune. How long is it going to take you to pay this off?"

Tim just smiled. "I'm glad you like it. I do too. It handles a lot more smartly than the BMW."

"So where are we going to go? You'll want to give the car a decent run."

"Yes I do. I thought we could take a drive along the East Lothian Touring Trail. What do you think?"

"East Lothian is a very pretty county and I love the coast road from Edinburgh through all the little towns and villages," Gillian said.

"We'll pass the beaches. I love to see the sea, and Guillane golf course too. Do you play golf, Gillian?"

"I've never tried. It's quite an expensive sport, isn't it? But I do like the views towards Dirleton Castle. Can we go past there?"

Tim laughed. "Of course, wherever you like, pet." Gillian sounded so excited just about going for a drive. But she was right, this was a great car. Well worth every penny, in his opinion. He wasn't entirely sure his mother would have approved of him spending so much money on another car, and that thought caused him a twinge of guilt, but the twinge didn't last long. After they had driven down the coast, Tim swung around and drove along the edge of the Lammermuir Hills. It was getting darker and the country roads did not offer much light, but Tim's headlights did. Beautiful.

"I don't know about you, Tim, but I'm beginning to get hungry," Gillian said.

"Yes, I think Longniddry is just coming up. We'll stop there shall we?"

"Thank you, It's a long time since I've been to the Longniddry Inn. It used to be one of our Sunday stops when I was a little girl," Gillian smiled.

Somebody standing outside smoking gave a wolf-whistle. Tim saw Gillian blush, but he wasn't sure whether the man was whistling at her or the car. He held the door open for her and they walked in. The restaurant was not as busy as he had expected, but it was warm, and a good-natured rumble of discussion rose from the tables.

Just as the waitress came to take their order, Tim looked up from the menu and noticed a familiar face across the other side of the room. The man gazed across at Tim, and recognition turned to horror in his eyes. He got up and started heading for the door.

"No you bloody don't!" Tim shouted. He nudged the surprised waitress out of the way and squeezed past an elderly couple to chase after the man. He almost knocked over the smoker in his haste, but the familiar face had gone, driving as fast as the red Volkswagen would take him. "Ha, ha, ha," Tim laughed. "You want a race, do you, Hamilton?"

He jumped into the new car and drove swiftly out of the car park. As his speed was increasing, Tim seemed to remember that John Hamilton had family in Tranent, not far from where they were, but he was driving in the opposite direction. It took Tim no time at all to catch up with Hamilton, but there was no safe place to pass and he couldn't bear the thought of smashing his shiny new car. Tim called the station on his hands-free phone. He was so glad he had that in this car.

Neil Larkin answered.

"Neil, it's Tim. I've found John Hamilton, he was in a restaurant in East Lothian. The idiot is still driving the same red Volkswagen that he took DI Wilson in. I'm following him, but I'll need back-up."

"Where are you, Tim?"

Tim gave Neil the co-ordinates from his GPS system and heard Neil put out a call to the local bobbies. "Thank goodness we are all Police Scotland now," Tim muttered.

Then Tim noticed Hamilton begin to swerve around in the road, to put Tim off. He sped up, he slowed down, he moved across the road. Hamilton almost met his end under a fuel lorry travelling in the other direction.

Tim felt the chase went on for far longer than it really did until, up ahead, Tim saw Hamilton slow down. The blue flashing lights ahead of them signalled the presence of uniformed officers only too happy to catch John Hamilton.

"Thanks a lot," Tim said to the local men as he jumped out of his car. "I didn't want to have to use my new car as a crash barrier."

"I'm not surprised. That's a fine motor. It must have cost a fair bit. Is it really yours?" one of the uniforms asked.

"Yes, I just picked it up today and I was taking it for a drive, when my girlfriend and I stopped for dinner. Oh God, my girlfriend!" Tim exclaimed. "I'll have to go."

"We'll want to book him for dangerous driving, then I understand a certain DI Wilson has dabs on him?" the other uniform asked.

"Oh fuck, no!" Hamilton shouted.

"Oh fuck yes, John, and I wouldn't want to be you at that meeting." Tim smiled.

"We'll get him up to Fettes tomorrow. That do you?" the first uniform said.

"Now that you are all one force, Police Scotland, can everything not be dealt with here, officers?" Hamilton asked.

"You know something, it probably could," the first uniform said.

"But, after all I've heard about you, where would be the fun in that for DI Wilson, I ask you that?" The second uniform grinned.

"Great. Thanks so much, I'll tell DI Wilson to expect him," Tim said.

***

By the time Tim got back to the Longniddry Inn, Gillian was tucking into the largest ice cream he had ever seen.

"I'm so sorry, pet," Tim said.

"I got two spoons," Gillian smiled.

Chapter Forty-Three

Mackay walked into the room, and the volume of conversations dropped from thunderous to an incessant murmur.

"Are you going to eat that bacon roll, Jane?" Bear asked.

"No. Do you want it?"

Bear lifted the roll, gazing at it lovingly. "Come to Daddy..."

"If you have quite finished robbing DS Renwick of her breakfast, DC Zewedu, perhaps we could hear about the latest news she has received from MIT," Mackay said.

Jane stood up and spoke clearly. "MIT have warned stations in the city about new people-traffickers who have started working in Edinburgh. We became aware of them when the fraud division got information about money-laundering through local betting shops. They think both the trafficking and the financial criminals are based in Eastern Europe or maybe Russia, but their investigations are ongoing. We just need to be vigilant."

"Maybe not too vigilant," Tim said. "I think I have been given information about this."

"Really? How did you come by that?" Hunter asked.

"I bought my new car from Thomson's Top Cars and picked it up yesterday," Tim began.

"From what I heard, that's not the only thing you picked up," Colin smiled.

"I'll talk about that later, but you're right that's true," Tim said. "What I wanted to mention, in light of Jane's information, is that Ian Thomson stayed open late for me, but not out of the goodness of his heart. He wanted to run something by me."

"What's he up to now?" Hunter asked.

"Ian bought the new bookies in Frederick Street and Lothian Road."

"Yes, Charlie Middleton mentioned something about that before he went on holiday. He was out with Neil a few days ago," Mackay commented.

"Exactly. Well, needless to say, Ian knew that he wasn't going to get a licence to run the betting shops himself, so he had to employ a manager without a criminal record. One that he felt he could trust," Tim said.

"Does Ian know anybody without a criminal record? Apart from you, big man?" Bear looked at Tim.

"Ha, ha, very funny. I asked him something similar, to be honest."

"Didn't Charlie say Arjun Mansoor's wife was working for Ian as manageress of one of the betting shops?" Hunter said.

"Yes, he did," Mackay agreed.

"He must be mad to have anything to do with Mansoor. Everything that man touches turns sour," Rachael said.

"She's actually manager of both his shops. And you're right, Rachael; that's exactly what has happened," Tim said. "It has all turned very sour. Ian asked her to keep two sets of books: one for him, and one for the taxman."

"He told you that?" Hunter asked.

"He showed them to me," Tim said.

"Ian does know that's illegal?" Jane laughed.

"He does, but what he found was worse," Tim said. "He didn't just find the two sets of books, he found four."

"Four!" Rachael exclaimed.

"Each one was easily identifiable: Thomson, HMRC, Ponomarenko and Mansoor." Tim looked around the room, pleased with the effect his news had had.

"Where does Ponomarenko fit in?" Hunter asked.

"Well, the money boffins at Gartcosh will need to confirm it, but to the naked eye, it looks like Ponomarenko is putting lumps of money into Ian's business, unbeknownst to Ian. Then they remove it, and Mansoor gets a twenty percent cut," Tim said.

"How much are we looking at?" Jane asked.

"Ian has identified sixty thousand in less than a month."

"Does he know where it's coming from?" Hunter asked.

"No, Boss. He just knows he's being used and he's furious," Tim said.

"You need to hand that information over to Jane and MIT to deal with this, Tim," Hunter said.

"Yes, Boss."

"And from what I hear, you and DS Renwick had another little run in with Mr Ponomarenko?" Mackay asked.

"Yes, Sir. He seems to have mistaken me for Brian Squires."

"That's not much of a compliment. Tall, light hair, big ugly mug. Right enough, easy mistake." Bear grinned and ducked as Tim took a good natured swipe at him.

"He approached me when I was standing alone in the Sheraton after Jane and I had interviewed Cameron." Tim nodded at Hunter. "He shoved a gun in my back. Nobody else saw it, but it made my blood run cold. Luckily Jane correctly deduced that I was not in a good situation, and called for back-up. I think we have Mr Ponomarenko here to interview today?"

"Yes. You and DI Wilson can attend to that," Mackay said. "But I understand that you broke with protocol and refused to get checked out at the hospital?"

"I did, Sir. But, to be fair, if I had gone to hospital, Ian wouldn't have given me those accounts and I wouldn't have seen John Hamilton." Tim smiled.

Hunter shook his head. "That's not really the point, lad," he said solemnly. "But how did you catch up with Hamilton, anyway?"

"I was taking Gillian for a run in the new car. It can move." Tim grinned.

"I want a shot," Mel said.

"No doubt you do, Mel!" Tim smiled. "Gillian and I took a drive through East Lothian and stopped for dinner at The Longniddry Inn."

"It makes sense you saw him in that part of the country,

because John's family are out by Tranent," Colin said.

"Hamilton probably saw me when I walked in. He was with a much older woman."

"Probably his fond farewell to his mother before he flees the country," Colin said sourly. "When he noticed that I had caught sight of him, he ran and I followed. He was fast, but my car was faster. Some local uniforms stopped him and I think they planned to book him for dangerous driving and then send him to us, Boss." Tim looked at Hunter.

"Yes, Colin had asked East Lothian stations to keep a look out for him. Seems Hamilton made it easy for them." Hunter smiled.

"Now, DI Wilson, I do not want you to be involved in that interview," Mackay said.

"Please let me, Sir," Colin asked.

"Good idea, DS Reid. You and DC Chan can play good cop/ bad cop."

"Such a fun game." Colin winked at Nadia.

"No guesses needed as to which part I get to play," Nadia said.

"What about Sheptytsky? Is he well enough to be interviewed?" Mackay asked.

"No word on that yet, Sir," Hunter said.

"Would you like me to speak to the hospital?" Tim asked.

"No, I would like you to keep well away from that, DC Myerscough. He is your girlfriend's boss," Mackay said. "Perhaps you could give the hospital a call and see what you can find out, DC Grant?"

Mel nodded. "Of course, Sir."

"Are we any further forward with who killed Ponomarenko's daughter?" Mackay asked.

"No, Sir." Rachael shook her head.

"I want you to go over the statements we have and work out what we're missing, DC Anderson, DC McKenzie," Mackay said to Rachael and Angus. "And DC Zewedu, you can assist DS Renwick and interview Ponomarenko."

***

"It's still nice and warm here, even in October," Jamie said.

"Aye, shall we have a coffee and then go and explore?" Harry asked.

"Tea for me," Gavin said. "The inside of my mouth feels like a cat's litter tray."

"Try shutting your mouth when you sleep. That way it'll no be so dry and you won't snore," Jamie complained.

Gavin shrugged and wandered through to the shower. "I want to smell good for the lassies."

As the boys came down the steps they saw Mrs Macnab wearing sensible walking shoes and carrying a large handbag. She called over to them.

"Good morning, boys. Did you sleep well?"

"Aye, aye we did. We're off to the beach now," Jamie said.

"It's lovely. Really nice views. I'm sure you'll enjoy it."

The boys grinned at each other and hurried on.

"I'm sure we'll enjoy the views," Harry joked meaningfully.

They did not have far to walk to the beach. It was pretty and the views across the sea were lovely, but the only people the boys could see were little family groups with small children digging purposefully into the sand. No doubt the girls were still in bed because they had been out late clubbing. The boys turned back from the beach and walked to the main street, where they bought a few essentials for the fridge. Bread, butter, ham, milk and beer. When they found a café, they stopped for breakfast and bought a good meal consisting of cake, coffee, cigarettes and beer.

Chapter Forty-Four

"You do know that if Ian Thomson had thought faster and not told you about the HMRC accounts, we'd have had nothing on him here at all, Tim? He would be the hero," Jane said.

"Yes, I know that, and he did ask if it might be possible for me to forget to pass those on."

"What did you say?"

"Well it was hard, because he protected my dad from the worst of the beatings while they were in jail together, but I said I couldn't do it." Tim shook his head. "I tell you, Jane, I did have a little devil sitting on my shoulder shouting 'Go on, nobody will ever know!' – but that's where the trouble starts, isn't it? I would know, and more importantly Ian would know that I had bent the rules – and he would have a hold over me if he slipped from the straight and narrow in the future. He could just bring that up."

"Of course, you're right." Jane smiled. "But I can understand the internal turmoil. Now, let's have a look and see what we have."

Jane and Tim pored over the paperwork that Tim had received from Ian Thomson. The figures they could see were vastly different, but as Jane thought about the sums involved she realised that it was almost as if there were two sets of two accounts. Those for Ian and HMRC went up and down in tandem, just showing a substantially lower figure to be issued to the taxman. Likewise, the books for Ponomarenko and Mansoor ran in parallel, with Mansoor creaming his cut off the money the Ukrainian brothers paid into the business. She noticed that that money never stayed for long enough to affect the monthly bottom line of the shops.

"Mansoor does bloody well for sitting around on his bum in

jail," Jane commented.

"He does. Maybe we're in the wrong job?" Tim laughed.

"As if you need to worry, Mr Moneybags," Jane teased. "I hope I'm getting a ride in your flash new car soon?"

"Of course. I'm thrilled with it, just name the day and I'll take you and Rache for a spin," Tim grinned.

"Sounds like a plan. Well, bearing in mind that these accounts don't show Ian Thomson in a pure white light, let me get them over to Gartcosh for the experts to examine them."

"Yes, I think they need an expert eye," Tim agreed.

Jane nodded. "They certainly seem to support the information Superintendent Miller gave me about money laundering through betting shops in the city."

***

"That is a fabulous sale to the young detective," Janice cooed in Ian's ear. "Maybe you could treat me to a nice Chanel bag or a bright yellow pair of Jimi Choos? I've always wanted a pair of really glamorous shoes. Where does that man get all his money? It's not as an honest copper."

"No, his mother was hugely wealthy and left her money between him and his sister," Ian said.

"Not to her husband?"

"I don't know! All I know is Tim can afford anything he wants and he wanted that car," Ian said in an exasperated voice.

"Don't shout at me, Ian, you know I don't like it," Janice whined.

"I'm sorry, darlin'. I've just got a lot on my mind."

"What's the matter? Can I help?" She nuzzled into the crook of his neck and patted his arm.

"Nobody can help, Janice."

"I can listen?"

"Well, you know I've got Mrs Mansoor working as my book-keeper in the betting shops?"

"Yes, I know. And that was a right bloody stupid idea, if you ask me. That Mansoor lot have never brought you anything but trouble. So have you decided what to do about the four sets of accounts?"

"Yes, I gave them all to Tim Myerscough yesterday," Ian said.

"Even the ones between you and HMRC? Are you daft?"

Chapter Forty-Five

Hunter drove from the station to the Edinburgh Royal Infirmary on the outskirts of the city, in Little France, where Sheptytsky was still under observation. It was a lovely, clear autumn day and the leaves on the trees were beginning to turn vibrant shades of gold, yellow, orange, red and brown. Hunter always revelled in the autumn colours of the deciduous trees with their leaves dancing like ballerinas as they fluttered to earth. He felt there was something special about his city on a brisk autumn day like today when the air was crisp, and people were beginning to wear their sweaters and scarves that had been discarded over the summer months.

The only parking space he could find was further away from the hospital entrance than he would have liked, but he and Mel wove swiftly in between the parked cars.

"We are going to ask the professor why he was visiting Mansoor as well as about his run-in with Ponomarenko, aren't we Boss?" Mel asked.

"Yes, we are. But let's start by being nice, shall we, Mel?" Hunter said as he held the door open for her and they followed the signs towards the ward.

"Professor Sheptytsky, I am DI Hunter Wilson, we have met before. This is my colleague DC Mel Grant. It is good to see you alert. The doctor says your condition is much improved and that you might be able to answer a few questions for me?"

"I am happy to tell you all I know, if it will help," Sheptytsky said.

Hunter watched Mel take out her notebook. Then he looked back at Sheptytsky and noticed that although the man was awake and had an English language newspaper in front of him, he still looked very pale and tired.

"What has your relationship with Oleksander Ponomarenko been like over the years you have known him?" Hunter asked.

"I wouldn't really say I knew him well enough to call it a relationship. His sister-in-law is my cousin, our fathers were brothers. So I would see Oleksander occasionally at larger family gatherings: my cousin's wedding, Xristina's baptism, my uncle's funeral, that sort of thing, so I have only met him on a handful of occasions."

"Did he contact you when Xristina decided to continue her studies in Edinburgh in your department?"

"Yes, he did. He asked me about the quality of teaching and the standing of Edinburgh University. He also asked about the safety of the city." Sheptytsky sighed. "I told him that Edinburgh was one of the most respected Universities in Britain and that I believed it to be a safe city. It is very small, for a city."

"It is quite a small city," Mel nodded.

"Of course, since that dreadful thing happened to Xristina, Oleksander is furious. Too angry to think reasonably. He is looking for someone to blame: me, the man who picked Xristina up from the airport and took her to the flat, the police, the university, anybody, anything. That's why he attacked me. He asked me who murdered Xristina and why, but I had no answer. If I had not been family, I think he would have killed me there and then. As it was, he left me there to die." Sheptytsky looked at Hunter with tears in his eyes. "Please find who is responsible before he kills me or some other innocent. Oleksander Ponomarenko is not a nice man at the best of times, but when he is angry, nothing but blood will stop him."

"I will try," Hunter replied softly.

Hunter let silence lie for a few moments as he looked around the room and gave Professor Sheptytsky time to compose himself. Sheptytsky was in a side room on his own within the ward; there was a shower room cubicle with a lavatory in a little room in the corner. Everything was white and clean and stark, except for the patient's hospital gown that was stamped all over in small green letters *Hospital Property*.

Hunter could not help but wonder who would want to remove the garment from the premises.

Hunter took a deep breath and began to speak. "Professor Sheptytsky, there is another matter I hope you can help me with."

"If I can."

"How well do you know Arjun Mansoor?" Hunter asked.

"Hardly at all."

"But you do know him?" Mel confirmed.

"I have met him once. He is in prison here."

"Yes, he is. Why did you go to visit him in prison?" Hunter asked.

"I studied for many years in Baghdad. Mr Mansoor is from Iraq and he has family in Baghdad. I got to know some members of his family when we were all at the university there." Sheptytsky paused. "We keep in touch, it is easy to do now with Skype, Facebook and Instagram, even just email. It is not like before."

"That's true, it is easier to keep in touch," Hunter said. In his head he thought that it didn't always happen, even with his own family. It was weeks since he had heard from his daughter, Alison. He glanced at Mel before he spoke again. He saw she was writing fast to try to ensure her notes were complete.

"Why did you go to HMP Edinburgh to visit Arjun Mansoor?" Hunter asked in a very cold voice.

"His family asked me to go. He only has his wife who is able to visit him. She sometimes goes with their son, but it upsets the boy, so often she goes alone."

Hunter nodded. "So yours was a humanitarian visit?"

"I suppose it was. I went to see him, to talk to him in his own language, so that I can tell his family how he is, that he is in good spirits and has food and time for prayer."

"Oh, he has plenty of time for prayer," Mel said sourly.

"Did he ask you to do anything for him?" Hunter asked.

"Like what?"

"Any business? Send money for him?"

"Inspector, I am a university professor. I have no head for

185

business and less for money. Mr Mansoor would be in a sorry state if he waited for me to arrange deals for him."

"Did he ask about Xristina?" Mel asked.

"He doesn't know Xristina. How could he ask about her? Why would he ask about her?"

"Did he mention Oleksander Ponomarenko?" Hunter asked.

"He told me he was doing business with two of my countrymen, Oleksander and Sergei Ponomarenko. I said they were gangsters."

"Did he talk about the other Ukrainian girls who have come to the city recently?"

"He said he didn't care, he was getting easy money by allowing them to launder money through a business his wife manages. The Ponomarenko brothers told them they were recruitments agents. I said they were more likely to be people-traffickers."

"What did Mansoor say to that?" Mel asked.

"He was horrified. One of his nieces was taken, only fourteen, and sold to Daesh as a bride."

"Disgusting," Hunter said.

"He told me to find out for him if it was true."

"Couldn't his wife find out for him?" Hunter asked.

"She told him payments were coming from The Edinburgh Massage Suite in Lothian Road. It made more sense for a man to go there than a woman. It is all too horrible. I went to see Mr Mansoor to do a nice thing for his family who were kind to me. We spoke about members of his family, the beauty of Baghdad before the troubles, the danger there now, and our favourite Iraqi food." Sheptytsky's voice got louder and louder. And then very softly he said, "Mr Mansoor misses home cooking, so he smokes too many cigarettes to try to forget the taste. I put twenty pounds of my own money into his prison account so that he could buy more cigarettes. That is the only money or talk of money that was exchanged."

"Did you learn anything from the staff at The Edinburgh Massage Suite?" Hunter asked.

Sheptytshky shook his head.

Hunter looked at Mel until she stopped writing. "Thank

you, Professor Sheptytsky."

"Now, I am very tired, please leave me."

***

Jane and Bear entered Interview Room 2 at the station. Jane was always struck by how stuffy and smelly these rooms were. It never seemed to matter how much disinfectant or furniture polish the cleaners used, they always smelled stale. When the room was painted, they used blue paint on the bottom half of the walls and grey on the top half and the ceiling. She didn't know why. Maybe it was meant to look more interesting than the plain grey that had been there before. However, over time, interviewees who were kept waiting longer than they felt they should have been had picked at the blue paint, leaving little grey pock-marks at table height.

The blue chairs were fixed to the floor, the table was fixed to the floor, and the audio-recording equipment was fixed to the table. Cameras for visual recording were fixed high on the walls almost at the ceiling. She looked up and noticed they were caked with dust.

Jane led and Bear into the room and they took their seats. Jane looked across the table at Oleksander Ponomarenko, his consular official and his solicitor, Andrew Barley. Jane liked Barley; he was a sensible man who knew the ropes and had been in his profession too long to still feel he had things to prove.

"Mr Ponomarenko, I am DS Jane Renwick and this is my colleague, DC Zewedu," she said.

"It's not Mr Ponomarenko, it's Attaché Ponomarenko. I should not be here. I am the trade attaché to the Ukrainian Consulate. I have diplomatic immunity."

"Before Attaché Ponomarenko says anything, I must insist that his right to diplomatic immunity has been recorded and it is acknowledged that he will face no charges for any crimes he may admit to or be charged with," Andrew Barley said.

"Even so, that doesn't mean you cannot assist us with enquiries," Bear said.

"It is true, but I do not have to 'help with enquiries'," he sneered. "Now let me leave before this becomes a diplomatic incident."

"I am surprised that you do not want us to solve your daughter's murder. But please, feel free to leave." Jane stood up and pointed to the door. "Good bye, Mr Ponomarenko."

"I, of course, I, indeed, I want the murder of my daughter to be solved. I will help with that, if I can," Ponomarenko said softly. His brusque demeanour had been replaced with the most miserable expression Jane had ever seen.

Jane frowned. "What did you think we were going to talk about that you do not want to talk about? Just so that I can be sure to avoid those subjects."

She noticed Andrew Barley crack a smile, but he said nothing.

"Just talk about Xristina," Ponomarenko said.

"Shall we start with why your daughter wanted to come here to study under Professor Sheptytsky? I believe he is your sister-in-law's cousin. A member of your extended family," Jane said.

"Not my family, my brother's family. Anyway, the man is a fool."

"A fool?" Bear asked in surprise. "He is a very clever fool. He speaks several languages, including English and Arabic, and he has a PhD."

"And what does he use his command of Arabic for? He goes to speak to Arjun Mansoor and rocks my boat!"

"How well do you know Arjun Mansoor, Mr Ponomarenko?" Jane asked.

"We have done business, but I have never met him: I do not know him."

"Would that business have anything to do with the money accounted for in your name at the betting shops known as Thomson's Bets?"

"I don't want to speak about this."

"How could Professor Sheptytsky rock your boat with Mr Mansoor?" Bear asked.

"He spoke more than he should about things that do not

concern him."

"What kind of things, Mr Ponomarenko? Was that why you attacked him at the university, or do you feel he was partly to blame for Xristina's death?" Jane asked quietly.

"Do you have children?" Ponomarenko asked.

Both Jane and Bear shook their heads.

"It is the best pleasure and the worst pain known to mankind. When they cry, you weep; when they are scratched, you bleed profusely; when they die, your own life ends, but you have to keep on living. I have seen much suffering in my life, but nothing is so bad as to witness the death of your own child. My only child. My treasure, my future, my world."

Jane watched Ponomarenko's head hit the table and he sobbed uncontrollably. She was not sure how to proceed, and was grateful when Andrew Barley spoke.

"DS Renwick, perhaps we could take a short break? I will accompany Attaché Ponomarenko and the consular official to your unforgettable canteen and we will restore ourselves with a cup of tea. You know my client is keen to assist in finding his daughter's murderer. We will not leave the building, and perhaps we could re-convene in thirty minutes?"

"An excellent idea, Mr Barley. Do you know your way?" Jane asked.

"All too well, I fear."

***

As Bear shut the door on the other three men he turned to Jane and stared at her.

"I don't know where to start. That was the softest most waffley interview I have ever witnessed. Why don't you follow up? Why are you so soft on him? Don't you want answers?" Bear slammed his hand on the table so hard that Jane jumped.

"I've never dealt with anybody with diplomatic immunity before. I don't want him to get up and walk away."

"You are surely not intimidated by that blustering buffoon, are you? That's just what he wants! Well, my father was

189

Ethiopian Ambassador before we sought asylum. He had diplomatic immunity when we first came here. I understand it, I've lived it, and it doesn't impress me at all. Do you want me to take over asking the questions?"

"I forgot about your Dad's position. Yes please, Bear. Give it a try."

When the men walked back in, Jane recommenced the interview and switched on the recorder.

Bear took a deep breath. "Attaché Ponomarenko, I know what it is like to lose people who are close to you. Believe me, I have been there too often. I also know what it is like to have diplomatic immunity: I come from a long line of diplomats. However, I trust that you are an *honourable* man, and as such would not abuse your diplomatic status to avoid answering our questions."

"Of course, to help find Xristina's murderer," Oleksander agreed purposefully.

"We do not yet know what information will lead us to her murderer, so, even if my questions embarrass you or implicate you, I expect you to answer them honestly. You may then claim your diplomatic privilege if you are charged with any crime. Do you understand, Attaché Ponomarenko?"

"Yes, ask what you want. I need to know who killed my girl."

"Why did you go to Edinburgh University?"

"I wanted to see where Xristina studied. What meant so much to her."

"Did you go to confront Professor Sheptytsky?"

"No, but he was there. I asked him if he knew what had happened to Xristina, or who had done it. He said he did not. He was very sorry for Xristina but it was justice for me – for what I do to the daughters of others. Then he laughed at me," Ponomarenko shouted, "He laughed at me!"

Bear looked away briefly. "What did he mean by that, 'what you do to the daughters of others'?"

"How do I know?"

"I don't know how you know, but you do. What did he mean?" Bear asked firmly.

"What did Professor Sheptytsky find out that you had been doing?" Jane asked.

"Yes, what did he mean?" Bear repeated.

"He went to visit Arjun Mansoor in prison. He told me that. When Zelay Sheptytsky studied in Baghdad he met members of Mansoor's family and when they learned he was to teach in Edinburgh, they asked him to visit. I doubt they can afford to come. I do business with Arjun Mansoor."

"What kind of business? Arjun Mansoor does not have a good reputation," Jane said.

"That was the problem. Mansoor had offered, agreed maybe, to arrange to allow me to pay money into a business his wife runs. He would take a small fee and I would get it out again."

"We call that money-laundering, Attaché Ponomarenko," Bear said. "It is frowned upon here. It is illegal."

Ponomarenko smiled. "Yes, well, I am still looking for the place it is strictly legal, but what can you do?"

"Pay your tax like everybody else?" Jane suggested sourly.

"So far so good: I sense there is more," Bear prompted.

"There is. Mansoor had learned from his wife the source of the funds. He may not have a good reputation, as you say, but even he was not happy with my business." Ponomarenko shrugged. "He asked Sheptytsky to go and visit the source and find out if his wife was correct."

"Why did Mansoor not ask his wife to go?" Jane asked.

"I doubt even the loyal Mrs Mansoor would want to visit The Edinburgh Massage Suite in Lothian Road."

"I doubt that too," Bear said. "And so that I do not jump to conclusions, just what is your business with The Edinburgh Massage Suite in Lothian Road?"

"I suppose you would call me a recruitment consultant for that business."

"Would I? I doubt that very much. Exactly who did you recruit?"

"Staff, just staff," Ponomarenko smiled broadly, but the smile did not reach his eyes.

"Now, Attaché Ponomarenko, we had been getting along so

191

well. Please do not try to obfuscate the issue. Which members of staff did you supply to the business?" Bear asked pointedly.

"As if we couldn't guess," Jane muttered.

Bear frowned at her and looked back to Ponomarenko. He noticed that both the consular official and Andrew Barley were looking distinctly uncomfortable. Bear realised that they had not been aware of Ponomarenko's 'business dealings', and from the look on their faces Bear could tell that they found the direction this conversation was going distinctly distasteful.

"The Edinburgh Massage Suite relies on the expertise of young women. Many want to leave my country for a more lucrative life in the West. I assist both parties to succeed in their aims." Ponomarenko held out his hands, palms upwards in supplication and smiled apologetically.

"So you supply young Ukrainian women to work in The Edinburgh Massage Suite?" Bear growled. "How do they make contact with you?"

"Well, that was part of the problem," Ponomarenko began.

"Before Attaché Ponomarenko says any more, I must reiterate that his right to diplomatic immunity has been recorded, and he will face no charges for any crimes he may admit to," Andrew Barley said.

Bear nodded curtly. "What part of the problem was it, Attaché Ponomarenko?"

"Mrs Mansoor had noticed that for the first three girls we supplied—"

"We?" Jane and Bear asked together.

"My brother Sergei and I run a business in Ukraine. He is still there, keeping things going while I am here to see about Xristina."

"Go on," Bear said.

"For the first three women, the price we were paid was only twenty thousand pounds each because they came to us from the local whorehouse in Kiev. Of course, the women paid something towards their journey, but not nearly enough to make it worth my while. Luckily, the owner of the massage parlour is a reasonable man. He even used to let the girls out to hand out vouchers to get business, but since Xristina's death that doesn't happen.

"However, most recently, my brother and I achieved very good much higher prices for an additional five girls. They are so young, so beautiful, so virginal." Ponomarenko gazed into the middle distance.

"And how did these young, beautiful girls get in touch with you?" Jane hissed.

"We bought them from the local orphanage. That is why we must get a higher price. It will be a good source of workers, I think," Ponomarenko said dreamily. "Mrs Mansoor noticed we were paid fifty thousand pounds each for these young girls. She told her husband before she wrote up the accounts. He sent his spy, Sheptytsky, to find out why, and all of a sudden I am the bad guy? Why should Mansoor worry? He'll get his cut!"

"Trafficking people is also illegal here, Attaché Ponomarenko," Bear whispered.

"So that is why I attacked Sheptytsky. For Xristina, and for him speaking badly about me finding work for these young women in the West as they wished."

Jane and Bear brought the interview to a close without further comment. Andrew Barley conferred with Ponomarenko and they agreed to return to discuss matters further the following day.

"He comes across as if he is the victim! Do you even think he believes that he is the one hard done by?" Jane asked Bear incredulously.

"I don't know what *he* believes," Bear said angrily, "but *I* believe I would like to rip his head from his shoulders."

Chapter Forty-Six

Jamie looked around the beach again. He could not understand it. There was no talent at all. The young families who had been playing in the sand all morning had left at lunchtime to avoid the heat of the day, and Jamie got quite excited. It must be the afternoon when the young folk came out to sunbathe. He lay on the warm sand with Gavin and Harry waiting for the fun to start, waiting for the babes in bikinis – or better still, topless.

One or two young couples arrived and put up parasols. Jamie noticed that these very definitely did not shade the owners from the sun. A couple of young men walked along the beach towards him. Jamie shouted to them, "Hey mate! Which is the best club here to go to tonight? The one with the most single birds?"

The men clearly did not speak much English. The taller of the two shook his head but patted his binoculars. "Birds and waves, lovely," he said.

"I don't think he's interested in the same kind of birds," Harry said. "Look, they're holding hands."

"Shit! Cuz, where are the birds?" Jamie moaned.

"I wonder where that San Antonio place is that the girls mentioned?" Gavin asked. "Look, there's old Mrs Macnab. If she's been here so often, she must know. Jamie, go and ask her."

"You go and ask her!"

Gavin looked at Jamie and Harry and shrugged his shoulders. "All right, I will. But I may not share the info with you two."

Jamie watched Gavin walk smartly over to Mrs Macnab. He couldn't hear what was said, but saw Gavin's posture change from his smart, military stance to his shoulders slumping.

Gavin put his hands into the pockets of his shorts then sat down beside Mrs Macnab. The old lady kept on talking, then showed Gavin a little book. Gavin looked as if he was going to burst into tears. He put his head in his hands. He sat like that for some minutes, then Jamie saw him shake Mrs Macnab by the hand and wander back.

"It doesn't look like it's good news, cuz," Jamie said to Harry.

"You're right, he looks awfy miserable," Harry replied.

They waited in silence until Gavin threw himself on the sand beside them.

"You will not bloody believe it!" Gavin said.

"Try us," Harry said.

"Do you want the good news or the bad news?"

"Good news!" Jamie shouted.

"There isn't any. There is bad news and worse news."

"Go on then, Gavin. Let's hear it," Harry said.

"There are no decent clubs here at all!"

"Yeh, right. This is Ibiza, man. It's only a wee island but there's nothing to do," Jamie said sarcastically.

"Except go clubbing and have fun," Harry added with a laugh.

"Maybe. Maybe in the big resorts like San Antonio, but no' here, lads. We managed to choose the quiet bit of the island." Gavin sighed.

"I didn't know there was a quiet bit of the island. But still, can we no' get a bus or a taxi to the big resorts, or even hire a car? I've got my driving licence with me," Jamie suggested.

Harry shook his head. "You're no' even twenty-one, cuz. But even if we could get a hire car, it'd cost us a fortune with insurance and that."

Gavin sighed. "A taxi would cost us an arm and a leg, and any buses there are don't run late enough. We should have stayed in Edinburgh and spent our money on seeing Olena and Symona. You could have had Anichka, Jamie."

"So what is there to do?" Jamie asked with a groan.

***

"You know, DC Anderson," Angus said, "nobody has really given much thought to how whoever killed Xristina got to her. I'm going to go back over the statements."

"That's a good idea, Angus. You do that, and I'll look over the post-mortem report and the information we got from forensics. And call me Rachael, we're the same rank." Rachael smiled.

"Shall I make us some tea before we get started?" Angus asked.

"Now you're talking. But I'll have coffee, with milk."

Rachael started reading the post-mortem report as Angus got up to make drinks. She noticed that the injuries to Xristina's head and face had been caused by a heavy, blunt object.

She flipped over to the forensics report. It said there was nothing lying near the victim that could have caused these injuries, but there was a cricket bat and a hockey stick just inside the front door. There were also old tools under the kitchen sink. All of these had been taken to be forensically examined. None of the items had revealed any fingerprints, but the hockey stick and one set of pliers had been cleaned. But not cleaned well enough to remove all the traces of Xristina's skin and blood.

The lock on the door of the flat had been tampered with, but it was only a Yale lock and not difficult to flip. Rachael sat and thought about all the information she had until she was disturbed by Angus coming back into the incident room, carrying two mugs.

"Thanks Angus," she said. "Can you check through the statements and see if there is any reference made to a cricket bat, a hockey stick and some tools under the sink? I think I need to know who those belong to."

"Of course, I'll let you know when I get to that."

Rachael began reading the forensic evidence again, and noticed that although the lock had been tampered with, there was a key under the mat. Whoever had broken in didn't know about that.

The two detectives made notes as they studied the

information to hand. After about two hours, when Rachael got up to make more drinks, she noticed that Angus was so engrossed that he didn't even notice her leave. When she came back, she suggested to him that they take a break.

"That's a good idea." Angus stood up and rubbed the back of his neck. "I think I might go outside for a few minutes for a change of scene and a fag. I'll be back in ten. I have some interesting facts here, but I want to get them straight in my head."

Rachael smiled and watched him leave the room. She then got up and went to the Ladies to splash some water on her face.

"Hello, Janey," Rachael said as she saw her partner leaning on a sink.

"Hi love," Jane said. "You will not believe what Bear and I have discovered about Ponomarenko."

"What?"

"Only that he's been busy people-trafficking and money-laundering. And because of his 'diplomatic immunity' he will get away with it!" Jane sounded exasperated.

"No way! That can't be true!"

"Of course it is! MIT had leads, but Ian Thomson found the evidence and gave it to Tim. Now Ponomarenko has just admitted it, in case it helps us find his daughter's killer. In fact, remember those three girls you and Charlie Middleton interviewed who were in the flat when Xristina was found dead?"

"Yes, pretty lassies," Rachael said.

"Well, they were the first three Ponomarenko brought from Ukraine to here. They paid him what money they had, but for him, it wasn't enough, so he says he sold them to The Edinburgh Massage Suite in Lothian Road. Twenty grand a time."

"You have got to be joking? That is really evil," Rachael said.

"He calls himself a 'recruitment consultant'. Isn't that sick?"

"Bad bastard!"

"He is that. And, apparently, the manager told him that the

girls used to get out now and again to hand out flyers and advertising cards, but after Xristina's death and their run-in with us, the owner doesn't let them out at all now. Supposedly they have debts to repay him."

"Why do I fear these poor bitches will never get those 'debts' repaid?" Rachael muttered.

"And that ghastly man tried to make it sound like he was the victim. I thought Bear might rip him apart when he came out with all this" Jane continued.

"I wish he had, except Bear would have got done."

"So those poor young women are working their butts off, literally, I'd guess," Jane said.

"They must hate Ponomarenko so much."

"I bet they do. Both brothers, because they are both involved in this sleazy business. Apparently even Arjun Mansoor disapproves. Let's face it, if you're on the wrong side of Arjun Mansoor, you must be a really nasty piece of work," Jane said. "Anyway, I have to go and write this up. Bear and I thought we might all go out to The Golf Pub in Bruntsfield before we go home?"

"I'll look forward to that." Rachael kissed Jane lightly on the lips and went back to find Angus waiting for her.

"Right, Let me tell you what I've found," he said. "Lucky Buchanan had confirmed that the cricket bat and hockey stick were his, from his university days when he lived in the flat. Cameron Wilson admitted to owning the tools under the sink. And the front door of the flat was open when Cameron got home from the night club with the two soldiers and their dates Olena and Symona. They all confirmed that."

"The Yale lock had been tampered with and the door damaged a bit, but there was a key under the mat," Rachael said. "Whoever broke in most likely didn't know about the key. So who did know about it?"

"Well the soldiers, Olena and Symona had only met Cameron, so they wouldn't know about the key, but they also wouldn't know where he lived. Cameron knew where the key was because he put it there." Angus said.

"So that leaves Lucky and Squires?"

"And possibly Professor What's-His-Name that Ponomarenko put in hospital," Angus said. "And remember, Tim's statement says he woke Lucky when he phoned him."

"Or Lucky pretended to have been woken up," Rachael said, "Of course, if Ponomarenko ever contacted the massage parlour, it's possible he told the owner that his daughter was studying in Edinburgh and where she was living," Jane mused.

"Why would he do that?" Angus asked.

"Boasting? Discussing plans to visit Edinburgh? Who knows? If he did, the three girls he trafficked here might have overheard him."

"They might have, and I doubt he's their favourite person," Angus said.

"Of course," Rachael said softly. "When you really want to hurt someone, you don't attack them, but someone they love..."

Chapter Forty-Seven

"This is all I bloody need," Hamilton said. "An interview with a tight-arsed, clean-living, do-gooder and the bitch who took my job! I just hope you're more broad-minded than him, lassie."

"Mr Hamilton, I am DS Colin Reid and this is my colleague DC Nadia Chan. Would you like a solicitor present for this interview?"

"Ooh, wee Colin got through his sergeants exams, did he? What did you do, take an apple for the teacher? I know fine who you are, Colin. And, no, I don't want a lawyer: I probably know the criminal law better than they do. Just get on with it."

Nadia cleared her throat and began to speak. She chose to speak softly so that Hamilton would have to listen carefully.

"Mr Hamilton, I have here a statement from a fellow-officer. It puts you inside his home without his permission. What do you have to say?"

"No comment."

"A glass in my colleague's home had traces of rohypnol in it. We have also identified your fingerprints on that same glass."

"You did not, I wiped them!"

Nadia smiled.

"But not the top of the glass inside," Colin said.

Hamilton sighed.

"My colleague's neighbour, Mrs Lamb, has identified you as having entered the premises when he was at work. She noticed that when you left with him some hours later, he did not seem well. Would you like to comment on that?"

"No comment."

"My colleague was found by a farmer on his land. He was

told by my colleague that he had come from a car being driven by you. My colleague also states that, as you had taken his shoes, he was obliged to borrow yours. Could you comment on that?" Nadia asked.

"No comment."

"The officers who attended the car found you and Mr Squires had both received injuries. You claimed my colleague had inflicted these. Why would he do that, Mr Hamilton?"

"Because he's a bloody psycho who's got it in for me, that's why."

"You and Mr Squires left hospital before being formally discharged," Nadia said.

"That's not a crime."

"No, it's not, but it is unwise. Do you know where Mr Squires is now, Mr Hamilton?" Nadia asked.

"No idea, not a scooby. And I wouldn't tell you if I did."

"Why did you run when you saw my colleague DC Tim Myerscough in The Longniddry Inn?" Colin asked.

"He's got a big ugly mug and I don't like looking at it. Anyway, it's not a crime to run away, wee Colin."

Colin stood up and glowered at Hamilton. "No, but dangerous driving, abduction and assault are crimes. DC Chan, charge him and then get uniform to take him to the cells. I don't fancy his chances in jail."

***

Frankie took the twins to their childminder. He had told his uncle Ian that he would be late to Thomson Top Cars today, but he didn't tell Ian how much he was looking forward to going back to the skin care salon for his appointment with Donna. Frankie felt much less anxious on this trip to the city centre. He did not have to wait outside the business entrance to gird up his courage before going in. It was an early appointment, and Frankie saw Donna leaning on the reception desk talking to other members of staff. As he walked in, the bell on the door rang and Donna looked up. She smiled at him.

"Good morning, Frankie," she said. "Tracy, this is my nine

o'clock. I'll take Mr Hope straight through. How are you today, Frankie?"

"Good, Donna, I'm okay." Frankie followed Donna into the treatment room.

She closed the door and then said, "That light treatment is definitely going to make a difference for you. Let me see." She put on the tight white gloves and ran her fingers over his skin. "You know, when we get this acne under control, you really won't know yourself. Right now, when you look in the mirror, you only see your condition. You don't see yourself, do you?"

"What do you mean?" Frankie asked nervously.

"You see spots. You don't see that you are a great-looking man: you have big brown eyes, great high cheek bones and thick dark hair. By the time I'm finished with you, I hope to be able to change that."

"Annie said things like that," Frankie said.

"Who's Annie?"

"She was my girlfriend. She died when our twins were born."

"That's so sad. But you have twins! You're young for that. Boys or girls or one of each?" Donna took out her instruments and quickly lanced the large pimple on Frankie's chin.

He winced. "Two girls."

"Don't worry. That's it for the pain," Donna said. "So what are the twins called?"

"Kylie-Ann and Dannii-Ann," Frankie got out his phone to show her pictures of his girls.

"They are beautiful, Frankie. And I bet you're a great dad."

"I try. It's all I can do. The family helps." Frankie smiled just thinking of the twins.

"You have a lovely smile."

"Thank you, Donna. You are really pretty and you have a lovely accent."

"I'm from Belfast," she smiled.

"I thought it was Ireland, somewhere, but I couldn't place it. Annie's Mum came from Donegal."

"Aye they talk quite differently down there, don't they?" Donna said.

"And what kind of light treatment worked best?" Frankie asked.

"As I thought, the red and blue pulsed lights worked best. That's what we'll use."

Frankie put on the ugly little eye shades she handed to him, and Donna applied the light to each portion of his face and neck in turn.

"You don't do it for long, do you?" Frankie asked.

"No. I'm starting off with fifteen seconds for each area. We'll extend it as your skin gets used to it. The maximum for you would be thirty seconds."

"Why not start off at that?" Frankie asked. "Wouldn't it work faster?"

"No, it would just harm your skin. You wouldn't thank me for that."

"Probably not," he smiled.

Frankie sat up at the end of the treatment session. While he felt Donna apply the moisturiser all over his face, an idea popped into his head.

"Look, just say no if it's not cool, but I was going to take the twins to the zoo on Sunday. You could always come with us, if you wanted to?" He hesitated. "No, look, that's a really stupid idea. I'm sorry."

"I'd love to come, thank you."

"Are you sure, Donna?"

"Of course, but there is one condition." She smiled.

"Oh. So what's that then?"

"We get an ice cream when we're there, and you let me push the buggy."

"That's two conditions." Frankie grinned as he took her face in his hands and kissed her tenderly on the lips.

Chapter Forty-Eight

Ian was surprised to see Frankie grinning broadly as he walked into the showroom. He walked slowly out of his office and towards his nephew. He knew that grin: it was the stupid, senseless grin that every young man, including himself many years ago, had worn in the first flush of love.

"Congratulations, Frankie boy!" Ian called over.

"Congratulations? For what?" Frankie's face assumed an air of innocence.

"You can't fool me, lad, that's your loved-up face: and it's too long since I've seen it!"

"Shut up, Uncle Ian." Frankie blushed.

"Make us a coffee, lad," Ian smiled.

"No problem, Uncle Ian." Frankie ran off.

"And then you can tell me all about her," Ian called after Frankie.

The two men sat chatting at the showroom reception, in case anybody came in."

"Donna's really nice and so pretty," Frankie said.

"I'm right glad for you, lad," Ian smiled as his nephew compared the girl to Annie, favourably. He was pleased that Frankie had decided just to include her in his usual routine with the twins rather than arrange an extravagant date. This was more like Frankie – and, Ian thought, if Donna doesn't take to Frankie's twins, no relationship would develop. He knew Frankie too well to think it would even have a chance.

"I wonder how the lads are getting on in Ibiza," Ian said.

"I bet they're out in the clubs and having a great time. I just couldn't leave the twins." Frankie picked up the mugs and took them back to the little kitchen near Ian's office.

"I know, Frankie. You take right good care of those wee

girls," Ian said. He watched Frankie as he walked to and from the kitchen. Never in a million years had he thought a teenage boy could make such a good fist of raising the twins, but Frankie's love and determination to do the right thing by Kylie-Ann and Dannii-Ann had meant he had more than risen to the challenge.

"Uncle Ian, did you hear any more about those extra accounts Mansoor's wife was keeping?" Frankie asked as he came back to the desk.

"No yet, but I've no doubt I will."

Almost as if they had been waiting outside for their cue, Ian saw Jane and Hunter walk into the showroom.

"I've been half-expecting you," Ian said. "Can we do this here, or are we going to the station?"

"It had better be the station, Mr Thomson," Hunter said.

"Oh, dear, I'm getting my Sunday name, it must be bad." Ian grimaced. "Frankie, can you manage here until closing?"

"Aye, we're no exactly run off our feet. Will you be home for tea?"

"That's unlikely, Frankie." Hunter answered for Ian as they walked with Jane towards the least glamorous car on the forecourt.

***

"Mr Thomson, for the tape, you have declined the services of a solicitor?"

"Yes, I have. What's the point? I gave you the stuff you're going to ask me about."

Hunter went on to make formal introductions for the interview.

"What's MIT?" Ian asked Jane.

"Since the regional forces in Scotland combined into one large police force covering the whole country, we do things slightly differently," she explained. "The MIT or Major Incident Team has been set up to investigate serious crime nationwide."

"And you work with them?"

205

"Yes. MIT had become aware of the money-laundering through your betting shops even before you spoke to DC Myerscough about it," Jane said.

"Yes, but I told you as soon as I knew about it. That must count for something?"

"It will, but having a separate account for the taxman is somewhat frowned upon," Hunter said quietly.

"Ah, but that was Mrs Mansoor. I had nothing to do with that, she did that all on her own."

"Indeed?" Hunter said. "Well, you can talk to your lawyer about that, if you choose to get one. In the meantime, perhaps you can help us by answering a few questions."

Ian listened as Jane explained briefly that MIT had become aware of the excessive sums going through the betting shops.

"How did they know?" Ian asked.

"To be honest, I don't know the source of the information, and even if I did, I couldn't tell you."

"I suppose not."

"We have since become aware that the funds come from payments made to Oleksander and Sergei Ponomarenko by The Edinburgh Massage Suite in Lothian Road," Jane went on.

"That's just along the road from one of my shops," Ian said.

"Yes. Do you know the Ponomarenko brothers?"

"No, but I've heard that name recently. There was a lassie killed, first night Harry was home. He was questioned about it."

"Do either of the Ponomarenko brothers have a legitimate interest in your business?" Jane asked.

"No. Not at all. And I honestly didn't know anything about their money going through the books. That smells of Arjun Mansoor. Even when I try to do the decent thing by his wife and give her a job when she needs one, he still tries to shaft me."

***

When the interview was over, Hunter was instructed by Superintendent Miller at MIT not to release Ian Thomson as

206

he'd breached his parole conditions by allowing the separate accounts for HMRC to be kept. Thomson was charged with intention to defraud Her Majesty's Revenue and Customs, and Miller made it clear that MIT wanted Ian detained.

"He'll probably have to serve at least the remainder of his sentence for the bank robbery," Mackay said.

Hunter felt quite sorry for Ian Thomson. But he knew Mackay was right. He allowed Ian to phone Janice and tell her he would not be home for dinner today, or any day in the foreseeable future.

It also looked as if Ponomarenko would get off because of his diplomatic immunity. That made Hunter very angry.

***

Hunter left Jane writing up the report for MIT and went to find somebody to accompany him to The Edinburgh Massage Suite. Tim and Bear both expressed a keen professional interest in attending, but Hunter recalled that Rachael had been involved in interviewing the three Ukrainian girls previously, and he thought it better to be accompanied by a female officer.

Travel through Edinburgh was slow because the afternoon rush-hour had started and vehicles were nose-to-tail in the city centre. Even as they approached Lothian Road, Hunter knew that parking would be an issue.

He decided to park in the Castle Terrace car-park and they would walk from there.

"So are we going to speak to the girls at their work or at the station, Boss?" Rachael asked.

"The owner made it clear that it was necessary to keep the meetings as brief as possible so that the girls take as little time off work as possible. We'll see them there."

"One at a time?"

"Yes, one at a time."

***

Hunter stood as Olena walked into the room. He noticed that, although she smiled, she sat in the chair furthest away from the detectives. Hunter made the introductions and sat down beside Rachael.

"Why did you come to Scotland?" Hunter asked.

"I didn't want to come here. I thought I was going to London. I paid to go to London to work as an actress in the shows. That is what the pigs Ponomarenko told me. I was told I would make big money to send to my family. Now I am here and the only acting I do is not to cry every day. They have a special cocktail that sends us to sleep if we do not do as they say. I am told if I do not work hard, my family will be tortured and killed."

"Who told you that?" Hunter asked softly.

"The big ugly pig who brought us from London. Anichka tried to run away, but he caught her. He hurt her bad."

"You have bruises too," Rachael said.

"From Oleksander Ponomarenko. He came here one time not so long ago. He was even worse than in Kiev." Olena sighed.

"You knew him in Kiev?" Hunter asked. "How well did you know him?"

"Everybody in Ukraine knows the brothers Ponomarenko. They are big business but bad news. Both would come to the club where I worked," Olena said solemnly.

"Oh dear. So where do you live?" Rachael asked.

"Here. We are not out since Ponomarenko's daughter was killed. Boss man says it is in case we get killed too. We are no good to him dead. That man shouts all the time. Why must he say everything in such loud voice?"

"How much do you get paid?" Rachael asked.

"Paid? Hah! A little less than it costs to live here and eat, it seems." Olena spat out her words.

"How often do you speak to your family back home?" Hunter asked softly.

He watched as Olena just shook her head. Tears ran down her cheeks. Hunter handed her a tissue and waited until she composed herself.

"You and Symona were at a club the night Xristina Ponomarenko was killed. How did that happen if you never get out?" Rachael asked.

"We did at first. Me, Symona and Anichka, we got out to promote this place and get men to come, but not now. Now if we want to go out they give us a drink and it puts us to sleep, so we don't ask."

"Did you know Xristina when you lived in Kiev?" Rachael asked.

"No, only her father and uncle used to come to the club, or maybe whore-house, where we worked. We knew them. They really are not nice men." She spat on the floor.

"How did you learn where Xristina lived?" Hunter asked. He noticed Rachael glance at him quizzically, but he just stared at her and shook his head almost imperceptibly.

"What makes you say that? You know something. How could I know that?" Olena stood up, stuck out her chin and glowered at Hunter. He knew he had hit a nerve.

"I don't know anything, yet, Olena. But I intend to find out," Hunter said.

Olena refused to comment further. and tThe interview with Symona told Hunter and Rachael nothing new, but Anichka seemed extremely nervous as she came into the room.

Hunter allowed Rachael to ask her a few questions to try to settle the young woman's nerves, and then he spoke.

"You were in Xristina's flat the night she died. How did you get in?"

"She opened the door."

"Did she? Did you see her killer?"

"No."

"What did you see?"

"Nothing., We were going to have a drink. Xristina just chose water. Then I thought I heard someone come in and I hid. I heard Xristina scream and shout and cry out. It went on so long, so I was afraid and I stayed hidden until Olena and Symona came in with their men."

Walking back to the car, Hunter asked, "Well, what did you think?"

"I think MIT should investigate the girls' arrival here," Rachael said. "It sounds like people-trafficking to me."

"And the conditions they are being kept in now sound like slavery to me," Hunter added. "Will you get those written up, Rachael? I've got a darts match tonight and I don't want to be late. But there is something that we were told tonight that I need to discuss with Meera. I'll phone her before I go out to The Persevere Bar."

"No problem, Boss. Who are you playing?"

"A Portobello pub team."

"Have you any chance of winning?"

"Ha, Ha. Thank you for that vote of confidence. They are traditional rivals of ours, but we beat them last time, so here's hoping we can do it again. Let's get back to the ranch, shall we?"

Chapter Forty-Nine

Hunter noticed that Tim arrived at the station especially early the following morning. His big BMW was difficult to miss. Hunter did not have car-envy, but even he could see that Tim's car was the smartest in the car park. It was not unusual for the young detective to be early, but it was almost an hour before he was due on shift. Hunter knew that meant there was something Tim wanted to speak about privately, so he just sat in his office, listening to Tim march along the corridor.

"Come in, young Myerscough." Hunter said, as Tim rapped smartly on the door.

"How did you know it was me, Boss?"

"Just a lucky guess. So what brings you here so early?"

"Well, I went for a run this morning, and after that, I thought I'd get here in good time."

"Aha. That's all?"

"Well, there was one thing I wanted to ask you, Boss."

"How can I help?"

"I wondered if I could get involved with interviewing Ponomarenko, Boss?"

"The man who followed you around the Sheraton Hotel and threatened you with a gun? Hmm. Now, let me ask you something, young Myerscough: on a scale of one to ten how likely do you think it is that I am going to agree to that?"

"Somewhere between zero and nil?"

"Correct. Now help yourself to a decent mug of coffee from my machine, then get out of my office." Hunter smiled wryly at Tim as he left, coffee mug in hand.

***

"Now where are we with everything?" Mackay asked as he banged a file on the desk to get some semblance of order into the room.

"Professor Sheptytsky admitted going to see Mansoor. He knows the family," Hunter said.

"He also went to The Edinburgh Massage Suite in Lothian Road to establish for Mansoor whether Ponomarenko was involved in people-trafficking," Bear added. "That line of business appalled both the Professor and Mansoor."

"Gosh, something even Mansoor frowns on? That's a first!" Colin exclaimed.

"Sir, the rohypnol used on DI Hunter and Xristina were not the same batch." Angus looked up from his notes. "So it may be that Squires was not involved in Xristina's murder?"

"DC McKenzie, what it means is that the drug used was not identical," Mackay said. "Therefore the attacks could have been conducted by the same people with two containers of the drug, or two different people. But it is interesting."

Rachael spoke. "Sir, Olena told us that the women working at The Edinburgh Massage Suite have been drugged to keep they quiet when they complain or get argumentative. The manager doesn't hit them."

"Doesn't want them bruised, I suppose," Hunter commented. "Rachael and I were told something else when we interviewed Anichka."

"The third girl?" Mackay clarified. "What did she say, Hunter?"

"She said that she got into the flat when Xristina opened the door for her."

"She said? You don't believe her? And how did she know where Xristina lived?" Mackay frowned.

"Ponomarenko said he told the manager of The Edinburgh Massage Suite, and Olena told us he speaks very loudly. Anichka or one of the other women probably overheard."

"I don't like that word probably, Hunter."

"I agree, Sir, but Anichka also told us that she did not see Xristina's attacker, but that she heard Xristina screaming and crying out. She said she hid until she was sure the attacker had gone."

Tim smiled. "That is very clever, Boss. Have you considered that Anichka couldn't have seen the attacker if she was the one who did the deed?"

"Yes, that thought occurred to me too, Tim," Hunter said.

"Forensics report that the hockey stick beside the front door has traces of hair and blood from Xristina on the end, and traces of skin on the grip," Rachael said.

"Anichka also wouldn't have known that there was a spare key under the mat," Hunter nodded.

"No, because she hadn't been there before," Rachael said.

"And I spoke to Doctor Sharma yesterday before I knocked off," Hunter went on. "She believes that Anichka couldn't have heard Xristina screaming and crying for a long time because the rohypnol would have kept Xristina quiet. In any case, that first blow to her head with the hockey stick probably knocked Xristina out, even if there had been no further blows. I want to take DNA from Anichka to see if it matches the traces of skin we found on and around the grip at the top of the stick. The attacker would have been holding it very tightly."

"Why cut Xristina's fingertips off?" Jane asked.

"To make identification more difficult," Hunter said.

"See if there is any matching DNA on the food bin where the CSIs found the fingertips," Jane said.

"Well thought, DS Renwick." But there's no sign of the glass that Xrisitina drank the water from. The murderer must have washed it and put it away. Do we have anything else?" Mackay asked.

"Well, I'll need to bring the three Ukrainian women in and interview them formally here, even if their manager objects," Hunter said. "But I'm pretty sure of what happened. I plan to interview Ponomarenko again today to try to tie up some of the loose ends in my mind."

"Any sign of Squires?" Colin asked.

"Not yet, Colin," Hunter said.

Nadia frowned. "How does a man that big hide in a country where the average height is five feet eight inches?"

"At least Hamilton is heading straight to jail," Colin said.

***

After the briefing, Sergeant Charlie Middleton phoned up from the front desk to let Hunter know that Ponomarenko and Andrew Barley had arrived.

"Oh, good holiday, Charlie?,"

"Grand thanks , Hunter, but too short."

"They all are, Charlie. Ponomarenko not got any consular official today?"

"No, Boss, just the two men."

"Show them into Interview Room 1, will you Charlie?" Hunter said. "Angus, you join DS Renwick and me for this interview. Just stand by the door and listen. It will be good experience for you to witness this."

"Yes, Boss. I'd like that." Angus smiled.

"Not quite the reaction I was expecting, Angus, but let's go. Ready, Jane?" Hunter led the way along the corridor.

"Three of you today?" Oleksander Ponomarenko said. "Why are you here, young man?" He asked Angus.

"I think you'll find that it's me who's asking the questions, Mr Ponomarenko," Hunter said, before Angus could say anything.

"Attaché Ponomarenko," Andrew Barley corrected Hunter.

"Of course. My apologies, Attaché Ponomarenko," Hunter said with exaggerated politeness. Then he explained the audio and visual recording as had been done the previous day, and, for the benefit of the recordings, he introduced everybody in the room.

"How can I assist you and your colleagues today, DI Wilson?" Ponomarenko asked. I cannot be here too long. I have a plane to catch."

"Indeed, where are you travelling to?" Jane asked.

"I return to Kiev to the breast of my family at this tragic time. The consulate will attend to the transfer of my daughter's body in due course. She must be buried at home," Ponomarenko said quietly.

"Of course," Jane said, equally quietly.

Hunter looked at Jane and then began his formal line of

questions. "Attaché Ponomarenko, my colleague, DC McKenzie, worked out the confusion about the flat your daughter lived in. Who did you ask to meet her and deliver her to Frederick Street?"

"I know hardly anybody in the city," Ponomarenko said. "I was grateful when my associate, Arjun Mansoor, offered to have his colleague, a Mr Brian Squires, I now believe, help Xristina to her new home. He said Squires was big and strong. Mr Mansoor suggested that I release one thousand pounds to ensure Xristina had enough money to settle in and buy food and books, but when I went to the flat the young man who lived there said he was only given five hundred pounds."

"That is correct," Hunter said. "And for the avoidance of doubt, I must clarify that the young man is my son, Cameron Wilson."

"I thought that when I saw the name," Andrew Barley said.

"It is a fine place for such a young man to live," Ponomarenko commented. "Not cheap."

"It belongs to Lord Lachlan Buchanan, whom you also met there, I believe," Hunter said. "My son lives in the flat as he is employed by Lord Buchanan as his driver."

"He is most fortunate." Ponomarenko said.

"Attaché Ponomarenko, is there anybody else who knew where Xristina was staying?" Hunter asked.

"Yes, of course. It wasn't a secret."

"Who knew? Anybody with whom you were on bad terms?"

"Nobody knows me here! How can I be on bad terms with anybody when I do not know them?" Ponomarenko stood up and shouted.

"Please sit down and do not shout at me, Attaché Ponomarenko," Hunter said. "I am trying to find out who had motive and opportunity to murder your daughter. Help me do that."

Hunter waited quietly while the Ukrainian man sat and composed himself. Then Hunter said, "Did the staff at Edinburgh University know where Xristina lived?"

"Yes, of course they must have her home address on file."

"And you did not get on well with Professor Sheptytsky. You know him. You attacked him and left him where there was every chance he would die," Jane commented.

"But that was after Xristina was killed," Ponomarenko said.

"It was, but my point is, that there are people in the city that you knew and with whom you were not on good terms," Hunter said. He stared silently at Oleksander Ponomarenko as he watched the penny drop and the man suddenly understood his meaning.

"Of course, what better way to hurt your enemy than to hurt the one they love and watch them suffer?" Ponomarenko sighed.

"Apart from Professor Sheptytsky, I have spoken to the three young women who work in The Edinburgh Massage Suite in Lothian Road. They all claim to have known you and your brother in Kiev. Is that true?"

"They are whores. My brother and I sometimes use the brothel. We like to have fun."

"But even whores have feelings and families, and I didn't get the impression they thought of their time with you as fun," Hunter said.

"It is their job. Do I care if they enjoy it?"

"Probably not," Jane said. "Could the girls have known where Xristina lived?"

"I did not tell them. But the manager of The Edinburgh Massage Suite knew. I told him on the phone the day Xristina left Kiev. I said he should take a note of the address and send anything there he needed to." Ponomarenko paused.

"Why did you do that?" Jane asked.

"You cannot trust the postal service in my country, and Xristina could scan and e-mail anything I needed quickly. But surely he would not discuss something like that with those bitches?"

"They could have overheard him. Or seen the note he made of Xristina's address? Or perhaps you had differences of opinions with him?" Hunter asked.

"None at all."

"So, they may have overheard him? Or read a note if he

wrote it down. They can hardly be your biggest fans," Jane said.

"But they wanted to come to Britain, and I got them here. They are just working to pay me back the costs," Ponomarenko whined.

"That's not quite true, is it, Attaché Ponomarenko?" Hunter asked. "They wanted to come to London to work as actresses and dancers on the West End Stage. Yet you have them in Edinburgh working in a massage suite of rather dubious repute."

Oleksander Ponomarenko shook his head and looked at the floor.

"Is there anything else you can tell me that might help me convict Xristina's killer?" Hunter asked.

"No, but when you find them, I ask you just give me five minutes alone in this room," Ponomarenko growled.

"You and I both know that is not going to happen, Attaché Ponomarenko. But we will not detain you further, if you have a plane to catch." Hunter nodded to Andrew Barley. "However, if you return to this country, I will charge you with both money-laundering and people-trafficking. And you will not be accepted as a diplomat here again, believe me."

"I will not return. I assure you," Oleksander Ponomarenko said.

"Best not, or you will stand trial for these very serious crimes. Your diplomatic immunity will not cover you then," Hunter said grimly. He explained the charges to Oleksander Ponomarenko, and informed him and Barley that the Ukrainian Consul and Embassy would be advised that Attaché Ponomarenko was required to return to Ukraine and was considered an unacceptable person to hold diplomatic office in Great Britain and Northern Ireland.

"I anticipated this," Ponomarenko said. "That is why my flight is today. I prefer to leave of my own accord." Oleksander clenched his fists and his jaw tightened. "So if we are finished here, I will take my leave of you, Inspector."

"Pleas get him out of here, Mr Barley," Hunter said to the lawyer.

"Yes, I think that time has come," Barley said.

Hunter got up and led Jane and Angus from the interview room.

Chapter Fifty

"I haven't been to the zoo for years, Frankie," Donna said. "I had forgotten what a steep hill this is. I'm quite glad to have the buggy to push."

"I like to start at the top of the hill and work my way down. You get great views across the city from up here right across towards Arthur's Seat, the big hill in Queen's park, and on towards Fife. Over here we can look out for zebras, antelopes and, see girls, those funny -looking birds are ostriches," Frankie said.

"Let's make sure we see the giant pandas and the penguins' parade too. I remember it from when I was a wee girl. They look so funny when they waddle along."

"Yes, the girls liked that when we came last year. It's quite expensive, so I can't bring them too often, but they do love those penguins." He smiled as Kylie-Ann pointed to a pigeon. "They're too wee to know a flying rat from an interesting animal."

"I suppose Annie had red hair?" Donna asked.

"Aye, she did. She and her mam both had red hair, and the twins have it too. So beautiful." Frankie smiled and ran his hand over the top of the twins' heads.

"I just have boring old brown hair," Donna fished quietly for a compliment.

"Nothing boring about you, Donna," Frankie said as she rewarded him with a kiss.

***

"Are you sure you're okay to come back to my place? It's just that the twins are so tired I need to get them their tea and to bed. I could order us a pizza, and there's always a few beers in the fridge once I've got them settled?"

"Good idea! Can I read the girls a story?"

Frankie smiled and kissed Donna again. He made a mental note to thank his aunt very much for the appointments she made for him at the salon.

"This is where you live?" Donna exclaimed as the taxi pulled up outside the house in Lauder Road.

"Yes. My uncle bought it. It's a long story. Do you like it?"

"It's very grand. Is your uncle a duke or something?"

"No nothing like that, believe me. Come in." Frankie unlocked the door.

"We don't have much furniture yet 'cos we just moved in, but have a seat on the sofa and I'll get the girls sorted. Maybe you could choose the pizza and phone to order it?"

***

Frankie turned to Donna. "You were really great with the twins at the zoo. Thank you."

"I really like kids. I wanted to be a nursery nurse, but I didn't get the right grades at school. Too thick, I suppose. You have the last piece of pizza," Donna said, handing him the box. "Okay for me to get us each another beer?"

"Okay to get another beer, not okay to say you're thick. You know lots of stuff. You could train to be a nursery nurse, if you wanted to," Frankie said defiantly.

As Donna returned from the kitchen with the beers, there was a thump on the front door and Frankie could hear an argument starting on the door step.

"What's that?" Donna asked with worry in her voice. She sat a little closer to Frankie on the couch.

"That's my bro', his pal and my cuz back from Ibiza. You better just excuse them in advance."

"Frankie, my boy! How's it goin' And who's this little beauty?" Harry said.

Frankie smiled and introduced Donna to Jamie, Harry and Gavin.

Jamie threw himself onto one of the leather reclining chairs. "So you're telling me we went all the way to Ibiza for no action at all, and you do the decent thing, stay home with the twins and bag yourself this gorgeous bird, Frankie?"

"There's no fuckin' justice, is there, Harry?" Gavin said.

"So, Donna, me and Gavin here are soldiers, what do you do?"

"I'm a beautician," she said.

"So how the fuck did you meet Frankie, he's no oil painting!" Jamie laughed.

"Right place, right time, lads," Donna smiled. She held her hand out to Frankie. "Shall we get to bed, love? We'll have a busy morning with the twins."

Frankie smiled and took Donna's hand as he led her to his part of the house. He was well aware of the other three men in the room staring at them as they walked.

"Goodnight, lads," he said.

"I can't believe that guy's luck!" Jamie said. "How does he do it? Annie wasn't bad looking either? What's wrong with me?"

"Do you want the long version or the short version?" Harry asked.

Just then Jamie's phone rang.

"Hello Mam. Aye, we're not long back from the airport. Ah well, no' quite what we expected, but a laugh with Harry and Gavin. Slow down, Mam. Slow down, I'm just no understanding you. My pop's what? Oh no! Whit fur?"

Jamie looked at Harry. His worried expression was mirrored in his cousin's face.

"What's going on, Jamie?" Harry asked. "Put yer mam on loudspeaker!"

Jamie did what Harry suggested. All three of the men in the room heard his mother say, "Your pop thinks he'll have to do the rest of his sentence. For breach of parole, but he told them about the bloody extra sets of books!"

"Oh Mam, this is just shit. He'll lose the betting shops, won't he?"

"Yes darlin'. He'll lose the betting shops. And he's told me that fine big house will have to go."

"Just as well Frankie's still got the house in West Mains Road," Jamie said. "We can move back there. It'll be a bit of a squash, Mam, but we'll manage."

"Don't worry about me, darlin'. I've had an offer I couldn't refuse."

"What do you mean, Mam?"

"Well that big, handsome friend of Lenny The Lizard's has swept me off my feet!"

"Who? You mean Brian Squires? He's a big ugly thug who don't have the brains he was born with, Mam. Last time I saw him he broke my arm. You dinny want to be with him, Mam," Jamie said, more in desperation than hope.

"Oh, Jamie, you know how much I need a man to care for me. I'm a physical woman with needs. I can't manage alone."

"You won't be alone, Mam. You'll have me and Frankie and the twins, and Harry, when he's home."

"Jamie, I am a woman with needs. You boys can't take care of *all* my needs, but my Brian baby is all man. He'll take care of me."

"Mam, you're mad," Jamie shouted. "This'll all end in tears, your tears. And it will kill Pop. You just can't leave him again."

"I'm not leaving him," Janice whined. "He's left me by being back in jail."

"Where are you going, Mam?"

"Brian baby can't stay here, the coppers are after him. We're going back to Spain. We'll run the bar Brian and Lenny The Lizard have there. You must come to Malaga and be with us, darlin'."

"No way! Mam, you're on your own." Jamie ended the call and switched his phone off.

"Shut up, Jamie, you'll wake the twins," Frankie said from the top of the stairs.

"That's the least of our problems, cuz," Jamie said, and went on to explain his mam's news.

Epilogue

Tim opened the door to Thomson's Top Cars and walked in, closely followed by Ailsa. He saw there was a new girl at the reception desk. Frankie and Jamie were standing chatting with a customer. He caught Jamie's eye and they exchanged a wave.

"Come on, Ailsa, let's have a look around and see what you want."

"This is decent of you, Tim. I don't need anything fancy, just something to get me about. But I want something green."

"I know, Sis, but just choose what you like. I'll buy it now and you can pay me back, or just buy me a new car when you get control of your trust fund."

"I think I'll pay you back. Your taste in cars is much more expensive than mine, Tim."

"So how can I help you today, Blondie?" Jamie said to Tim as he walked towards him.

"Jamie, this is my sister, Doctor Ailsa Myerscough. She needs a car to get her about the city."

"I can do that. What are you looking for, Doc?"

"I quite like that Prius over there, Jamie."

"You know it's a hybrid, like Blondie's BMW?"

"Yes, that's one of the reasons I like it. Do they do it in green?"

"For a beautiful lady like you, Doc, I'll get it green and purple stripes with orange dots." Jamie grinned.

Ailsa smiled. "Hmm, I think just plain green will do."

While Ailsa was looking at shades of green, Frankie walked over and the three men spoke quietly.

"Well, I suppose the good news is my pop can look out for yours again, Blondie. He's been given three years," Jamie said.

"Will that run concurrently with the remainder of his first sentence?" Tim asked.

"At the same time? Yes, that's right."

"The betting shops have gone. But Frankie and I are sorta used to running this place, aren't we cuz?"

"Yep. Had to get used to it didn't we?" Frankie smiled. "My girlfriend, Donna, does reception Thursdays and Saturdays. The rest of the week she's at college. Going to be a nursery nurse."

"That's really good, Frankie. How are the twins?" Tim asked.

"They're doing great. Me and Jamie have moved back to West Mains Road."

"Aye, Frankie and Donna have the big room, I'm in the back bedroom and we've got twin beds in the wee room for the girls," Jamie said. "It'll be a bit of a squash whenever Harry is home on leave, but we'll manage."

"I heard your mother made off with Brian Squires? How do you feel about that?" Tim asked Jamie.

"Least said, Blondie, least said. I think she's a fool, and she's broke my pop's heart again. I can't forgive her this time."

"Jamie, can I have it in this bright metallic green?" Ailsa called over.

"Anything for you, Doc," Jamie smiled.

***

When Tim got back to the station later in the day, he saw his team sitting in the briefing room.

"What sentence did those Ukrainian girls that killed Xristina get, Boss?" Rachael asked.

"Olena and Symona each got four years, and Anichka got five and a half," Hunter said.

"It doesn't seem much for conspiracy and murder," Nadia commented.

"With all that Xristina's family had put them through, the Crown accepted a lesser plea," Hunter said.

"They're lucky," Colin said. "They got hold of the rohypnol, found out Xristina's address and even drew straws as to which of them would attack her."

"When you put it like that, it all sounds pretty premeditated to me," Mel said.

"I know, Mel, but what kind of life have they had because of the Ponomarenko brothers?" Rachael said.

"Yes, I don't really blame them, because of that," Mel said. "The three girls that were brought over here by Xristina's father were so incensed by the way he treated them and cheated them that they decided to get their own back by hurting his daughter. They felt it was justice because he hurt other people's daughters."

"They didn't just hurt her, Mel, they killed her," Bear said. "And Xristina wasn't guilty of anything."

"But the plan wasn't to kill her," Hunter said. "Anichka was unlucky that Xristina wouldn't finish drinking the water because it tasted funny to her. I wish I'd noticed the same when Hamilton laced my drink. Anyway, Anichka looked around and saw the hockey stick by the front door. She grabbed it and whacked Xristina so hard that Doctor Sharma believes the first blow was probably fatal."

"Anichka certainly thought it was," Colin said.

"She did," Hunter said. "Then she panicked and tried to disfigure Xristina and used Cameron's tools from under the kitchen sink to cut off her fingertips so Xristina's identity would not be discovered."

"Has nobody here got anything better to do than sit around and blether?" DCI Mackay said as he looked into the room.

"Yes, Sir, of course," Hunter said. "Back to work, team."

DI Hunter Wilson will return soon in
Hunter's Blood

Fantastic Books
Great Authors

CROOKED
CAT

Meet our authors and discover
our exciting range:

- Gripping Thrillers
- Cosy Mysteries
- Romantic Chick-Lit
- Fascinating Historicals
- Exciting Fantasy
- Young Adult and Children's
  Adventures
- Non-Fiction

Visit us at:
www.crookedcatbooks.com

Join us on facebook:
www.facebook.com/crookedcatbooks